P9-ELQ-692

GREAT CASES
OF
THE THINKING MACHINE

JACQUES FUTRELLE (1875–1912)

GREAT CASES
OF
THE THINKING MACHINE

by Jacques Futrelle

WITH AN INTRODUCTION BY

E. F. BLEILER

DOVER PUBLICATIONS, INC.
NEW YORK

Published in Canada by General Publishing Company, Ltd., 30 Lesmill Road, Don Mills, Toronto, Ontario.
Published in the United Kingdom by Constable and Company, Ltd., 10 Orange Street, London WC 2.

Great Cases of The Thinking Machine, first published by Dover Publications, Inc., in 1976, is a new selection of stories by Jacques Futrelle. E. F. Bleiler has written an Introduction especially for the Dover edition.

International Standard Book Number: 0-486-23335-9
Library of Congress Catalog Card Number: 76-9182

Manufactured in the United States of America
Dover Publications, Inc.
180 Varick Street
New York, N.Y. 10014

CONTENTS

INTRODUCTION

Someone has commented that the great British detectives Sherlock Holmes and Dr. John Evelyn Thorndyke never (or almost never) communicate by telephone. They prefer instead all sorts of evasions and expedients: messenger boys, telegrams, the mails or even the agony columns of the newspapers.

The great American detective, The Thinking Machine, on the other hand, makes such proficient use of the phone that he might well be subtitled The Phoning Machine. Story after story is resolved when Professor Augustus S. F. X. Van Dusen (with more honorary degrees after his name than it is convenient to list) withdraws into a small side room and emerges a little later, answer achieved by logic—and the telephone.

Professor Van Dusen, one of the best-imagined detectives in the American literature, was the creation of Jacques Futrelle (1875-1912), an American newspaperman, who at the time of Van Dusen's appearance worked for the Boston *American*, the local Hearst newspaper.

Futrelle, a Georgian by birth, had worked at being a stage manager and at assorted other jobs before becoming an editor for the *American* and settling in the Boston area. After his newspaper stint he worked as a freelance writer, with many books and much magazine literature to his credit. He died on the *Titanic*, on the night of April 14-15, 1912, after pushing his wife to safety in a lifeboat.

Today, despite the wide range of his work—sport stories, romances, mysteries, westerns, society stories—Futrelle is remembered only for the tales about The Thinking Machine. That peculiarly exasperating and fascinating man was first conceived in 1905, when "The Problem of Cell 13" appeared as a week-long serial in the *American*, with the prize to the reader who worked out the solution best.

All in all Futrelle wrote 45 stories about The Thinking Machine.

These included a short novel, *The Chase of the Golden Plate*, which appeared in book form in 1906, and a succession of short stories, most of which first appeared in newspapers of the day. Some of these stories were collected into two volumes, *The Thinking Machine* (1906) and *The Thinking Machine on the Case* (1907). Others remain uncollected.

Futrelle's earlier stories, such as those in the first Dover collection*, were concerned mostly with the word that The Thinking Machine dislikes so much: the Impossible. Impossible events and situations had to be shifted into the realm of possibility. A perfect alibi opposed to a perfect incrimination; a motor car that disappeared into thin air along a country road that was watched at both ends; a series of footprints that end in the middle of a snowfield—these were the situations of the earlier stories. In a sense these stories are quasi-scientific, in that an idea or fact serves as the basis for a story in some cases: the properties of illuminating gas, the optics of mirrors.

In the later stories, such as are mostly represented in this volume, Futrelle was much less concerned with the Impossible. Instead he delighted in positing a mystifying situation, out of which an explanatory story must develop. It is the role of The Thinking Machine to evoke such stories.

What is the crime that will explain a runaway speedboat with a corpse at the controls, a corpse dressed like a French admiral, with no easily perceived cause of death? Why does a young society burglar harass his victim by systematically destroying his overcoats? Why was an actor kidnaped and forced to enact a deathbed scene, and how can the incident be traced? Why does a young lady badger a surgeon into amputating a perfectly healthy finger?

This new direction in The Thinking Machine stories had obvious repercussions. It probably enabled Jacques Futrelle to sell his work to a wider market than the more scientific stories, since societal situations were more popular than germinal ideas. This redirection may be a gain for the modern reader, if he likes to examine the weird values of the denizens of the Gold Coast. In a larger sense, however, it was a loss, for it removed Futrelle's later work from the direct track of the evolving modern American detective story. By and large the detective story does not flourish in the Back Bay and on Beacon Hill.

Whether Futrelle might have returned to the mood of the Impossible stories, or turned in still another direction, is problematic, since his life ended abruptly.

***Best "Thinking Machine" Detective Stories* by Jacques Futrelle. Dover Publications, 1973.

This second collection of stories about the irritable little scientist has been taken, with one exception, from the *Sunday Magazine*, a syndicated feature that was issued with certain large newspapers. The stories appeared there from 1906 through 1908, in two series, at irregular intervals.

"The Haunted Bell" is the single exception to this group. It was printed as a supplement to the later editions of Futrelle's novel *The Diamond Master*. I have not been able to locate an earlier publication in periodicals, although the chances are that it first appeared in a magazine or newspaper. It is unusual in being a venture in cross-forms, where Futrelle brought a new element into his detective stories. The Thinking Machine provides an explanation, but he does not have the last word. Some readers may regard this as a minor sacrilege; others may find it a resolution with a refreshing shock. Let each reader decide.

E. F. BLEILER

GREAT CASES
OF
THE THINKING MACHINE

THE SILVER BOX

"Really great criminals are never found out, for the simple reason that the greatest crimes—their crimes—are never discovered," remarked Professor Augustus S. F. X. Van Dusen positively. "There is genius in the perpetration of crime, Mr. Grayson, just as there must be in its detection, unless it is the shallow work of a bungler. In this latter case there have been instances where even the police have uncovered the truth. But the expert criminal, the man of genius—the professional, I may say—regards as perfect only that crime which does not and cannot be made to appear a crime at all; therefore one that can never involve him, or anyone else."

The financier, J. Morgan Grayson, regarded this wizened little man of science—The Thinking Machine—thoughtfully, through the smoke of his cigar.

"It is a strange psychological fact that the casual criminal glories in his crime beforehand and from one to ten minutes afterward," The Thinking Machine continued. "For instance, the man who kills for revenge wants the world to know it is his work; but at the end of ten minutes comes fear, abject terror, and then, paradoxically enough, he will seek to hide his crime and protect himself by some transparent means utterly inadequate, because of what he has said or done in the passion which preceded the act. With fear comes panic, with panic irresponsibility, and then he makes the mistake—hews a pathway which the trained mind follows from motive to a prison cell.

"These are the men who are found out. But there are men of genius, Mr. Grayson, professionally engaged in crime. We never hear of them, because they are never caught, and we never even suspect them, because they make no mistake—they are men of genius. Imagine the great brains as turned to crime. Well, there are today brains as great as any of these which make a profession of it; there is murder and theft and robbery under our noses that we never dream of. If I, for instance, should become an active criminal, can you see——" He paused.

Grayson, with a queer expression on his face, puffed steadily at his cigar.

"I could kill you now, here in this room," The Thinking Machine went on calmly, "and no one would ever know, never even suspect. Why not? Because I would make no mistake. In other words, I would immediately take rank with the criminals of genius who are never found out."

It was not a boast as he said it; it was merely a statement of fact. Grayson appeared to be a little startled. Where there had been only impatient interest in his manner, there was now something else—fascination, perhaps.

"How would you kill me, for instance?" he inquired curiously.

"With any one of a dozen poisons, with virulent germs, or even with a knife or revolver," replied the scientist placidly. "You see, I know how to use poisons. I know how to inoculate with germs; I know how to produce suicidal appearance perfectly with either a revolver or knife. And I never make mistakes, Mr. Grayson. In the sciences we must be exact—not approximately so, but absolutely so. We must know. It isn't like carpentry. A carpenter may make a trivial mistake in a joint, and it will not weaken his house; but if the scientist makes one mistake, the whole structure tumbles down. We must know. Knowledge is progress. We gain knowledge by observation and logic—inevitable logic. And logic tells us that while two and two make four, it is not only sometimes but all the time."

Grayson flicked the ashes of his cigar thoughtfully, and little wrinkles appeared about his eyes as he stared into the drawn, inscrutable face of the scientist. The enormous, straw-yellow head was cushioned against the chair, the squinting, watery blue eyes turned upward, and the slender white fingers at rest, tip to tip. The financier drew a long breath. "I have been informed that you were a remarkable man," he said at last, slowly. "I believe it. Quinton Frazer, the banker who gave me the letter of introduction to you, told me how you once solved a remarkable mystery, in which——"

"Yes, yes," interrupted the scientist shortly, "the Ralston bank robbery—I remember."

"So I came to you to enlist your aid in something which is more inexplicable than that." Grayson went on hesitatingly. "I know that no fee I might offer would influence you, yet it is a case which——"

"State it," interrupted The Thinking Machine again.

"It isn't a crime—that is, a crime that can be reached by law," Grayson hurried on—"but it has cost me millions and——"

For one instant The Thinking Machine lowered his squint eyes to those of his visitor, then raised them again. "Millions!" he repeated. "How many?"

"Six, eight, perhaps ten," was the reply. "Briefly, there is a leak in my office. My plans become known to others almost by the time I have perfected them. My plans are large; I have millions at stake; and the greatest secrecy is absolutely essential. For years I have been able to preserve this secrecy; but half a dozen times in the last eight weeks my plans have become known, and I have been caught. Unless you know the Street, you can't imagine what a tremendous disadvantage it is to have someone know your next move to the minutest detail, and knowing it, defeat you at every turn."

"No, I don't know your world of finance, Mr. Grayson," remarked The Thinking Machine. "Give me an instance."

"Well, take this last case," suggested the financier earnestly. "Briefly, without technicalities, I had planned to unload the securities of the P., Q., and X. railway, protecting myself through brokers, and force the outstanding stock down to a price where other brokers, acting for me, could buy far below the actual value. In this way I intended to get complete control of the stock. But my plans became known, and when I began to unload, everything was snapped up by the opposition, with the result that instead of gaining control of the road I lost heavily. The same thing has happened, with variations, half a dozen times."

"I presume that this is strictly honest?" inquired the scientist mildly.

"Honest?" repeated Grayson. "Certainly—of course. It's business."

"I shall not pretend to understand all that," said The Thinking Machine curtly. "It doesn't seem to matter, anyway. You want to know where the leak is. Is that right?"

"Precisely."

"Well, who is in your confidence?"

"No one, except my stenographer."

"Of course there is an exception. Who is he, please?"

"It's a woman—Miss Evelyn Winthrop. She has been in my employ for six years in the same capacity—more than five years before this leak appeared—and I trust her absolutely."

"No man knows your business?"

"No," replied the financier grimly. "I learned years ago that no one could keep my secrets as I do—there are too many temptations—therefore I never mention my plans to anyone—never—to anyone!"

"Except your stenographer," corrected the scientist.

"I work for days, weeks, sometimes months, perfecting plans, and it's all in my head, not on paper—not a scratch of it," explained Grayson. "Therefore, when I say that she is in my confidence, I mean that she knows my plans only half an hour or less before the machinery is put into motion. For instance, I planned this P., Q., and X. deal. My brokers didn't know of it; Miss Winthrop never heard of it until twenty minutes before the Stock Exchange opened for business. Then I dictated to her, as I always do, some short letters of instructions to my agents. That is all she knew of it."

"You outlined the plan in those letters?"

"No; they merely told my brokers what to do."

"But a shrewd person, knowing the contents of all those letters, could have learned what you intended to do?"

"Yes; but no one person knew the contents of all the letters. No one broker knew what was in the other letters—many of them were unknown to each other. Miss Winthrop and I were the only two human beings who knew all that was in them."

The Thinking Machine sat silent for so long that Grayson began to fidget in his chair. "Who was in the room besides you and Miss Winthrop before the letters were sent?" he asked at last.

"No one," responded Grayson emphatically. "For an hour before I dictated those letters, until at least an hour afterward, after my plans had gone to smash, no one entered that room. Only she and I work there."

"But when she finished the letters, she went out?" insisted The Thinking Machine.

"No," declared the financier. "She didn't even leave her desk."

"Or perhaps sent something out—manifolds of the letters?"

"No."

"Or called up a friend on the telephone?" continued The Thinking Machine quietly.

"Nor that," retorted Grayson.

"Or signaled to some one through the window?"

"No," said the financier again. "She finished the letters, then remained quietly at her desk, reading a book. She didn't move for two hours."

The Thinking Machine lowered his eyes and glared straight into those of the financier. "Some one listened at the window?" he went on after a moment.

"No. It is six stories up, fronting the street, and there is no fire escape."

"Or the door?"

"If you knew the arrangement of my offices, you would see how utterly impossible that would be, because——"

"Nothing is impossible, Mr. Grayson," snapped the scientist abruptly. "It might be improbable, but not impossible. Don't say that. It annoys me exceedingly." He was silent for a moment. Grayson stared at him blankly. "Did either you or she answer a call on the phone?"

"No one called; we called no one."

"Any apertures—holes or cracks in your flooring, or walls or ceilings?" demanded the scientist.

"Private detectives whom I had employed looked for such an opening, and there was none," replied Grayson.

Again The Thinking Machine was silent for a long time. Grayson lighted a fresh cigar and settled back in his chair patiently. Faint cobwebby lines began to appear on the domelike brow of the scientist, and slowly the squint eyes were narrowing.

"The letters you wrote were intercepted?" he suggested at last.

"No," exclaimed Grayson flatly. "Those letters were sent direct to the brokers by a dozen different methods, and every one of them had been delivered by five minutes of ten o'clock, when 'Change begins business. The last one left me at ten minutes of ten."

"Dear me! Dear me!" The Thinking Machine rose and paced the length of the room thrice.

"You don't give me credit for the extraordinary precautions I have taken, particularly in this last P., Q., and X. deal," Grayson continued. "I left positively nothing undone to insure absolute secrecy. And Miss Winthrop I know is innocent of any connection with the affair. The private detectives suspected her at first, as you do, and she was watched in and out of my office for weeks. When she was not under my eyes, she was under the eyes of men to whom I had promised an extravagant sum of money if they found the leak. She didn't know it, and doesn't know it now. I am heartily ashamed of it all, because the investigation proved her absolute loyalty to me. On this last day she was directly under my eyes for two hours; and she didn't make one movement that I didn't note, because the thing means millions to me. That proved beyond all question that it was no fault of hers. What could I do?"

The Thinking Machine didn't say. He paused at a window, and for minute after minute stood motionless there, with eyes narrowed down to mere slits.

"I was on the point of discharging Miss Winthrop," the financier went on, "but her innocence was so thoroughly proved to me by this last affair that it would have been unjust, and so——"

Suddenly the scientist turned upon his visitor. "Do you talk in your sleep?" he demanded.

"No," was the prompt reply. "I had thought of that, too. It is beyond all ordinary things, professor. Yet there is a leak that is costing me millions."

"It comes down to this, Mr. Grayson," The Thinking Machine informed him crabbedly enough. "If only you and Miss Winthrop knew those plans, and no one else, and they did leak, and were not deduced from other things, then either you or she permitted them to leak, intentionally or unintentionally. That is as pure logic as that two and two make four; there is no need to argue it."

"Well, of course, I didn't," said Grayson.

"Then Miss Winthrop did," declared The Thinking Machine finally, positively, "unless we credit the opposition, as you call it, with telepathic gifts hitherto unheard of. By the way, you have referred to the other side only as the opposition. Do the same men, the same clique, appear against you all the time, or is it only one man?"

"It's a clique," explained the financier, "with millions back of it, headed by Ralph Matthews, a young man to whom I give credit for being the prime factor against me." His lips were set sternly.

"Why?" demanded the scientist.

"Because every time he sees me, he grins," was the reply. Grayson seemed suddenly discomfited.

The Thinking Machine went to a desk, addressed an envelope, folded a sheet of paper, placed it inside, then sealed it. At length he turned back to his visitor. "Is Miss Winthrop in your office now?"

"Yes."

"Let us go there, then."

A few minutes later the eminent financier ushered the eminent scientist into his private office on the Street. The only other person there was a young woman—a woman of twenty-six or seven, perhaps—who turned, saw Grayson, and resumed reading. The financier motioned to a seat. Instead of sitting, however, The Thinking Machine went straight to Miss Winthrop and extended a sealed envelope to her.

"Mr. Ralph Matthews asked me to hand you this," he said.

The young woman glanced up into his face frankly, yet with a certain timidity, took the envelope, and turned it curiously in her hand.

"Mr. Ralph Matthews," she repeated, as if the name was a strange one. "I don't think I know him."

The Thinking Machine stood staring at her aggressively, insolently even, as she opened the envelope and drew out the sheet of paper. There was no expression save surprise—bewilderment, rather—to be read on her face.

"Why, it's a blank sheet!" she remarked, puzzled.

The scientist turned away suddenly toward Grayson, who had witnessed the incident with frank astonishment in his eyes. "Your telephone—a moment please," he requested.

"Certainly; here," replied Grayson.

"This will do," remarked the scientist.

He leaned forward over the desk where Miss Winthrop sat, still gazing at him in a sort of bewilderment, picked up the receiver, and held it to his ear. A few moments later he was talking to Hutchinson Hatch, reporter.

"I merely wanted to ask you to meet me at my apartments in an hour," said the scientist. "It is very important."

That was all. He hung up the receiver, paused for a moment to admire an exquisitely wrought silver box—a "vanity" box—on Miss Winthrop's desk, beside the telephone, then took a seat beside Grayson and began to discourse almost pleasantly on the prevailing meteorological conditions. Grayson merely stared; Miss Winthrop continued her reading.

Professor Augustus S. F. X. Van Dusen, distinguished scientist, and Hutchinson Hatch, newspaper reporter, were poking round among the chimney pots and other obstructions on the roof of a skyscraper. Far below them the slumber-enshrouded city was spread out like a panorama, streets dotted brilliantly with arc lights, and roofs hazily visible through the mists of night. Above, the infinite blackness hung like a veil, with star points breaking through here and there.

"Here are the wires," Hatch said at last, and he stopped.

The Thinking Machine knelt on the roof beside him, and for several minutes they remained thus in the darkness, with only the glow of an electric flash to indicate their presence. Finally The Thinking Machine rose.

"That's the wire you want, Mr. Hatch," he said. "I'll leave the rest of it to you."

"Are you sure?" asked the reporter.

"I am always sure," was the tart response.

Hatch opened a small hand satchel and removed several queerly shaped tools. These he spread on the roof beside him; then, kneeling again, began his work. For half an hour or so he labored in the gloom, with only the electric flash to aid him, and then he rose.

"It's all right," he said.

The Thinking Machine examined the work that had been done, grunted his satisfaction, and together they went to the skylight, leaving a thin, insulated wire behind them, stringing along to mark their path.

They passed down through the roof, and into the darkness of the hall of the upper story. Here the light was extinguished. From far below came the faint echo of a man's footsteps as the watchman passed through the silent, deserted building.

"Be careful!" warned The Thinking Machine.

Along the hall to a room in the rear they went, and still the wire trailed behind. At the last door they stopped. The Thinking Machine fumbled with some keys, then opened the way. Here an electric light was on. The room was bare of furniture, the only sign of recent occupancy being a telephone instrument on the wall.

Here The Thinking Machine stopped and stared at the spool of wire which he had permitted to wind off as he walked, and his thin face expressed doubt.

"It wouldn't be safe," he said at last, "to leave the wire exposed as we have left it. True, this floor is not occupied; but some one might pass up this way and disturb it. You take the spool, go back to the roof, winding the wire as you go, then swing the spool down to me over the side so I can bring it in the window. That will be best. I shall catch it here, and thus there will be nothing to indicate any connection."

Hatch went out quietly and closed the door.

Twice the following day The Thinking Machine spoke to the financier over the telephone. Grayson was in his private office, Miss Winthrop at her desk, when the first call came.

"Be careful in answering my questions," warned The Thinking Machine when Grayson answered. "Do you know how long Miss Winthrop has owned the little silver box which is now on her desk, near the telephone?"

Grayson glanced around involuntarily to where the girl sat idly turning over the leaves of her book. "Yes," he answered; "for seven months. I gave it to her last Christmas."

"Ah!" exclaimed the scientist. "That simplifies matters. Where did you buy it?"

Grayson mentioned the name of a well known jeweler.

"Good by," came the voice of the scientist, and the connection was broken.

Considerably later in the day The Thinking Machine called Grayson to the telephone again.

"What make of typewriter does she use?" came the querulous voice over the wire.

Grayson named it.

"Good by."

While Grayson sat with deeply perplexed lines in his face, the diminutive scientist called upon Hutchinson Hatch at his office. The reporter was just starting out.

"Do you use a typewriter?" demanded The Thinking Machine.

"Yes."

"What kind?"

"Oh, four or five kinds—we have half a dozen varieties in the office. I can use any of them."

They passed along through the city room, at that moment

practically deserted, until finally the watery blue eyes settled upon a typewriter with the name emblazoned on the front.

"That's it!" exclaimed The Thinking Machine. "Write something on it," he directed Hatch.

"What shall I write?" inquired the reporter, and he sat down.

"Anything you like," was the terse response. "Just write something."

Hatch drew up a chair and rolled off several lines of the immortal practice sentence beginning, "Now is the time for all good men——"

The Thinking Machine sat beside him, squinting off across the room in deep abstraction, and listening intently. His head was turned away from the reporter, and his ear was within a few inches of the machine. For a minute he sat there listening, then shook his head.

"Strike your vowels," he commanded, "first slowly, then rapidly."

Again Hatch obeyed, while the scientist listened. And again he shook his head. Then in turn every make of machine in the office was tested the same way. At the end The Thinking Machine rose and went his way. There was an expression nearly approaching bewilderment on his face as he went out.

For hour after hour that night The Thinking Machine half lay in a huge chair in his laboratory, with eyes turned uncompromisingly upward, and an expression of complete concentration on his face. There was no change either in his position or his gaze as minute succeeded minute; the brow was deeply wrinkled now, and the thin line of the lips was drawn taut. The tiny clock in the reception room struck ten, eleven, twelve, and finally one. At just half-past one The Thinking Machine rose suddenly.

"Positively, I am getting stupid!" he grumbled half aloud. "Of course! Of course! Why couldn't I have thought of that in the first place!"

So it came about that Grayson did not go to his office on the following morning at the usual time. Instead, he called again upon The Thinking Machine in eager, expectant response to a note which had reached him at his home just before he started to his office.

"Nothing yet," said The Thinking Machine as the financier entered. "But here is something you must do today. What time does the Stock Exchange close?"

"Three o'clock," was the reply.

"Well, at one o'clock," the scientist went on, "you must issue orders for a gigantic deal of some sort; and you must issue them precisely as you have issued them in the past; there must be no variation. Dictate the letters as you have always done to Miss Winthrop; but don't send them. When they come to you, keep them until you see me."

"You mean that the deal must be purely imaginary?" inquired the financier.

"Precisely," was the reply. "But make your instructions circumstantial; give them enough detail to make them absolutely convincing."

"And hold the letters?"

"Hold the letters," the other repeated. "The leak comes before you receive them. I don't want to know or have an idea of what mythical deal it is to be; but issue your orders at one o'clock."

Grayson asked a dozen questions, answer to which was curtly denied, then went to his office. The Thinking Machine again called Hatch to the telephone.

"I've got it," he announced briefly. "I want the best telegraph operator you know. Bring him along and meet me in a room on the top floor where the telephone is, at precisely fifteen minutes of one o'clock today."

"Telegraph operator?" Hatch repeated.

"That's what I said—telegraph operator," replied the scientist irritably. "Good by."

Hatch smiled whimsically at the other end as he heard the receiver banged on the hook—smiled because he knew the eccentric ways of this singular man, whose mind so accurately illuminated every problem to which it was directed. Then he went out to the telegraph room and borrowed the principal operator. They were in the little room on the top floor at precisely fifteen minutes of one.

The operator glanced about in astonishment. The room was still unfurnished, save for the telephone box on the wall.

"What do I do?" he asked.

"I'll tell you when the time comes," responded the scientist, as he glanced at the watch.

At three minutes of one o'clock he handed a sheet of blank paper to the operator, and gave his final instructions. "Hold the telephone receiver to your ear and write on this what you hear," he directed. "It may be several minutes before you hear anything. When you do, tell me so."

There was ludicrous mystification on the operator's face, but he obeyed orders, grinning cheerfully at Hatch as he tilted his cigar up to keep the smoke out of his eyes. The Thinking Machine stood impatiently looking on, watch in hand. Hatch didn't know what was happening; but he was tremendously interested.

And at last the operator heard something. His face suddenly became alert. He continued to listen for a moment, and then came a smile of recognition as he turned to the scientist.

"It's good old Morse, all right," he announced, "but it's the queerest sort of sounder I ever read."

"You mean the Morse telegraphic code?" demanded The Thinking Machine.

"Sure," said the operator.

"Write your message."

Within less than ten minutes after Miss Winthrop had handed over the typewritten letters of instruction to Grayson for signature, and while he still sat turning them over in his hands, the door opened and The Thinking Machine entered. He tossed a folded sheet of paper on the desk before Grayson, and went straight to Miss Winthrop.

"So you did know Mr. Ralph Matthews after all?" he inquired.

The girl rose from her desk, and a flash of some subtle emotion passed over her face. "What do you mean, sir?" she demanded.

"You might as well remove the silver box," The Thinking Machine went on mercilessly. "There is no further need for the connection."

Miss Winthrop glanced down at the telephone extension on her desk, and her hand darted toward it. The silver vanity box was underneath the receiver, supporting it, so that all weight was removed from the hook, and the line was open. She snatched the box, the receiver dropped back on the hook, and there was a faint tinkle of a bell somewhere below. The Thinking Machine turned to Grayson.

"It was Miss Winthrop," he said.

"Miss Winthrop!" exclaimed Grayson, and he rose. "I cannot believe it."

"It doesn't matter whether you believe it or not," retorted the scientist. "But if your doubt is very serious, you might ask her."

Grayson turned toward the girl and took a couple of steps forward. There was more than surprise in his face; there was doubt, and perhaps regret.

"I don't know what it's about," she protested feebly.

"Read the paper I gave you, Mr. Grayson," directed The Thinking Machine coldly. "Perhaps that will enlighten her."

The financier opened the sheet, which had remained folded in his hand, and glanced at what was written there. Slowly he read it aloud: "Goldman.—Sell ten thousand shares L. & W. at 97. McCracken Co.—Sell ten thousand shares L. & W., 97." He read on down the list, bewildered. Then gradually, as he realized the import of what he read, there came a hardening of the lines about his mouth.

"I understand, Miss Winthrop," he said at last. "This is the substance of the orders I dictated, and in some way you made them known to persons for whom they were not intended. I don't know how you did it, of course; but I understand that you did do it, so—" He stepped to the door and opened it with grave courtesy. "You may go now. I am sorry."

Miss Winthrop made no plea—simply bowed and went out. Grayson stood staring after her for a moment, then turned to The Thinking Machine, and motioned him to a chair. "What happened?" he asked briskly.

"Miss Winthrop," replied The Thinking Machine, "is a tremendously clever woman. She neglected to tell you, however, that besides being a stenographer and typist, she was a telegraph operator. She is so expert in each of her lines that she combined the two, if I may say it that way. In other words, in writing on the typewriter, she was clever enough to be able to give the click of the machine the sound of the Morse telegraphic code, so that another telegraph operator who heard her machine could translate it into words."

Grayson sat staring at him incredulously.

"I still don't understand," he finally said.

"Here," and The Thinking Machine rose and went to Miss Winthrop's desk—"here is an extension telephone with the receiver on the hook. It just happens that the little silver box which you gave Miss Winthrop is tall enough to support this receiver clear of the hook, and the minute the receiver is off the hook, the line is open. When you were at your desk and she was here, you couldn't see this telephone; therefore, it was a simple matter for her to lift the receiver, and place the silver box beneath, thus holding the line open permanently. That being true, the sound of the typewriter would go over the open wire to whoever was listening at the other end, wouldn't it? Then, if that typewriter was made to sound the telegraphic code, and an operator held the receiver at the other end, that operator could read a message written at the same moment your letters were being written. That is all. It requires extreme concentration to do the thing—cleverness."

"Oh, I see!" exclaimed Grayson at last.

"When we knew that the leak in your office was not in the usual way," continued The Thinking Machine, "we looked for the unusual. First I was inclined to believe that there was a difference in the sounding keys as they were struck, and some one was clever enough to read that. I had Mr. Hatch make experiments, however, which instantly proved that was out of the question—unless this typewriter had been tuned, I may say. The logic of the thing had convinced me, meanwhile, that the leak must be by way of the telephone line, and Mr. Hatch and I tapped it one night. He is an electrician, as well as a newspaper reporter. Then I saw the possibility of holding the line open, as I explained; but for hour after hour the actual method of communication eluded me. At last I found it—the telegraphic code. Then it was all simple.

"When I telephoned to you to find out how long Miss Winthrop had had the silver box, and you said seven months, I knew that it was always at hand. When I asked you where you got it, I went there and saw a duplicate. There I measured the box and tested my belief that it would just support the receiver clear of the hook. When I requested you to dictate those orders today at one o'clock, I had a telegraph operator listening at a telephone on the top floor of this building. There is nothing very mysterious about it, after all—it's merely clever."

"Clever!" repeated Grayson, and his jaws snapped. "It is more than that. Why, it's criminal! She should be prosecuted."

"I shouldn't advise that, Mr. Grayson," returned the scientist coldly. "If it is honest—merely business—to juggle stocks as you told me you did, this is no more dishonest. And besides, remember that Miss Winthrop is backed by the people who have made millions out of you, and—well, I wouldn't prosecute. It is betrayal of trust, certainly, but——" He rose as if that was all, and started toward the door. "I would advise you, if you want to stop the leak, to discharge the person in charge of your office exchange here," he said.

"Was she in the scheme?" demanded Grayson. He rushed out of the private office into the main office. At the door he met a clerk coming in.

"Where is Miss Mitchell?" demanded the financier hotly.

"I was just coming to tell you she went out with Miss Winthrop just now without giving any explanation," replied the clerk. "The telephone is without an attendant."

"Good day, Mr. Grayson," said The Thinking Machine.

The financier nodded his thanks, then stalked back into his room, banging the door behind him.

In the course of time The Thinking Machine received a check for ten thousand dollars, signed, "J. Morgan Grayson." He glared at it for a little while, then endorsed it in a crabbed hand, "Pay to Trustees Home for Crippled Children," and sent Martha out to mail it.

THE SUPERFLUOUS FINGER

She drew off her left glove, a delicate, crinkled suede affair, and offered her bare hand to the surgeon.

An artist would have called it beautiful, perfect, even; the surgeon, professionally enough, set it down as an excellent structural specimen. From the polished pink nails of the tapering fingers to the firm, well moulded wrist, it was distinctly the hand of a woman of ease—one that had never known labor, a pampered hand Dr. Prescott told himself.

"The forefinger," she exclaimed calmly. "I should like to have it amputated at the first joint, please."

"Amputated?" gasped Dr. Prescott. He stared into the pretty face of his caller. It was flushed softly, and the red lips were parted in a slight smile. It seemed quite an ordinary affair to her. The surgeon bent over the hand with quick interest. "Amputated!" he repeated.

"I came to you," she went on with a nod, "because I have been informed that you are one of the most skilful men of your profession, and the cost of the operation is quite immaterial."

Dr. Prescott pressed the pink nail of the forefinger then permitted the blood to rush back into it. Several times he did this, then he turned the hand over and scrutinized it closely inside from the delicately lined palm to the tips of the fingers. When he looked up at last there was an expression of frank bewilderment on his face.

"What's the matter with it?" he asked.

"Nothing," the woman replied pleasantly. "I merely want it off from the first joint."

The surgeon leaned back in his chair with a frown of perplexity on his brow, and his visitor was subjected to a sharp, professional stare. She bore it unflinchingly and even smiled a little at his obvious perturbation.

"Why do you want it off?" he demanded.

The woman shrugged her shoulders a little impatiently.

"I can't tell you that," she replied. "It really is not necessary that you should know. You are a surgeon, I want an operation performed. That is all."

There was a long pause; the mutual stare didn't waver.

"You must understand, Miss—Miss—er——" began Dr. Prescott at last. "By the way, you have not introduced yourself?" She was silent. "May I ask your name?"

"My name is of no consequence," she replied calmly. "I might, of course, give you a name, but it would not be mine, therefore any name would be superfluous."

Again the surgeon stared.

"When do you want the operation performed?" he inquired.

"Now," she replied. "I am ready."

"You must understand," he said severely, "that surgery is a profession for the relief of human suffering, not for mutilation—willful mutilation I might say."

"I understand that perfectly," she said. "But where a person submits of her own desire to—to mutilation as you call it, I can see no valid objection on your part."

"It would be criminal to remove a finger where there is no necessity for it," continued the surgeon bluntly. "No good end could be served."

A trace of disappointment showed in the young woman's face, and again she shrugged her shoulders.

"The question after all," she said finally, "is not one of ethics but is simply whether or not you will perform the operation. Would you do it for, say, a thousand dollars?"

"Not for five thousand dollars," blurted the surgeon.

"Well, for ten thousand then?" she asked, quite casually.

All sorts of questions were pounding in Dr. Prescott's mind. Why did a young and beautiful woman desire—why was she anxious even—to sacrifice a perfectly healthy finger? What possible purpose would it serve to mar a hand which was as nearly perfect as any he had ever seen? Was it some insane caprice? Staring deeply into her steady, quiet eyes he could only be convinced of her sanity. Then what?

"No, madam," he said at last, vehemently, "I would not perform the operation for any sum you might mention, unless I was first convinced that the removal of that finger was absolutely necessary. That, I think, is all."

He arose as if to end the consultation. The woman remained seated and continued thoughtful for a minute.

"As I understand it," she said, "you *would* perform the operation if I could convince you that it was absolutely necessary?"

"Certainly," he replied promptly, almost eagerly. His curiosity was aroused. "Then it would come within the range of my professional duties."

"Won't you take my word that it is necessary, and that it is impossible for me to explain why?"

"No. I must know why."

The woman arose and stood facing him. The disappointment had gone from her face now.

"Very well," she remarked steadily. "You *will* perform the operation if it is necessary, therefore if I should shoot the finger off, perhaps——?"

"Shoot it off?" exclaimed Dr. Prescott in amazement. "Shoot it off?"

"That is what I said," she replied calmly. "If I should shoot the finger off you would consent to dress the wound? You would make any necessary amputation?"

She held up the finger under discussion and looked at it curiously. Dr. Prescott himself stared at it with a sudden new interest.

"Shoot it off?" he repeated. "Why you must be mad to contemplate such a thing," he exploded, and his face flushed in sheer anger. "I—I will have nothing whatever to do with the affair, madam. Good day."

"I should have to be very careful, of course," she mused, "but I think perhaps one shot would be sufficient; then I should come to you and demand that you dress it?"

There was a question in the tone. Dr. Prescott stared at her for a full minute, then walked over and opened the door.

"In my profession, madam," he said coldly, "there is too much possibility of doing good and relieving actual suffering for me to consider this matter or discuss it further with you. There are three persons now waiting in the ante-room who *need* my services. I shall be compelled to ask you to excuse me."

"But you will dress the wound?" the woman insisted, undaunted by his forbidding tone and manner.

"I shall have nothing whatever to do with it," declared the surgeon, positively, finally. "If you need the services of any medical man permit me to suggest that it is an alienist and not a surgeon."

The woman didn't appear to take offense.

"Someone would have to dress it," she continued insistently. "I should much prefer that it be a man of undisputed skill—you I mean; therefore I shall call again. Good day."

There was a rustle of silken skirts and she was gone. Dr. Prescott stood for an instant gazing after her in frank wonder and annoyance in his eyes, his attitude, then he went back and sat down at the desk. The crinkled suede glove still lay where she had left it. He examined it gingerly then with a final shake of his head dismissed the affair and turned to other things.

Early next afternoon Dr. Prescott was sitting in his office writing when the door from the ante-room where patients awaited his leisure was thrown open and the young man in attendance rushed in.

"A lady has fainted, sir," he said hurriedly. "She seems to be hurt."

Dr. Prescott arose quickly and strode out. There, lying helplessly back in her chair with white face and closed eyes, was his visitor of the day before. He stepped toward her quickly, then hesitated as he recalled their conversation. Finally, however, professional instinct, the desire to relieve suffering, and perhaps curiosity, too, caused him to go to her. The left hand was wrapped in an improvised bandage through which there was a trickle of blood. He glared at it with incredulous eyes.

"Hanged if she didn't do it," he blurted angrily.

The fainting spell, Dr. Prescott saw, was due only to loss of blood and physical pain, and he busied himself trying to restore her to consciousness. Meanwhile he gave some hurried instructions to the young man who was in attendance in the ante-room.

"Call up Professor Van Dusen on the 'phone," he directed, "and ask him if he can assist me in a minor operation. Tell him it's rather a curious case and I am sure it will interest him."

It was in this manner that the problem of the superfluous finger first came to the attention of The Thinking Machine. He arrived just as the mysterious woman was opening her eyes to consciousness from the fainting spell. She stared at him glassily, unrecognizingly; then her glance wandered to Dr. Prescott. She smiled.

"I knew you'd have to do it," she murmured weakly.

After the ether had been administered for the operation, a simple and an easy one, Dr. Prescott stated the circumstances of the case to The Thinking Machine. The scientist stood with his long, slender fingers resting lightly on the young woman's pulse, listening in silence.

"What do you make of it?" demanded the surgeon.

The Thinking Machine didn't say. At the moment he was leaning over the unconscious woman, squinting at her forehead. With his disengaged hand he stroked the delicately pencilled eye-brows several times the wrong way, and again at close range squinted at them. Dr. Prescott saw and seeing, understood.

"No, it isn't that," he said and he shuddered a little. "I thought of it myself. Her bodily condition is excellent, splendid."

It was some time later when the young woman was sleeping lightly, placidly under the influence of a soothing potion, that The Thinking Machine spoke of the peculiar events which had preceded the operation. Then he was sitting in Dr. Prescott's private office. He had picked up a woman's glove from the desk.

"This is the glove she left when she first called, isn't it?" he inquired.

"Yes."

"Did you happen to see her remove it?"

"Yes."

The Thinking Machine curiously examined the dainty, perfumed trifle, then, arising suddenly, went into the adjoining room where the woman lay asleep. He stood for an instant gazing down admiringly at the exquisite, slender figure; then, bending over, he looked closely at her left hand. When at last he straightened up, it seemed that some unspoken question in his mind had been answered. He rejoined Dr. Prescott.

"It's difficult to say what motive is back of her desire to have the finger amputated," he said musingly. "I could perhaps venture a conjecture but if the matter is of no importance to you beyond mere curiosity I should not like to do so. Within a few months from now, I daresay, important developments will result and I should like to find out something more about her. That I can do when she returns to wherever she is stopping in the city. I'll 'phone to Mr. Hatch and have him ascertain for me where she goes, her name and other things which may throw a light on the matter."

"He will follow her?"

"Yes, precisely. Now we only seem to know two facts in connection with her. First, she is English."

"Yes," Dr. Prescott agreed. "Her accent, her appearance, everything about her suggests that."

"And the second fact is of no consequence at the moment," resumed The Thinking Machine. "Let me use your 'phone please."

Hutchinson Hatch, reporter, was talking.

"When the young woman left Dr. Prescott's, she took the cab which had been ordered for her and told the driver to go ahead until she stopped him. I got a good look at her, by the way. I managed to pass just as she entered the cab and walking on down got into another cab, which was waiting for me. Her cab drove for three or four blocks aimlessly, and finally stopped. The driver stooped down as if to listen to someone inside, and my cab passed. Then the other cab turned across a side street and after going eight or ten blocks, pulled up in front of an apartment house. The young woman got out and went inside. Her cab went away. Inside I found out that she was Mrs. Frederick Chevedon Morey. She came there last Tuesday—this is Friday—with her husband, and they engaged——"

"Yes, I knew she had a husband," interrupted The Thinking Machine.

"——engaged apartments for three months. When I had learned

this much I remembered your instructions as to steamers from Europe landing on the day they took apartments or possibly a day or so before. I was just going out when Mrs. Morey stepped out of the elevator and preceded me to the door. She had changed her clothing and wore a different hat.

"It didn't seem to be necessary then to find out where she was going, for I knew I could find her when I wanted to, so I went down and made inquiries at the steamship offices. I found, after a great deal of work, that none of the three steamers which arrived the day the apartments were rented had brought a Mr. and Mrs. Morey, but a steamer on the day before had brought a Mr. and Mrs. David Girardeau from Liverpool. Mrs. Girardeau answered Mrs. Morey's description to the minutest detail, even to the gown she wore when she left the steamer. It was the same gown she wore when she left Dr. Prescott's after the operation."

That was all. The Thinking Machine sat with his enormous yellow head pillowed against a high-backed chair and his long slender fingers pressed tip to tip. He asked no questions and made no comment for a long time, then:

"About how many minutes was it from the time she entered the house until she came out again?"

"Not more than ten or fifteen," was the reply. "I was still talking casually to the people down stairs trying to find out something about her."

"What do they pay for their apartment?" asked the scientist, irrelevantly.

"Three hundred dollars a month."

The Thinking Machine's squint eyes were fixed immovably on a small discolored spot on the ceiling of his laboratory.

"Whatever else may develop in this matter, Mr. Hatch," he said after a time, "we must admit that we have met a woman with extraordinary courage—nerve, I daresay you'd call it. When Mrs. Morey left Dr. Prescott's operating room, she was so ill and weak from the shock that she could hardly stand, and now you tell me she changed her dress and went out immediately after she returned home."

"Well, of course——" Hatch said, apologetically.

"In that event," resumed the scientist, "we must assume also that the matter is one of the utmost importance to her, and yet the nature of the case had led me to believe that it might be months, perhaps, before there would be any particular development in it."

"What? How?" asked the reporter.

"The final development doesn't seem, from what I know, to belong on this side of the ocean at all," explained The Thinking Machine. "I imagine it is a case for Scotland Yard. The problem of course is: What made it necessary for her to get rid of that finger? If we admit her sanity, we can count the possible answers to this question on one hand, and at least three of these answers take the case back to England." He paused. "By the way, was Mrs. Morey's hand bound up in the same way when you saw her the second time?"

"Her left hand was in a muff," explained the reporter. "I couldn't see, but it seems to me that she wouldn't have had time to change the manner of its dressing."

"It's extraordinary," commented the scientist. He arose and paced back and forth across the room. "Extraordinary," he repeated. "One can't help but admire the fortitude of women under certain circumstances, Mr. Hatch. I think perhaps this particular case had better be called to the attention of Scotland Yard, but first I think it would be best for you to call on the Moreys tomorrow—you can find some pretext—and see what you can learn about them. You are an ingenious young man—I'll leave it all to you."

Hatch did call at the Morey apartments on the morrow, but under circumstances which were not at all what he expected. He went there with Detective Mallory, and Detective Mallory went there in a cab at full speed because the manager of the apartment house had 'phoned that Mrs. Frederick Chevedon Morey had been found murdered in her apartments. The detective ran up two flights of stairs and blundered, heavy-footed into the rooms, and there he paused in the presence of death.

The body of the woman lay on the floor and some one had mercifully covered it with a cloth from the bed. Detective Mallory drew the covering down from over the face and Hatch stared with a feeling of awe at the beautiful countenance which had, on the day before, been so radiant with life. Now it was distorted into an expression of awful agony and the limbs were drawn up convulsively. The mark of the murderer was at the white, exquisitely rounded throat—great black bruises where powerful, merciless fingers had sunk deeply into the soft flesh.

A physician in the house had preceded the police. After one glance at the woman and a swift, comprehensive look about the room Detective Mallory turned to him inquiringly.

"She has been dead for several hours," the doctor volunteered, "possibly since early last night. It appears that some virulent, burning poison was administered and then she was choked. I gather this from an examination of her mouth."

These things were readily to be seen; also it was plainly evident for many reasons that the finger marks at the throat were those of a man, but each step beyond these obvious facts only served further to bewilder the investigators. First was the statement of the night elevator boy.

"Mr. and Mrs. Morey left here last night about eleven o'clock," he said. "I know because I telephoned for a cab, and later brought them down from the third floor. They went into the manager's office leaving two suit cases in the hall. When they came out I took the suit cases to a cab that was waiting. They got in it and drove away."

"When did they return?" inquired the detective.

"They didn't return, sir," responded the boy. "I was on duty until six o'clock this morning. It just happened that no one came in after they went out until I was off duty at six."

The detective turned to the physician again.

"Then she couldn't have been dead since early last night," he said.

"She has been dead for several hours—at least twelve, possibly longer," said the physician firmly. "There's no possible argument about that."

The detective stared at him scornfully for an instant, then looked at the manager of the house.

"What was said when Mr. and Mrs. Morey entered your office last night?" he asked. "Were you there?"

"I was there, yes," was the reply. "Mr. Morey explained that they had been called away for a few days unexpectedly and left the keys of the apartment with me. That was all that was said; I saw the elevator boy take the suit cases out for them as they went to the cab."

"How did it come, then, if you knew they were away that some one entered here this morning, and so found the body?"

"I discovered the body myself," replied the manager. "There was some electric wiring to be done in here and I thought their absence would be a good time for it. I came up to see about it and saw—that."

He glanced at the covered body with a little shiver and a grimace. Detective Mallory was deeply thoughtful for several minutes.

"The woman is here and she's dead," he said finally. "If she is here, she came back here, dead or alive last night between the time she went out with her husband and the time her body was found this morning. Now that's an absolute fact. But *how* did she come here?"

Of the three employees of the apartment house only the elevator boy on duty had not spoken. Now he spoke because the detective glared at him fiercely.

"I didn't see either Mr. or Mrs. Morey come in this morning," he explained hastily. "Nobody came in at all except the postman and some delivery wagon drivers up to the time the body was found."

Again Detective Mallory turned on the manager.

"Does any window of this apartment open on a fire escape?" he demanded.

"Yes—this way."

They passed through the short hallway to the back. Both the windows were locked on the inside, so it appeared that even if the woman had been brought into the room that way, the windows would not have been fastened unless her murderer went out of the house the front way. When Detective Mallory reached this stage of the investigation, he sat down and stared from one to the other of the silent little party as if he considered the entire matter some affair which they had perpetrated to annoy him.

Hutchison Hatch started to say something, then thought better of it and turning, went to the telephone below. Within a few minutes The Thinking Machine stepped out of a cab in front and paused in the lower hall long enough to listen to the facts developed. There was a perfect network of wrinkles in the dome-like brow when the reporter concluded.

"It's merely a transfer of the final development in the affair from England to this country," he said enigmatically. "Please 'phone for Dr. Prescott to come here immediately."

He went on to the Morey apartments. With only a curt nod for Detective Mallory, the only one of the small party who knew him, he proceeded to the body of the dead woman and squinted down without a trace of emotion into the white pallid face. After a moment he dropped on his knees beside the inert body and examined the mouth and the finger marks about the white throat.

"Carbolic acid and strangulation," he remarked tersely to Detective Mallory who was leaning over watching him with something of hopeful eagerness in his stolid face. The Thinking Machine glanced past him to the manager of the house. "Mr. Morey is a powerful, athletic man in appearance?" he asked.

"Oh, no," was the reply. "He's short and slight, only a little larger than you are."

The scientist squinted aggressively at the manager as if the description were not quite what he expected. Then the slightly puzzled expression passed.

"Oh, I see," he remarked. "Played the piano." This was not a question; it was a statement.

"Yes, a great deal," was the reply, "so much so in fact that twice we had complaints from other persons in the house despite the fact that they had been here only a few days."

"Of course," mused the scientist abstractedly. "Of course. Perhaps Mrs. Morey did not play at all?"

"I believe she told me she did not."

The Thinking Machine drew down the thin cloth which had been thrown over the body and glanced at the left hand.

"Dear me! Dear me!" he exclaimed suddenly, and he arose. "Dear me!" he repeated. "That's the ——" He turned to the manager and the two elevator boys. "This is Mrs. Morey beyond any question?"

The answer was a chorus of affirmation accompanied by some startling facial expressions.

"Did Mr. and Mrs. Morey employ any servants?"

"No," was the reply. "They had their meals in the café below most of the time. There is no housekeeping in these apartments at all."

"How many persons live in the building?"

"A hundred, I should say."

"There is a great deal of passing to and fro, then?"

"Certainly. It was rather unusual that so few persons passed in and out last night and this morning, and certainly Mrs. Morey and her husband were not among them, if that's what you're trying to find out."

The Thinking Machine glanced at the physician who was standing by silently.

"How long do you make it that she's been dead?" he asked.

"At least twelve hours," replied the physician. "Possibly longer."

"Yes, nearer fourteen, I imagine."

Abruptly he left the group and walked through the apartment and back again slowly. As he re-entered the room where the body lay, the door from the hall opened and Dr. Prescott entered, followed by Hutchinson Hatch. The Thinking Machine led the surgeon straight to the body and drew the cloth down from the face. Dr. Prescott started back with an exclamation of astonishment, recognition.

"There's no doubt about it at all in your mind?" inquired the scientist.

"Not the slightest," replied Dr. Prescott positively. "It's the same woman."

"Yet, look here!"

With a quick movement The Thinking Machine drew down the cloth still more. Dr. Prescott together with those who had no idea of what to expect, peered down at the body. After one glance the surgeon dropped on his knees and examined closely the dead left hand. The forefinger was off at the first joint. Dr. Prescott stared, stared incredulously. After a moment his eyes left the maimed hand and settled again on her face.

"I have never seen—never dreamed—of such a startling——" he began.

"That settles it all, of course," interrupted The Thinking Machine. "It solves and proves the problem at once. Now, Mr. Mallory, if we can go to your office or some place where we will be undisturbed I will——"

"But who killed her?" demanded the detective abruptly.

"Let us find a quiet place," said The Thinking Machine in his usual irritable manner.

Detective Mallory, Dr. Prescott, The Thinking Machine, Hutchinson Hatch and the apartment house physician were seated in the front room of the Morey apartments with all doors closed against prying, inquisitive eyes. At the scientist's request Dr. Prescott repeated the circumstances leading up to the removal of a woman's left forefinger, and there The Thinking Machine took up the story.

"Suppose, Mr. Mallory," and the scientist turned to the detective, "a woman should walk into *your* office and say she must have a finger cut off, what would you think?"

"I'd think she was crazy," was the prompt reply.

"Naturally, in your position," The Thinking Machine went on, "you are acquainted with many strange happenings. Wouldn't this one instantly suggest something to you? Something that was to happen months off?"

Detective Mallory considered it wisely, but was silent.

"Well, here," declared The Thinking Machine. "A woman whom we now know to be Mrs. Morey wanted her finger cut off. It instantly suggested three, four, five, a dozen possibilities. Of course, only one, or possibly two in combination, could be true. Therefore which one? A little logic now to prove that two and two always make four—not *some* times but *all* the time.

"Naturally the first supposition was insanity. We pass that as absurd on its face. Then disease—a taint of leprosy perhaps which had been visible on the left forefinger. I tested for that, and that was eliminated. Three strong reasons for desiring the finger off, either of which is strongly probable, remained. The fact that the woman was unmistakably English was obvious. From the mark of a wedding ring on her glove and a corresponding mark on her finger—she wore no such ring—we could safely surmise that she was married. These were the two first facts I learned. Substantiative evidence that she was married and not a widow came partly from her extreme youth and the lack of mourning in her attire.

"Then Mr. Hatch followed her, learned her name, where she lived and later the fact that she had arrived with her husband on a steamer a day or so before they took apartments here. This was proof that she was English, and proof that she had a husband. They came over on the steamer as Mr. and Mrs. David Girardeau—here they were Mr. and Mrs. Frederick Chevedon Morey. Why this difference in name? The circumstance in itself pointed to irregularity—crime committed or contemplated. Other things made me think it was merely contemplated and that it could be prevented; for then absence of every fact gave me no intimation that there would be murder. Then came the murder presumably of—Mrs. Morey?"

"Isn't it Mrs. Morey?" demanded the detective.

"Mr. Hatch recognized the woman as the one he had followed, I recognized her as the one on which there had been an operation, Dr. Prescott also recognized her," continued The Thinking Machine. "To convince myself, after I had found the manner of death, that it was the woman, I looked at her left hand. I found that the forefinger was gone—it had been removed by a skilled surgeon at the first joint. And this fact instantly showed me that the dead woman was not Mrs. Morey at all, but somebody else; and incidentally cleared up the entire affair."

"How?" demanded the detective. "I thought you just said that you had helped cut off her forefinger?"

"Dr. Prescott and I cut off that finger yesterday," replied The Thinking Machine calmly. "The finger of the dead woman had been cut off months, perhaps years, ago."

There was blank amazement on Detective Mallory's face, and Hatch was staring straight into the squint eyes of the scientist. Vaguely, as through a mist, he was beginning to account for many things which had been hitherto inexplicable.

"The perfectly healed wound on the hand eliminated every possibility but one," The Thinking Machine resumed. "Previously I had been informed that Mrs. Morey did not—or said she did not—play the piano. I had seen the bare possibility of an immense insurance on her hands, and some trick to defraud the insurance company by marring one. Of course, against this was the fact that she had offered to pay a large sum for the operation; that their expenses here must have been enormous, so I was beginning to doubt the tenability of this supposition. The fact that the dead woman's finger was off removed that possibility completely, as it also removed the possibility of a crime of some sort in which there might have been left behind a tell-tale print of that forefinger. If there had been a serious crime with the trace of the finger as evidence, its removal would have been necessary to her.

"Then the one thing remained—that is that Mrs. Morey or whatever her name is—was in a conspiracy with her husband to get possession of certain properties, perhaps a title—remember she is English—by sacrificing that finger so that identification might be in accordance with the description of an heir whom she was to impersonate. We may well believe that she was provided with the necessary documentary evidence, and we know conclusively—we don't conjecture but we *know*—that the dead woman in there is the woman whose rights were to have been stolen by the so-called Mrs. Morey."

"But that is Mrs. Morey, isn't it?" demanded the detective again.

"No," was the sharp retort. "The perfect resemblance to Mrs. Morey and the finger removed long ago makes that clear. There is, I imagine, a relationship between them—perhaps they are cousins. I can hardly believe they are twins because the necessity, then of one impersonating the other to obtain either money or a title, would not have existed so palpably, although it is possible that Mrs. Morey, if disinherited or disowned, would have resorted to such a course."

There was silence for several minutes. Each member of the little group was turning over the stated facts mentally.

"But how did she come here—like this?" Hatch inquired.

"You remember, Mr. Hatch, when you followed Mrs. Morey here you told me she dressed again and went out?" asked the scientist in turn. "It was not Mrs. Morey you saw then—she was ill and I knew it from the operation—it was Miss Rossmore. The manager says a hundred persons live in this house—that there is a great deal of passing in and out. Can't you see that when there is such a startling resemblance Miss Rossmore could pass in and out at will and always be mistaken for Mrs. Morey? That no one would ever notice the difference?"

"But who killed her?" asked Detective Mallory, curiously. "How? Why?"

"Morey killed her," said The Thinking Machine flatly. "How did he kill her? We can fairly presume that first he tricked her into drinking the acid, then perhaps she was screaming with the pain of it, and he choked her to death. I imagined first he was a large, powerful man, because his grip on her throat was so powerful that he ruptured the jugular inside; but instead of that he plays the piano a great deal, which would give him the hand-power to choke her. And why? We can suppose only that it was because she had in some way learned of their purpose. That would have established the motive. The crowning delicacy of the affair was Morey's act in leaving his keys with the manager here. He did not anticipate that the apartments would be entered for several days—after they were safely away—while there was a chance that if neither of them had been seen here and their disappearance was unexplained the rooms would have been opened to ascertain why. That is all, I think."

"Except to catch Morey and his wife," said the detective grimly.

"Easily done," said The Thinking Machine. "I imagine, if this murder is kept out of the newspapers for a couple of hours you can find them about to sail for Europe. Suppose you try the line they came over on?"

It was just three hours later that the accused man and wife were taken prisoner. They had just engaged passage on the steamer which sailed at half past four o'clock.

Their trial was a famous one and resulted in conviction after an astonishing story of an attempt to seize an estate and title belonging rightfully to a Miss Evelyn Rossmore who had mysteriously disappeared years before, and was identified with the dead woman.

THE MOTOR BOAT

Captain Hank Barber, master mariner, gripped the bow-rail of the *Liddy Ann* and peered off through the semi-fog of the early morning at a dark streak slashing along through the gray-green waters. It was a motor boat of long, graceful lines; and a single figure, that of a man, sat upright at her helm staring uncompromisingly ahead. She nosed through a roller, staggered a little, righted herself and sped on as a sheet of spray swept over her. The helmsman sat motionless, heedless of the stinging splash of wind-driven water in his face.

"She sure is a-goin' some," remarked Captain Hank, reflectively. "By Ginger! If she keeps it up into Boston Harbor, she won't stop this side o' the Public Gardens."

Captain Hank watched the boat curiously until she was swallowed up, lost in the mist, then turned to his own affairs. He was a couple of miles out of Boston Harbor, going in; it was six o'clock of a gray morning. A few minutes after the disappearance of the motor boat Captain Hank's attention was attracted by the hoarse shriek of a whistle two hundred yards away. He dimly traced through the mist the gigantic lines of a great vessel—it seemed to be a ship of war.

It was only a few minutes after Captain Hank lost sight of the motor boat that she was again sighted, this time as she flashed into Boston Harbor at full speed. She fled past, almost under the prow of a pilot boat, going out, and was hailed. At the mess table later the pilot's man on watch made a remark about her.

"Goin'! Well, wasn't she though! Never saw one thing pass so close to another in my life without scrubbin' the paint offen it. She was so close up I could spit in her, and when I spoke the feller didn't even look up—just kept a-goin'. I told *him* a few things that was good for his soul."

Inside Boston Harbor the motor boat performed a miracle. Pursuing a course which was singularly erratic and at a speed more than dangerous she reeled on through the surge of the sea regardless alike of fog, the proximity of other vessels and the heavy wash from larger craft. Here she narrowly missed a tug; there she skimmed by a slow-moving tramp and a warning shout was raised; a fisherman swore at her as only a fisherman can. And finally when she passed into a clear space, seemingly headed for a dock at top speed, she was the most unanimously damned craft that ever came into Boston Harbor.

"Guess that's a through boat," remarked an aged salt, facetiously as he gazed at her from a dock. "If that durned fool don't take some o' the speed offen her she'll go through all right—wharf an' all."

Still the man in the boat made no motion; the whizz of her motor, plainly heard in a sudden silence, was undiminished. Suddenly the tumult of warning was renewed. Only a chance would prevent a smash. Then Big John Dawson appeared on the string piece of the dock. Big John had a voice that was noted from Newfoundland to Norfolk for its depth and width, and possessed objurgatory powers which were at once the awe and admiration of the fishing fleet.

"You ijit!" he bellowed at the impassive helmsman. "Shut off that power an' throw yer hellum."

There was no response; the boat came on directly toward the dock where Big John and his fellows were gathered. The fishermen and loungers saw that a crash was coming and scattered from the string piece.

"The *durned* fool," said Big John, resignedly.

Then came the crash, the rending of timbers, and silence save for the grinding whir of the motor. Big John ran to the end of the wharf and peered down. The speed of the motor had driven the boat half way upon a float which careened perilously. The man had been thrown forward and lay huddled up face downward and motionless on the float. The dirty water lapped at him greedily.

Big John was the first man on the float. He crept cautiously to the huddled figure and turned it face upward. He gazed for an instant into wide staring eyes then turned to the curious ones peering down from the dock.

"No wonder he didn't stop," he said in an awed tone. "The durned fool is dead."

Willing hands gave aid and after a minute the lifeless figure lay on the dock. It was that of a man in uniform—the uniform of a foreign navy. He was apparently forty-five years old, large and powerful of frame with the sun-browned face of a seaman. The jet black of mustache and goatee was startling against the dead color of the face. The hair was tinged with gray; and on the back of the left hand was a single letter—"D"—tattooed in blue.

"He's French," said Big John authoritatively, "an' that's the uniform of a Cap'n in the French Navy." He looked puzzled a moment as he stared at the figure. "An' they ain't been a French man-o'-war in Boston Harbor for six months."

After awhile the police came and with them Detective Mallory, the big man of the Bureau of Criminal Investigation; and finally Dr. Clough, Medical Examiner. While the detective questioned the fishermen and those who had witnessed the crash, Dr. Clough examined the body.

"An autopsy will be necessary," he announced as he arose.

"How long has he been dead?" asked the detective.

"Eight or ten hours, I should say. The cause of death doesn't appear. There is no shot or knife wound so far as I can see."

Detective Mallory closely examined the dead man's clothing. There was no name or tailor mark; the linen was new; the name of the maker of the shoes had been ripped out with a knife. There was nothing in the pockets, not a piece of paper or even a vagrant coin.

Then Detective Mallory turned his attention to the boat. Both hull and motor were of French manufacture. Long, deep scratches on each side showed how the name had been removed. Inside the boat the detective saw something white and picked it up. It was a handkerchief—a woman's handkerchief, with the initials "E. M. B." in a corner.

"Ah, a woman's in it!" he soliloquized.

Then the body was removed and carefully secluded from the prying eyes of the press. Thus no picture of the dead man appeared. Hutchinson Hatch, reporter, and others asked many questions. Detective Mallory hinted vaguely at international questions—the dead man was a French officer, he said, and there might be something back of it.

"I can't tell you all of it," he said wisely, "but my theory is complete. It is murder. The victim was captain of a French man-of-war. His body was placed in a motor boat, possibly a part of the fittings of the warship and the boat set adrift. I can say no more."

"Your theory is complete then," Hatch remarked casually, "except the name of the man, the manner of death, the motive, the name of his ship, the presence of the handkerchief and the precise reason why the body should be disposed of in this fashion instead of being cast into the sea."

The detective snorted. Hatch went away to make some inquiries on his own account. Within half a dozen hours he had satisfied himself by telegraph that no French war craft had been within five hundred miles of Boston for six months. Thus the mystery grew deeper; a thousand questions to which there seemed no answer arose.

At this point, the day following the events related, the problem of the motor boat came to the attention of Professor Augustus S. F. X. Van

Dusen, The Thinking Machine. The scientist listened closely but petulantly to the story Hatch told.

"Has there been an autopsy yet?" he asked at last.

"It is set for eleven o'clock today," replied the reporter. "It is now after ten."

"I shall attend it," said the scientist.

Medical Examiner Clough welcomed the eminent Professor Van Dusen's proffer of assistance in his capacity of M.D., while Hatch and other reporters impatiently cooled their toes on the curb. In two hours the autopsy had been completed. The Thinking Machine amused himself by studying the insignia on the dead man's uniform, leaving it to Dr. Clough to make a startling statement to the press. The man had not been murdered; he had died of heart failure. There was no poison in the stomach, nor was there a knife or pistol wound.

Then the inquisitive press poured in a flood of questions. Who had scratched off the name of the boat? Dr. Clough didn't know. Why had it been scratched off? Still he didn't know. How did it happen that the name of the maker of the shoes had been ripped out? He shrugged his shoulders. What did the handkerchief have to do with it? Really he couldn't conjecture. Was there any inkling of the dead man's identity? Not so far as he knew. Any scar on the body which might lead to identification? No.

Hatch made a few mental comments on officials in general and skilfully steered The Thinking Machine away from the other reporters.

"Did that man die of heart failure?" he asked, flatly.

"He did not," was the curt reply. "It was poison."

"But the Medical Examiner specifically stated that there was no poison in the stomach," persisted the reporter.

The scientist did not reply. Hatch struggled with and suppressed a desire to ask more questions. On reaching home the scientist's first act was to consult an encyclopedia. After several minutes he turned to the reporter with an inscrutable face.

"Of course the idea of a natural death in this case is absurd," he said, shortly. "Every fact is against it. Now, Mr. Hatch, please get for me all the local and New York newspapers of the day the body was found—not the day after. Send or bring them to me, then come again at five this afternoon."

"But—but——" Hatch blurted.

"I can say nothing until I know all the facts," interrupted The Thinking Machine.

Hatch personally delivered the specified newspapers into the hands of The Thinking Machine—this man who never read newspapers—and went away. It was an afternoon of agony; an agony of impatience.

Promptly at five o'clock he was ushered into Professor Van Dusen's laboratory. The scientist sat half smothered in newspapers, and popped up out of the heap aggressively.

"It was murder, Mr. Hatch," he exclaimed, suddenly. "Murder by an extraordinary method."

"Who—who is the man? How was he killed?" asked Hatch.

"His name is——" the scientist began, then paused. "I presume your office has the book *Who's Who In America*? Please 'phone and ask them to give you the record of Langham Dudley."

"Is he the dead man?" Hatch demanded quickly.

"I don't know," was the reply.

Hatch went to the telephone. Ten minutes later he returned to find The Thinking Machine dressed to go out.

"Langham Dudley is a ship owner, fifty-one years old," the reporter read from notes he had taken. "He was once a sailor before the mast and later became a ship owner in a small way. He was successful in his small undertakings and for fifteen years has been a millionaire. He has a certain social position, partly through his wife whom he married a year and a half ago. She was Edith Marston Belding, a daughter of the famous Belding family. He has an estate on the North Shore."

"Very good," commented the scientist. "Now we will find out something about how this man was killed."

At North Station they took train for a small place on the North Shore, thirty-five miles from Boston. There The Thinking Machine made some inquiries and finally they entered a lumbersome carry-all. After a drive of half an hour through the dark they saw the lights of what seemed to be a pretentious country place. Somewhere off to the right Hatch heard the roar of the restless ocean.

"Wait for us," commanded The Thinking Machine as the carry-all stopped.

The Thinking Machine ascended the steps, followed by Hatch, and rang. After a minute or so the door was opened and the light flooded out. Standing before them was a Japanese—a man of indeterminate age with the graven face of his race.

"Is Mr. Dudley in?" asked The Thinking Machine.

"He has not that pleasure," replied the Japanese, and Hatch smiled at the queerly turned phrase.

"Mrs. Dudley?" asked the scientist.

"Mrs. Dudley is attiring herself in clothing," replied the Japanese. "If you will be pleased to enter."

The Thinking Machine handed him a card and was shown into a reception room. The Japanese placed chairs for them with courteous precision and disappeared. After a short pause there was a rustle of silken skirts on the stairs, and a woman—Mrs. Dudley—entered. She was not pretty; she was stunning rather, tall, of superb figure and crowned with a glory of black hair.

"Mr. Van Dusen?" she asked as she glanced at the card.

The Thinking Machine bowed low, albeit awkwardly. Mrs. Dudley sank down on a couch and the two men resumed their seats. There was a little pause; Mrs. Dudley broke the silence at last.

"Well, Mr. Van Dusen, if you——" she began.

"You have not seen a newspaper for several days?" asked The Thinking Machine, abruptly.

"No," she replied, wonderingly, almost smiling. "Why?"

"Can you tell me just where your husband is?"

The Thinking Machine squinted at her in that aggressive way which was habitual. A quick flush crept into her face, and grew deeper at the sharp scrutiny. Inquiry lay in her eyes.

"I don't know," she replied at last. "In Boston, I presume."

"You haven't seen him since the night of the ball?"

"No. I think it was half past one o'clock that night."

"Is his motor boat here?"

"Really, I don't know. I presume it is. May I ask the purpose of this questioning?"

The Thinking Machine squinted hard at her for half a minute. Hatch was uncomfortable, half resentful even, at the agitation of the woman and the sharp, cold tone of his companion.

"On the night of the ball," the scientist went on, passing the question, "Mr. Dudley cut his left arm just above the wrist. It was only a slight wound. A piece of court plaster was put on it. Do you know if he put it on himself? If not, who did?"

"I put it on," replied Mrs. Dudley, unhesitatingly, wonderingly.

"And whose court plaster was it?"

"Mine—some I had in my dressing room. Why?"

The scientist arose and paced across the floor, glancing once out the hall door. Mrs. Dudley looked at Hatch inquiringly and was about to speak when The Thinking Machine stopped beside her and placed his slim fingers on her wrist. She did not resent the action; was only curious if one might judge from her eyes.

"Are you prepared for a shock?" the scientist asked.

"What is it?" she demanded in sudden terror. "This suspense——"

"Your husband is dead—murdered—poisoned!" said the scientist with sudden brutality. His fingers still lay on her pulse. "The court plaster which you put on his arm and which came from your room was covered with a virulent poison which was instantly transfused into his blood."

Mrs. Dudley did not start or scream. Instead she stared up at The Thinking Machine a moment, her face became pallid, a little shiver passed over her. Then she fell back on the couch in a dead faint.

"Good!" remarked The Thinking Machine complacently. And then as Hatch started up suddenly: "Shut that door," he commanded.

The reporter did so. When he turned back, his companion was leaning over the unconscious woman. After a moment he left her and went to a window where he stood looking out. As Hatch watched he saw the color coming back into Mrs. Dudley's face. At last she opened her eyes.

"Don't get hysterical," The Thinking Machine directed calmly. "I know you had nothing whatever to do with your husband's death. I want only a little assistance to find out who killed him."

"Oh, my God!" exclaimed Mrs. Dudley. "Dead! Dead!"

Suddenly tears leaped from her eyes and for several minutes the two men respected her grief. When at last she raised her face her eyes were red, but there was a rigid expression about the mouth.

"If I can be of any service——" she began.

"Is this the boat house I see from this window?" asked The Thinking Machine. "That long, low building with the light over the door?"

"Yes," replied Mrs. Dudley.

"You say you don't know if the motor boat is there now?"

"No, I don't."

"Will you ask your Japanese servant, and if he doesn't know, let him go see, please?"

Mrs. Dudley arose and touched an electric button. After a moment the Japanese appeared at the door.

"Osaka, do you know if Mr. Dudley's motor boat is in the boat house?" she asked.

"No, honorable lady."

"Will you go yourself and see?"

Osaka bowed low and left the room, closing the door gently behind him. The Thinking Machine again crossed to the window and sat down staring out into the night. Mrs. Dudley asked questions, scores of them, and he answered them in order until she knew the details of the finding of her husband's body—that is, the details the public knew. She was interrupted by the reappearance of Osaka.

"I do not find the motor boat in the house, honorable lady."

"That is all," said the scientist.

Again Osaka bowed and retired.

"Now, Mrs. Dudley," resumed The Thinking Machine almost gently, "we know your husband wore a French naval costume at the masked ball. May I ask what you wore?"

"It was a Queen Elizabeth costume," replied Mrs. Dudley, "very heavy with a long train."

"And if you could give me a photograph of Mr. Dudley?"

Mrs. Dudley left the room an instant and returned with a cabinet photograph. Hatch and the scientist looked at it together; it was unmistakably the man in the motor boat.

"You can do nothing yourself," said The Thinking Machine at last, and he moved as if to go. "Within a few hours we will have the guilty person. You may rest assured that your name will be in no way brought into the matter unpleasantly."

Hatch glanced at his companion; he thought he detected a sinister note in the soothing voice, but the face expressed nothing. Mrs. Dudley ushered them into the hall; Osaka stood at the front door. They passed out and the door closed behind them.

Hatch started down the steps but The Thinking Machine stopped at the door and tramped up and down. The reporter turned back in astonishment. In the dim reflected light he saw the scientist's finger raised, enjoining silence, then saw him lean forward suddenly with his ear pressed to the door. After a little he rapped gently. The door was opened by Osaka, who obeyed a beckoning motion of the scientist's hand and came out. Silently he was led off the veranda into the yard; he appeared in no way surprised.

"Your master, Mr. Dudley, has been murdered," declared The Thinking Machine quietly, to Osaka. "We know that Mrs. Dudley killed him," he went on as Hatch stared, "but I have told her she is not suspected. We are not officers and cannot arrest her. Can you go with us to Boston, without the knowledge of anyone here and tell what you know of the quarrel between husband and wife to the police?"

Osaka looked placidly into the eager face.

"I had the honor to believe that the circumstances would not be recognized," he said finally. "Since you know, I will go."

"We will drive down a little way and wait for you."

The Japanese disappeared into the house again. Hatch was too astounded to speak, but followed The Thinking Machine into the carry-all. It drove away a hundred yards and stopped. After a few minutes an impalpable shadow came toward them through the night. The scientist peered out as it came up.

"Osaka?" he asked softly.

"Yes."

An hour later the three men were on a train, Boston bound. Once comfortably settled the scientist turned to the Japanese.

"Now if you will please tell me just what happened the night of the ball?" he asked, "and the incidents leading up to the disagreement between Mr. and Mrs. Dudley?"

"He drank elaborately," Osaka explained reluctantly, in his quaint English, "and when drinking he was brutal to the honorable lady. Twice with my own eyes I saw him strike her—once in Japan where I entered his service while they were on a wedding journey, and once here. On the night of the ball he was immeasurably intoxicated, and when he danced, he fell down to the floor. The honorable lady was chagrined and angry—she had been angry before. There was some quarrel which I am not comprehensive of. They had been widely divergent for several months. It was, of course, not prominent in the presence of others."

"And the cut on his arm where the court plaster was applied?" asked the scientist. "Just how did he get that?"

"It was when he fell down," continued the Japanese. "He reached to embrace a carved chair and the carved wood cut his arm. I assisted him to his feet and the honorable lady sent me to her room to get court plaster. I acquired it from her dressing table and she placed it on the cut."

"That makes the evidence against her absolutely conclusive," remarked The Thinking Machine, as if finally. There was a little pause, and then: "Do you happen to know just how Mrs. Dudley placed the body in the boat?"

"I have not that honor," said Osaka. "Indeed I am not comprehensive of anything that happened after the court plaster was put on except that Mr. Dudley was affected some way and went out of the house. Mrs. Dudley, too, was not in the ball room for ten minutes or so afterwards."

Hutchinson Hatch stared frankly into the face of The Thinking Machine; there was nothing to be read there. Still deeply thoughtful Hatch heard the brakeman bawl "Boston" and mechanically followed the scientist and Osaka out of the station into a cab. They were driven immediately to Police Headquarters. Detective Mallory was just about to go home when they entered his office.

"It may enlighten you, Mr. Mallory," announced the scientist coldly, "to know that the man in the motor boat was not a French naval officer who died of natural causes—he was Langham Dudley, a millionaire ship owner. He was murdered. It just happens that I know the person who did it."

The detective arose in astonishment and stared at the slight figure before him inquiringly; he knew the man too well to dispute any assertion he might make.

"Who is the murderer?" he asked.

The Thinking Machine closed the door and the spring lock clicked.

"That man there," he remarked calmly, turning on Osaka.

For one brief moment there was a pause and silence; then the detective advanced upon the Japanese with hand outstretched. The agile Osaka leapt suddenly, as a snake strikes; there was a quick, fierce struggle and Detective Mallory sprawled on the floor. There had been just a twist of the wrist—a trick of jiu jitsu—and Osaka had flung himself at the locked door. As he fumbled there, Hatch, deliberately and without compunction, raised a chair and brought it down on his head. Osaka sank down without a sound.

It was an hour before they brought him around again. Meanwhile the detective had patted and petted half a dozen suddenly acquired bruises, and had then searched Osaka. He found nothing to interest him save a small bottle. He uncorked it and started to smell it when The Thinking Machine snatched it away.

"You fool, that'll kill you!" he exclaimed.

Osaka sat, lashed hand and foot to a chair, in Detective Mallory's office—so placed by the detective for safe keeping. His face was no longer expressionless; there were fear and treachery and cunning there. So he listened, perforce, to the statement of the case by The Thinking Machine who leaned back in his chair, squinting steadily upward and with his long, slender fingers pressed together.

"Two and two make four, not *some* times but *all* the time," he began at last as if disputing some previous assertion. "As the figure 'two,' wholly disconnected from any other, gives small indication of a result, so is an isolated fact of little consequence. Yet that fact added to another, and the resulting fact added to a third, and so on, will give a final result. That result, if every fact is considered, *must* be correct. Thus any problem may be solved by logic; logic is inevitable.

"In this case the facts, considered singly, might have been compatible with either a natural death, suicide or murder—considered together they proved murder. The climax of this proof was the removal of the maker's name from the dead man's shoes, and a fact strongly contributory was the attempt to destroy the identity of the boat. A subtle mind lay back of it all."

"I so regarded it," said Detective Mallory. "I was confident of murder until the Medical Examiner——"

"We prove a murder," The Thinking Machine went on serenely. "The method? I was with Dr. Clough at the autopsy. There was no shot, or knife wound, no poison in the stomach. Knowing there was murder I sought further. Then I found the method in a slight, jagged wound on the left arm. It had been covered with court plaster. The heart showed constriction without apparent cause, and while Dr. Clough examined it I took off this court plaster. Its odor, an unusual one, told me that poison had been transfused into the blood through the wound. So two and two had made four.

"Then—what poison? A knowledge of botany aided me. I recognized faintly the trace of an odor of an herb which is not only indigenous to, but grows exclusively in Japan. Thus a Japanese poison. Analysis later in my laboratory proved it was a Japanese poison, virulent, and necessarily slow to act unless it is placed directly in an artery. The poison on the court plaster and that you took from Osaka is identical."

The scientist uncorked the bottle and permitted a single drop of a green liquid to fall on his handkerchief. He allowed a minute or more for evaporation then handed it to Detective Mallory who sniffed at it from a respectful distance. Then The Thinking Machine produced the bit of court plaster he had taken from the dead man's arm, and again the detective sniffed.

"The same," the scientist resumed as he touched a lighted match to the handkerchief and watched it crumble to ashes, "and so powerful that in its pure state mere inhalation is fatal. I permitted Dr. Clough to make public his opinion—heart failure—after the autopsy for obvious reasons. It would reassure the murderer for instance if he saw it printed, and besides Dudley did die from heart failure; the poison caused it.

"Next came identification. Mr. Hatch learned that no French warship had been within hundreds of miles of Boston for months. The one seen by Captain Barber might have been one of our own. This man was supposed to be a French naval officer, and had been dead less than eight hours. Obviously he did not come from a ship of his own country. Then from where?

"I know nothing of uniforms, yet I examined the insignia on the arms and shoulders closely after which I consulted my encyclopedia. I learned that while the uniform was more French than anything else, it was really the uniform of *no country*, because it was not correct. The insignia were mixed.

"Then what? There were several possibilities, among them a fancy dress ball was probable. Absolute accuracy would not be essential there. Where had there been a fancy dress ball? I trusted to the newspapers to tell me that. They did. A short dispatch from a place on the North Shore stated that on the night before the man was found dead there had been a fancy dress ball at the Langham Dudley estate.

"Now it is as necessary to remember *every* fact in solving a problem as it is to consider every figure in arithmetic. Dudley! Here was the 'D' tattooed on the dead man's hand. *Who's Who* showed that Langham Dudley married Edith Marston Belding. Here was the 'E. M. B.' on the handkerchief in the boat. Langham Dudley was a ship owner, had been a sailor, was a millionaire. Possibly this was his own boat built in France."

Detective Mallory was staring into the eyes of The Thinking Machine in frank admiration; Osaka to whom the narrative had thus far been impersonal, gazed, gazed as if fascinated. Hutchinson Hatch, reporter, was drinking in every word greedily.

"We went to the Dudley place," the scientist resumed after a moment. "This Japanese opened the door. Japanese poison! Two and two were still making four. But I was first interested in Mrs. Dudley. She showed no agitation and told me frankly that she placed the court plaster on her husband's arm, and that it came from her room. There was instantly a doubt as to her connection with the murder; her immediate frankness aroused it.

"Finally, with my hand on her pulse—which was normal—I told her as brutally as I could that her husband had been murdered. Her pulse jumped frightfully and as I told her the cause of death it wavered, weakened and she fainted. Now if she had known her husband was dead—even if she had killed him—a mere statement of his death would not have caused that pulse. Further I doubt if she could have disposed of her husband's body in the motor boat. He was a large man and the manner of her dress even, was against this. Therefore she was innocent.

"And then? The Japanese, Osaka, here. I could see the door of the boat house from the room where we were. Mrs. Dudley asked Osaka if Mr. Dudley's boat were in the house. He said he didn't know. Then she sent him to see. He returned and said the boat was not there, *yet he had not gone to the boat house at all.* Ergo, he knew the boat was not there. He may have learned it from another servant, still it was a point against him."

Again the scientist paused and squinted at the Japanese. For a moment Osaka withstood the gaze, then his eyes shifted and he moved uncomfortably.

"I tricked Osaka into coming here by a ludicrously simple expedient," The Thinking Machine went on steadily. "On the train I asked if he knew just how Mrs. Dudley got the body of her husband into the boat. Remember at this point he was not supposed to know that the body had been in a boat at all. He said he didn't know and by that very answer admitted that he knew the body had been placed in the boat. He knew because he put it there himself. He didn't merely throw it in the water because he had sense enough to know if the tide didn't take it out, it would rise, and possibly be found.

"After the slight injury Mr. Dudley evidently wandered out toward the boat house. The poison was working, and perhaps he fell. Then this man removed all identifying marks, even to the name in the shoes, put the body in the boat and turned on full power. He had a right to assume that the boat would be lost, or that the dead man would be thrown out. Wind and tide and a loose rudder brought it into Boston Harbor. I do not attempt to account for the presence of Mrs. Dudley's handkerchief in the boat. It might have gotten there in one of a hundred ways."

"How did you know husband and wife had quarrelled?" asked Hatch.

"Surmise to account for her not knowing where he was," replied The Thinking Machine. "If they had had a violent disagreement it was possible that he would have gone away without telling her, and she would not have been particularly worried, at least up to the time we saw her. As it was, she presumed he was in Boston; perhaps Osaka here gave her that impression?"

The Thinking Machine turned and stared at the Japanese curiously.

"Is that correct?" he asked.

Osaka did not answer.

"And the motive?" asked Detective Mallory, at last.

"Will you tell us just why you killed Mr. Dudley?" asked The Thinking Machine of the Japanese.

"I will not," exclaimed Osaka, suddenly. It was the first time he had spoken.

"It probably had to do with a girl in Japan," explained The Thinking Machine, easily. "The murder had been a long cherished project, such a one as revenge through love would have inspired."

It was a day or so later that Hutchinson Hatch called to inform The Thinking Machine that Osaka had confessed and had given the motive for the murder. It was not a nice story.

"One of the most astonishing things to me," Hatch added, "is the complete case of circumstantial evidence against Mrs. Dudley, beginning with the quarrel and leading to the application of the poison with her own hands. I believe she would have been convicted on the actual circumstantial evidence had you not shown conclusively that Osaka did it."

"Circumstantial fiddlesticks!" snapped The Thinking Machine. "I wouldn't convict a dog of stealing jam on circumstantial evidence alone, even if he had jam all over his nose." He squinted truculently at Hatch for a moment. "In the first place well behaved dogs don't eat jam," he added more mildly.

THE INTERRUPTED WIRELESS

Seven bells sounded. The door of the wireless telegraph office on the main deck of the transatlantic liner *Uranus* was opened quietly, and a man thrust his head out. One quick glance to his right, along the narrow, carpeted passage, showed it to be deserted; another glance to his left showed a young woman approaching, with steps made uncertain by the rolling and pitching of the ship. In one hand she carried a slip of paper, folded once. The man paused only to see this much, then withdrew his head and closed the door abruptly.

The young woman paused opposite the wireless office, and thoughtfully conned over something on the slip of paper. Finally she leaned against the wall, erased a word with a pencil, wrote in another, then laid a hand on the knob of the door as if to enter. The door was locked. She hesitated for an instant, then rapped. There was a pause, and she rapped the second time.

"What is it?" came a man's voice from inside.

"I wish to send a message," responded the young woman.

"Who is that?" came another query.

"It's Miss Bellingdame," was the impatient response. "I desire to get a wireless to a friend on the *Breslin* which has just been sighted to the north."

Again there was a pause. "It's impossible to send any message now," came the short, harsh answer at last. "It may not be possible to send it at all."

"Why?" demanded Miss Bellingdame. "It's a matter of the utmost importance. I must send it!"

"Can't be done—it's out of the question," came the positive, quick spoken answer. "There has been an—an accident."

Miss Bellingdame was silent for a moment, as she seemed to ponder a note of deep concern, excitement even, in the voice.

"Well, can't it be sent after the accident has been repaired?" she asked at last.

There was no answer.

"Is that Mr. Ingraham talking?" Miss Bellingdame demanded.

Still there was no answer. She remained there for a minute, perhaps, staring at the locked door, then turned and retraced her steps. A few minutes later she was reclining in a deck chair, gazing thoughtfully out over the treacherous, dimpling Atlantic with a troubled expression on her face.

At just about the moment she sat down, the telephone buzz in the Captain's cabin sounded, and Captain Deihl impatiently laid aside a remarkably promising pinochle hand to answer it.

"Captain Deihl?" came a short, sharp query over the wire.

"Yes."

"This is Mr. Tennell, sir. I'm in the wireless office. Can you come at once, and have some one send Dr. Maher?"

"What's the matter?" demanded the Captain gruffly.

"I can't very well tell you over the 'phone, sir," came the response; "but you and Dr. Maher are needed immediately."

With a slightly puzzled expression on his bronzed face, Captain Deihl turned to Dr. Maher, the ship's surgeon, who had been his opponent in the pinochle game and now sat staring idly out of the window.

"Tennell wants both of us down in the wireless office at once," the Captain explained. "He won't say what's the matter."

"Wants me?" inquired Dr. Maher. "Somebody hurt?"

"I don't know. Come along."

Captain Deihl led the way along the hurricane deck, down to the main deck, and along the narrow passage to the wireless office. The door was still locked. He rapped sharply, impatiently.

"Who's there?" came from inside.

"Captain Deihl. Open the door!"

The key turned in the lock, and First Officer Tennell's white face—white even beneath the deep tan—appeared.

"What's the matter, Mr. Tennell?" demanded the Captain brusquely.

"Please step inside, sir," and the first officer opened the door. "There's what's the matter!"

With a gesture the first officer indicated the corner of the cabin where the wireless operator's desk stood. Sitting before it, as if he had dropped back utterly exhausted, was the operator, Charles Ingraham. His head had fallen forward on his breast, and the arms hung straight down, flabbily. His back was toward them, and against the white of his shirt, just beneath the left arm, a heavy-handled knife showed. A thin line of scarlet dyed the shirt just below the knife handle.

Captain Deihl stood stockstill for one instant, then turning suddenly closed and locked the door behind him. Dr. Maher took two steps forward, wrested the knife from the wound with a slight effort, flung it on the floor, then dropped on his knees beside the chair.

"What is all this, Mr. Tennell?" demanded Captain Deihl at last.

"I don't know, sir," was the reply. "I found him like that."

Dr. Maher rose after a moment, with a hopeless shake of his head, and minutely examined the wound. It was a clean-cut incision; the knife had been driven in and allowed to remain. The blade had passed between the ribs and had reached the heart. Dr. Maher noted these things, then stooped and picked up the knife. It was a long, heavy, broad-bladed, dangerous looking weapon. After satisfying himself, the surgeon passed it to Captain Deihl.

"It was murder," he said tersely. "He could not have stabbed himself in that position. You keep the knife; it may be the only clue."

"Murder!" the Captain repeated involuntarily. "How long has—has he been dead?"

"Perhaps ten minutes—certainly not more than twenty," was the surgeon's reply. "The body is still warm, and the blood flows."

"Murder!" repeated Captain Deihl. "Who could have killed him? What could have been the motive?"

He stood staring at the knife silently for a time, then lifted two keen, inquisitive eyes to those of his first officer. Dr. Maher too was staring straight into Tennell's face, and slowly, under the sharp scrutiny, the blood mounted again to the tanned cheeks.

"What are your orders, sir?" inquired the first officer steadily.

"How long were you in this room, Tennell, before you called me?" asked Captain Deihl.

"Two or three minutes," was the reply. "I was in my cabin forward, preparing the dispatches which were to go ashore, according to your order, sir. The wireless was going then; for I could hear it. I noticed after a time that it stopped; so, having completed my dispatches, I brought them here directly. I found Mr. Ingraham just as you see him."

"H'm!" mused the Captain. He was still staring thoughtfully into the other's face. "Was the door locked?"

"No, sir. It was closed."

"And this knife, Mr. Tennell?" The Captain examined it again and then passed it to his first officer. "Do you know it? Have you ever seen it before?"

Without any apparent reason the first officer's face whitened again and he dropped down on the bench, with hands gripping each other fiercely. Dr. Maher was staring at him; Captain Deihl seemed surprised.

"You know whose knife it is then?" asked the Captain finally.

"Yes," and the first officer's head dropped forward. "It's mine!"

There was a long dead silence. The hands of the first officer were working nervously, with heavy fingers threading in and out. Dr. Maher turned away suddenly and idly fingered some papers on the operator's desk.

Captain Deihl's heavy face grew set and stern. "Did you kill him, Tennell?" he asked.

"No!" Tennell burst out. "No!"

"But it is your knife?"

"It would be useless for me to deny it, sir," replied the first officer, and he rose. "It was given to me by Mr. Forbes, the second officer, only a few weeks ago, and he could identify it instantly. I lost the knife yesterday, and last night—I shall ask you to corroborate this, sir—I posted a notice in the fo'c'sle offering a reward to anyone who should find it and return it to me."

Dr. Maher turned suddenly upon them. "And isn't it true, Mr. Tennell," he demanded, "that you and Ingraham had some—some serious disagreement a few days ago?"

Again the first officer's face blanched. "That is true, yes," he replied steadily. "It was a matter of ship's discipline. This was Mr. Ingraham's second trip with us, and on other ships he had been allowed certain liberties which the discipline of this ship compelled me to curtail. There was a disagreement, yes."

Dr. Maher nodded as if satisfied, and turned again to the desk.

Captain Deihl stood staring straight into the eyes of his first officer for a time, and then cleared his throat. "I want to believe you, Tennell," he admitted at last. "I have known you and believed in you for fourteen years. Now tell me why you call me here, show me this, and then admit things which—which you must confess make it look black for you. Now, Harry Tennell, if you ever in your life told me the truth, tell it now—man to man!"

The first officer read the friendliness behind the stern, commanding voice, and there was a grateful softening of the glaring eyes. "Man to man, John Deihl, I'll tell you the truth; but it's hard to believe, and I doubt if you will understand it," he said slowly, deliberately. "I did have a row with this man," and he indicated the crumpled figure in the chair, "a nasty row in the hearing of half a dozen of the crew. That was several days ago. Today I came here in the course of my duties, and found him like this. I recognized the knife instantly as mine—the one I had lost. I am not a coward, John Deihl—no man knows that better than you do—yet for a moment I was overcome by a feeling of terror. Here was the fact of the quarrel, my knife as the weapon of death, myself alone in the cabin with this man while the body was still warm. It all flashed across my mind in an instant—I was frightened at the utter helplessness of my position. No one had seen me enter this cabin, I knew, and the thought came that perhaps I might leave it without being seen, keep my mouth shut, and allow some one else to discover this." The first officer paused and sought vainly to read the expressions on the faces of the two men before him.

"I even went so far as to draw the knife out of the wound, with the purpose of flinging it overboard," the first officer continued slowly; "then my senses came back. I knew my duty again. I replaced the knife in the wound, precisely as I found it, and called you. You are a severe man, but you're a just man, John Deihl, and you know I am not the man to stab another in the back; you know, John Deihl, that fourteen years with me as shipmate and fellow officer has never shown you a weak spot in my courage; you know me, John Deihl, and I know you." The voice dropped suddenly. "That's all."

Captain Deihl had stood motionless, with stern, set face and keen, cold eyes searching those of the first officer. At last he reached out a hand and gripped the one that met it. "I believe you, Harry," he said quietly.

Dr. Maher turned quickly and regarded the two with a slight cynical uplifting of his lip. "I understand then," he said unpleasantly, "that this is to be a matter of friendship rather than of evidence?"

The first officer's face flamed, and he took one step toward the surgeon, with clenched fists.

"Go to your cabin, Mr. Tennell!" ordered Captain Deihl curtly. "Remain there till further orders come from me!"

The first officer paused, involuntarily straightened himself, and lifted one hand to his cap. "Yes, sir," he said.

"And you are not to mention this matter to anyone," Captain Deihl directed.

"I understand, sir."

But news travels quickly aboard ship; so that within less than an hour the tragedy had become a matter of general discussion. Miss Bellingdame was reclining comfortably in a deck chair, when a casual acquaintance, Clarke Matthews, dropped into a seat beside her, and informed her of it. She struggled to her feet, stood staring at him dully for an instant with whitening face, swayed, and fell prone to the deck. It was fully half an hour before the stewardess and her assistants saw the eyelids flutter and open weakly; and at the end of another half hour the stewardess sought out the Captain. She found him at his desk in his cabin, with Second Officer Forbes.

"We must get those dispatches off, Mr. Forbes," the Captain was saying. "Have the ship canvassed, first and second cabin, steerage and crew, to see if by any chance there is a man, woman, or child aboard who can operate the wireless. Attend to it at once!"

Forbes touched his cap and went out. The Captain turned to the stewardess inquiringly.

"Please, sir, Miss Bellingdame is almost insane from the shock of the murder," the stewardess informed him. "It's hard to make her keep in her state room, let alone the berth. Dr. Maher doesn't seem to be able to do her any good. She insists on seeing the body."

"Why?" asked Captain Deihl in surprise. "Was she acquainted with Ingraham?"

"She was engaged to be married to him, sir," replied the stewardess. "Poor child! I don't know what to do for her."

Captain Deihl stared at her blankly for an instant, then rose suddenly and accompanied her to Miss Bellingdame's state room. She was sitting up in her berth, pallid as the sheets about her. One of the stewardess's assistants sat near trying to soothe her.

"Is it true, Captain?" she demanded.

Captain Deihl nodded grimly.

She extended her hands convulsively and clutched his arm, then her head sank forward against it and she sobbed bitterly. "Do you know who—who did it?" she asked at last.

"We don't know, madam," he replied gently. "We are doing all we can; but——"

"Somebody told me your first officer had been arrested," she interrupted suddenly. "He is tall and dark, with a heavy mustache, isn't he?"

"Yes," replied the Captain. "Why?"

For a little while she was silent as she struggled to regain control of her voice, and then: "May I say something to you in private, Captain?"

"Do you know—do you suspect——?" he began.

"I must!" she insisted.

At a gesture from Captain Deihl the stewardess and her assistant left them alone together. Fifteen minutes later he emerged and summoned Second Officer Forbes to his cabin.

"Mr. Forbes, proceed at once to Mr. Tennell's cabin and formally place him under arrest," he ordered shortly. "You had better put him in irons, and keep an armed guard beside him day and night until we land. Don't take any chances with him."

"Yes, sir."

Two hours later Second Officer Forbes appeared in the cabin again. "We have canvassed the ship, sir," he reported. "There is not a wireless operator aboard, or even a telegraph operator."

"What is our speed?"

"A little better than seventeen knots, sir."

"We should land then about five o'clock tomorrow afternoon," the Captain mused. "Very well, Mr. Forbes; we shall have to do without an operator."

Captain Deihl paced slowly, thoughtfully, back and forth across the bridge. Above the stars glittered coldly down upon the silent, sinister sea as it slid past the *Uranus* in green, oily swells. The encompassing night was unbroken by a single glint of light save that which Nature gave grudgingly. The Captain gazed upon it all with unseeing eyes and grimly set lips.

Two bells sounded—one o'clock. As the echo of the last stroke was borne away on the wind, Captain Deihl suddenly became conscious of the sharp, venomous hiss of the wireless. The wireless! He paused incredulously, and glanced aloft. A spark sputtered at the top of the foremast, winked and flashed and spat viciously in the rhythmic dots and dashes of the Continental code. The wireless was working! Some one was sending! The Captain knew that no sound accompanied the receipt of a message, even with the automatic attachment; therefore that sputtering and hissing was some one sending, and if that was true it meant——

He ran down the ladder to the hurricane deck, and disappeared down a companion-way to the deck below.

Professor Augustus S. F. X. Van Dusen listened to Captain Deihl's recital of the circumstances surrounding the murder of Charles Ingraham, with a slight frown of annoyance on his wizened face. As he talked, the man of the sea turned from time to time to Dr. Maher for confirmation of the facts. Each time such corroboration was given with a short nod of the head.

"Now, there are a few other little things," Captain Deihl continued deliberately, "that are not known to Dr. Maher here. For instance, I personally went to the fo'c'sle to see if Tennell had posted a notice there offering a reward for the knife on the night before the murder, and found that statement correct. Here is the notice. You will see the description fits perfectly the knife with which the murder was committed."

The Thinking Machine accepted a sheet of paper which Deihl offered, glanced at it, then handed it back.

"I don't know if Dr. Maher even knows just why I ordered Tennell under arrest," continued the Captain. "Miss Bellingdame's story decided me. She was going to the wireless office to send a message, when she saw a man—it was First Officer Tennell—thrust his head out the door and look around, as if he contemplated escape. She thought it rather curious that he should slam the door when he saw her; but it meant nothing particularly. Then, at a time when we now know Ingraham was dead, she carried on a conversation with some one in the wireless office, through the locked door. Tennell had not mentioned this to me, and coming as it did, it seemed so conclusive that I ordered his arrest."

"It was conclusive from the first," remarked Dr. Maher.

"And then hearing the wireless that night after I had taken pains to assure myself that there was no operator aboard!" Captain Deihl resumed, and his face reflected his bewilderment. "I went straight from the bridge to the wireless office, to find it silent, dark, and the door locked. I called. There was no answer, and I smashed in the door. There was no sign of anyone having been in there—everything was precisely as we left it when the body was removed."

For a long time there was silence. Dr. Maher drummed impatiently on the arm of his chair; The Thinking Machine sat motionless, his slender figure all but engulfed in the huge chair.

"As I understand it," remarked The Thinking Machine at last, "Tennell is now in the hands of the police, and the body is——"

"Ashore awaiting burial," the Captain supplied. "Miss Bellingdame has asked permission of the authorities to take charge of it."

Dr. Maher rose and went to the window, where he stood looking out. The Thinking Machine lowered his squint eyes and stared steadily at the ship's surgeon.

"The case against the first officer seems perfectly clear thus far," said the scientist after a pause. "Why do you come to me?"

Captain Deihl's bronzed face reddened as if he was embarrassed, and he cleared his throat. "Because I know Harry Tennell," he said bluntly. "Circumstances are compelling me to believe that he is a murderer, and my reason won't let me believe it. Why, man, I've known him for years, and I simply can't make myself believe what I have to believe! The police are deaf to the bare suggestion of his innocence, and I—I came here."

"All of which is rather to the credit of your heart than to your head," interposed Dr. Maher cynically.

"Have you any cause to suspect anyone but Tennell, Captain?" inquired The Thinking Machine. He was squinting at the back of Dr. Maher's head. "Can you imagine any other motive than the apparent one?"

"No," replied Captain Deihl. "I can imagine nothing; but I would gamble my right arm that Harry Tennell didn't kill him."

Again there was silence. The Captain was gazing vainly into the drawn, inscrutable face of the diminutive scientist, who lay back with finger tips pressed together and eyes turned steadily upward.

"Dr. Maher," inquired the scientist at last, "the wound was made by a knife. Was it clean cut?"

"Yes."

"Was the knife driven to the hilt?"

"Yes. It required considerable strength."

"And I believe Captain Deihl says there was a thin trickle of blood from the wound before you pulled the knife out?"

"That's correct," was the short answer.

"Therefore it is a point for Tennell, as it shows the knife had been withdrawn and replaced. And so the real problem is to find what message Ingraham was sending when he was murdered," said the scientist quietly. "Neither of you happens to know?"

"The same thought came to me while Captain Deihl was talking to Tennell," said Dr. Maher quickly. "It was shortly after seven bells in the afternoon—that is, half-past three o'clock—when the crime was discovered. Now, the last message to be sent, according to the time check on it, was sent shortly after twelve. Yet, if we believe Tennell, the operator was sending a message just before he was struck down, or possibly at that moment. Well, there was nothing to show for that message—no scrap of paper—nothing."

The Thinking Machine glanced at Dr. Maher as if surprised. "Therefore the message Ingraham was sending," he put in, "was either stolen or was being composed as he sent it. Is that clear?"

There was a pause. Captain Deihl nodded, and Dr. Maher began drumming on the window sill.

"That being true," the scientist went on incisively, "the next step is to learn who aboard the *Uranus* could read the code—the Continental code too, mind you, not the Morse—as a message was being sent. Is that clear?"

"Yes; go on," said Captain Deihl.

"When we find the person who could read the Continental code, we also find the person who in all probability was operating the wireless at one o'clock the night of the murder. Is that clear?"

"Yes, yes."

"And when we find the person who operated the wireless, logic shows us incontrovertibly that we have either the murderer of Ingraham, or some one who was in the plot. Remember, the ship had been canvassed in a search for an operator. None came forward; therefore we know that the operator—an operator—was aboard, but for divers reasons preferred to remain unknown. We know that as certainly as that two and two make four, not *some*time but *all* the time."

Dr. Maher turned and dropped back into his chair, with a new interest evident in every line of his face.

"With these facts in hand it is a simple matter, albeit perhaps a tedious one, to find what message was sent from the ship both by the operator and by the unknown at night," The Thinking Machine resumed. He was silent for a moment, then rose and left the room. He was gone for perhaps ten minutes. "Now, Captain Deihl, and you, Dr. Maher, have you formed any opinion as to the exact method of the murder? Was the murderer inside the cabin with Ingraham, or was he killed by a knife thrust through an open window? You know the arrangement of the place better than I. What is your opinion?"

Captain Deihl considered the matter carefully as he sought to recall every minute detail of the cabin as he found it. "Since you have brought up the question," he said slowly at last, "it seems to me that he must have been stabbed by some one outside, through the window. His left side was toward the window, and the window was open, as it was warm, and he was in his shirt sleeves. Yes, it was within easy reach, and I'm inclined to believe—What do you think, Maher?"

"I agree with you perfectly," was the prompt response. "The angle of the knife indicates that an arm had been dropped inside the state room, and there was an upward thrust, where if a person had been in the room the natural angle would have been downward, unless that person had been lying on the floor."

"All of which being true, is a point in favor of Tennell," said The Thinking Machine curtly. "You found him inside the cabin with the body, and we must suppose from your own statement, Dr. Maher, that he would have had to lie down to inflict the wound. I may say that the strongest point in his favor is the fact that he did not throw away the knife. He knew it to be his; had opportunity to get rid of it, but didn't; therefore——" He shrugged his shoulders and was silent for a moment.

"All things depend on the point of view, gentlemen," he continued after a time. "There are half a dozen casual facts, several of which I have specified, which incline me to a belief in Tennell's innocence; and only two against him, these being the motive and the knife. Strong, you say? Yes; but the knife is turned in his favor. Now let us assume Tennell's innocence for a moment, and build our hypothesis on facts that we know. It is always possible to reconstruct a happening by the logic of its units. Let us see this rule applied to this case.

"We are reasonably certain that whatever message Ingraham was sending just before, or at the moment of his death, was not a written message. I have your word, Dr. Maher, that there was not a trace of any message after the one about noon. Shall we suppose that there was a written message and it was stolen from his desk by the hand that slew? Hardly. Let us take the simple view first. He was sending a message somewhere as he composed it. Now, anyone aboard that ship who knew the Continental code could have read that message, because the wireless has that fault. That being true, we shall admit that somebody did read it, or was reading it as it went.

"Right here we come to what may prove to be the solution. It was necessary for the person who read the message as it went to stop it, and perhaps to silence the man who sent it, even at the cost of a life. Therefore, the importance of the message to the person who read it was life and death. A blow was struck; the message was stopped. But the knife? Tennell says he lost it; anyone might have found it.

"The message is stopped; the man is dead. The next vital necessity which the murderer feels is self protection. How? Can a message be sent which will counteract the one which was stopped by the murder? If this can be done, it is vitally necessary. Some one then—the murderer—takes another tremendous chance, enters the office, and is sending another message, possibly a continuation of the interrupted message, when Captain Deihl becomes aware of it. He goes to investigate, and the probabilities are that the unknown operator escapes by way of the window and regains a state room unobserved.

"That's clear, isn't it? Well, now, what possible motive might lie back of it all? Well, one for instance. Suppose the English police, after the *Uranus* sailed, had reason to suspect there was some person aboard who was wanted there; they could have reached the *Uranus* by wireless. But no such report reached the *Uranus*, you say, Captain? That is, no such report reached you, you mean. The operator might have received such a report; but for reasons of his own kept it to himself. Do you see?

"Let us conjecture a bit. What if a big reward was offered for some person aboard the *Uranus*, and a statement of the fact reached it by wireless? What if the operator was that peculiar type of man who would hold that information to himself on the chance of discovering and delivering over that person who was wanted to the police of this country, thus holding the reward all to himself? Do you see the possibilities? Now, what if that person who was wanted was an operator as well, and able to read the unwritten message the regular operator was sending—a message, understand, which meant capture and punishment—is that a motive for murder?

"This is all partly conjecture, partly fact—merely a discussion of the possibilities. Still, our murderer is unknown. As I have said, the capture of the guilty person may be simple; but it may be tedious. When I hear from——"

There was a sharp ringing of the telephone bell in the next room. The scientist rose abruptly and went out. After a few minutes he returned.

"You allowed Miss Bellingdame to leave the *Uranus* on a motor boat, I understand, before you docked?" he inquired placidly.

"Yes," replied Captain Deihl. "She requested it, and Dr. Maher suggested that it would perhaps be best as she was very ill and weak from the shock following the tragedy."

"I shall be able to put my conjectures to a test at once then," said The Thinking Machine as he put on his hat. "First, I must ask some questions of Miss Bellingdame, however. Suppose you gentlemen wait for me at police headquarters? I shall be there in an hour or so."

The Thinking Machine and Hutchinson Hatch, reporter, were sitting together in a small reception room adjoining the telegraph office in the Hotel Teutonic. Opposite them was Miss Bellingdame, still pale and weary looking, with traces of grief on her face.

"Our close relationship with Mr. Ingraham prompted us to call upon you and offer our condolences at this time," The Thinking Machine was saying glibly; "and at the same time to ask if we could be of any service to you?"

"I appreciate the feeling; but hardly think there is anything you can do," Miss Bellingdame responded; "unless, indeed, it is to relieve me of the painful task of taking charge of the body, and——"

"Just what I was going to suggest," interrupted the little scientist. "With your permission I shall send a telegram at once to friends at home and tell them to make the preparations. If you will excuse me?" and he rose.

Miss Bellingdame nodded, and he went to the small window of the telegraph office, wrote a dispatch, and handed it in. After a moment he resumed his seat.

"It is singular that Charlie should never have mentioned your name in his letters home," continued The Thinking Machine as he dropped back into his chair.

"Well, our acquaintance was rather brief," replied Miss Bellingdame. "I met him abroad, and at his suggestion came directly over with him. Now that everything has happened, I hardly know just what I shall do next."

The telegraph sounder clicked sharply, and distinctly.

"And when were you to have been married?" interrupted the scientist gently.

Miss Bellingdame was listening intently. "Married?" she repeated absently. "Oh, yes, we were to have been married, to be sure."

Hatch strove vainly to read the expression which was creeping into her face. She was leaning forward, gripping the arms of the chair in which she sat with wide, staring, frightened eyes, and every instant her face grew whiter. Suddenly she rose.

"Really you must pardon me," she gasped hurriedly. "I am ill!"

She turned quickly and almost ran out of the room. The Thinking Machine walked out and into the arms of Detective Mallory in the lobby.

"Are your men placed?" demanded the scientist abruptly.

"Yes," was the complacent answer. "Did it work?"

"It worked," replied The Thinking Machine enigmatically. "Come on. Let us go to headquarters."

The Thinking Machine's conjecture was faulty only in one point, and that was his surmise that the message which had been sent at night from the *Uranus* after the murder had been to counteract the message which Ingraham was sending when he was killed. Instead, Miss Bellingdame, herself an operator, had picked up the wireless station ashore and ordered a motor boat out to meet her and take her off. Every other statement was correct as he had stated it.

"And simple," he told Hatch and Captain Deihl. "Mr. Hatch, to whom I telephoned while you, Captain, were with me, was able to find the interrupted message at sea; in fact, it had been relayed in to the station here for information. It stated that Miss Florence Hogarth, wanted for poisoning in England, and for whom there was a reward of one thousand pounds, was aboard the *Uranus* as Miss Bellingdame, and that instead of having dark hair her hair was straw blond, as the result of a little peroxide. You see, therefore, the logic of the units was correct. It is always so. She went to pieces when she read the sounder at the hotel, which was a prearranged affair in the hands of a Continental operator. The message I sent was a dummy."

Subsequent developments proved that instead of being engaged to the murdered operator, Miss Bellingdame, or Miss Hogarth, had never seen him until she came aboard the *Uranus*. It never appeared just how Ingraham had discovered her identity.

THE THREE OVERCOATS

Under the influence of that singular feeling of someone's being in the room with him, Carroll Garland opened his eyes suddenly from sound sleep. The intuition was correct: there was someone in the room with him—a man whose back was turned. At that particular moment he was examining the clothing Garland had discarded on retiring. Garland raised himself on one elbow, and the bed creaked a little.

"Don't disturb yourself," said the man, without turning. "I'll be through in a minute."

"Through what?" demanded Garland. "My pockets?"

The stranger straightened up and turned towards him. He was a tall, lithe, clean-cut young man, with crisp, curly hair, and a quizzical expression about his eyes and lips. He was in evening dress, and Garland could only admire the manner in which it fitted him. He wore an opera hat, and a lightweight Inverness coat.

"I didn't mean to wake you, really," the stranger apologized pleasantly. "I'm sure I didn't make any noise."

"No. I dare say you didn't," replied Garland. "What do you want?"

The stranger picked up an overcoat, which lay across a chair, and deftly, with a penknife, slit the lining on each side. He did something then which Garland couldn't see, after which he carefully folded the coat again, and laid it across the chair. "I have taken what you won at bridge at your club this evening," he remarked. "It will save me the trouble of cashing a check."

Garland gazed at this imperturbable, audacious person with a sort of admiration. "I trust you found the amount correct," he said sarcastically.

"Yes, thirteen hundred and forty-seven dollars. That will do very nicely, thank you. I am leaving two hundred and some odd dollars of your own."

"Oh, take it all," said Garland magnanimously, "because I am going to make you return it anyway."

The stranger laughed pleasantly. "I am going now," he said; "but before I go, I should like to tell you that you play a really excellent game of bridge, except, perhaps, you are a little reckless on no trumps."

"Thank you," said Garland, and started to get out of bed.

"Now, don't get up," advised the stranger, still pleasantly. "I have something here in my pocket which I should dislike very much to have to use, but I will use it if necessary."

Garland kept right on getting out of bed. "You are not such a fool as to shoot," he said quietly. "You couldn't get out of this hotel to save your life, if you did. It is only half-past eleven o'clock, there are people passing in the halls, and always at this time there are a great many people in the lobby. You would have to go that way. So now I'll trouble you for the money."

The stranger drew a glistening, shining object from his pocket, examined it casually, then went over and stood beside the call button. There was a glitter of determination in his eyes, and the smile had gone from his lips. "I certainly have no intention of returning the money—now," he said. "It would be best for both of us, of course, not to attract anyone's attention."

Garland was coming straight toward him.

"Now, don't do anything foolish," the stranger warned, not unkindly. "You can't reach the call button unless you go over me; you won't shout, because if you do, I shall have to use this revolver, and take my chances below. You don't happen to need this money, and I do. It was simply a pick-up for you at the club. If you give an alarm when I go out, it will be disagreeable for me."

Garland stared at him in frank amazement for a moment. The stranger steadily returned the gaze.

"I'll just take one whirl out of you, anyhow," declared Garland grimly. "I don't happen to have a gun, but——"

And Garland sent in a vicious right swing, which would have been highly effective had the stranger's head remained stationary. Instead, it ducked suddenly, and a left hand landed jarringly on one of Garland's eyes. Instantly he forgot all about the burglarious intentions of his visitor; it was man to man, and Garland happened to be dexterous in the science of pugilism—Mike Donovan had taught him.

After four blows had been exchanged, Garland became suddenly convinced that the stranger's teacher in the gentle art of bruising was more gifted than Mike, because in all the freedom of his pajamas, Garland got in only one blow for two, on a man who was hampered by overcoat and evening dress. A stinging jab to Garland's mouth made him clinch, and in trying to reach the stranger's throat, he forgot all the ethics of the game.

At this close range the stranger delivered one short-arm punch, and as Garland reeled and the world grew dark about him, he recalled the blow as being identical with one which was made famous in Carson City, at the time a world's championship changed hands. Dazzling lights danced before his eyes for a moment, and then all was dark.

The stranger stood looking down at him, planted his opera hat more firmly on his head, drew on his gloves, opened the door, and went out. He sauntered through the lobby carelessly, paused to light a cigar, and disappeared through the revolving doors. At the curb outside, an automobile was waiting. In it sat a veiled woman, and a very much begoggled chauffeur.

"Well?" the woman asked quickly.

The stranger shook his head, climbed in beside her, and the car rushed away.

When Garland recovered consciousness, he had the impression of having experienced a remarkably vivid nightmare. But one look into the mirror at his bulbous black eye, and the absence of thirteen hundred and forty-seven dollars from his pockets, convinced him of the reality of it all. Incidentally he examined the two knife cuts in the overcoat lining, and shook his head in bewilderment.

"What the deuce did he cut those for?" he asked himself.

On the following morning Garland returned the overcoat to its owner, Hal Dickson. There is a freemasonry among roommates at college by which one acknowledges that whatever he owns belongs equally to the other. Garland had exercised certain rights which had accrued to him by reason of the comradeship upon his arrival in the city the day before. He had been wearing a light-weight tan coat, entirely too thin for the extreme cold which set in immediately upon his arrival; so he borrowed a heavier coat, a thick frieze affair from his old chum, and left his own light coat with him.

"I want to tell you something about this, Hal," he said, and recited in detail the events of the night before. "Now look here where my friend cut your coat," he said in conclusion.

Together they examined the long slits, after which they stared at each other in blank wonderment.

"Send it down to your tailor and have it relined," remarked Garland. "Tell him to send the bill to me."

Dickson continued to stare at the coat lining.

"What did he want to cut it for?" he asked.

Garland shook his head. "Give me my own coat," he said. "I've got to go back home at two-thirty, and can manage with this light coat until I get there, and may not have a chance to come here again."

Garland was just about to put on his own coat, when he stopped in fresh amazement. "Well! Look at that!" he exclaimed.

Dickson looked. The lining of the coat was slit wide open on each side, as if with a sharp knife.

Ten minutes later the young men were on their way to police headquarters. Detective Mallory received them. The coats were laid under his official eyes, and he scrutinized them carefully.

Mallory listened, with his feet on his desk and his cigar clenched between his teeth. "What did the thief look like?" he asked at the end.

"He had every appearance of a gentleman."

"Just like me and you, eh?"

"Well, a little more like me," replied Garland innocently.

"I shall put my men on it at once," said the detective.

Garland caught the two-thirty train for a run of an hour and a half to a small city.

At fifteen minutes before five o'clock Detective Mallory was called to the long-distance telephone.

"That Mr. Mallory?" came an excited voice. "Well, this is Carroll Garland. Yes, I am at home. Just as soon as I got here, I went straight to my room to get a heavier overcoat. I was putting it on, when I found that the lining had been ripped open just like those other two. Now, what does that mean?"

For the first time in his life a question had been asked to which Mallory would confess that he didn't know the answer. He scratched his head thoughtfully, then stopped doing that to tug violently at his bristly moustache. Finally he hung up the receiver with a bang, and went out personally to look into an affair which had not attracted more than passing interest at the time it was reported.

"I can readily understand," Hutchinson Hatch was saying, "why the burglar took the money; but why did he slit the lining of the overcoat? Who was the veiled woman the doorman saw in the car?"

The Thinking Machine did not say.

"Then why did he go to Dickson's room and slit the lining of an overcoat which Garland left there?"

Still The Thinking Machine was silent.

"And, finally, why did he go to Garland's home, in another city, forty miles away, and slit the lining of another overcoat there?"

Professor Augustus S. F. X. Van Dusen receded still farther into the depths of a huge chair, and sat for a long time with his squint eyes turned upward, and fingertips pressed together. At last he broke the silence. "You have given me every known fact?"

"Everything," the reporter answered.

"There is really no problem in it at all," The Thinking Machine declared, "unless one of the units remains undiscovered. If all are known, the solution is obvious. When the money is returned to Garland, it will definitely prove the only possible hypothesis that may be advanced."

"When the money is returned?" gasped the reporter.

"That is what I said!" snapped the scientist crustily. "If Garland does not care to lose that thirteen hundred and forty-seven dollars, it would be wise not to press the investigation just now. If you will keep in communication with him, and inform me immediately when he receives the money, I shall undertake to close up the affair. Until then it is really not worth my attention."

Nearly a week elapsed before there was another development in the mystery—the return of thirteen hundred and forty-seven dollars, by express from Denver. Accompanying the money was an unsigned note of thanks for the use of it, and a line or two, which might have been construed into an apology for the stranger's conduct in Garland's room.

The police were astounded. This was against all the rules of the game. Garland was more than a little astounded, and at the same time delighted at the generosity of the thief. It was not possible to develop any fact as to the identity of the intruder from the express records. Obviously the sender had used a fictitious name in Denver. When Hatch explained this point to The Thinking Machine, it was dismissed with a wave of one slender hand.

"It is really of no consequence," declared the scientist. "Garland knows the name of the man who took the money and cut the overcoat."

"But he says he doesn't," Hatch remonstrated.

"There may be circumstances which make it necessary for him to say that," continued the scientist.

"He is prepared to swear that he never saw the man before."

"That might be quite true," was the curt rejoinder, "but I dare say he does know the name. The next time Garland comes to the city, let me know."

"He is here now," the reporter informed him. "He came in today to consult with Detective Mallory about the return of the money."

"That simplifies matters," said the scientist. "We'll see him at once."

Garland was in. Hatch introduced the distinguished man of science, and he came immediately to business.

"Tell me something of your love affairs, Mr. Garland," The Thinking Machine began abruptly.

"My love affairs? I have no love affairs at all."

"Oh, I see. Married."

Garland gazed straight into the squinting eyes, with a quizzical expression about his mouth. "I don't see that it is absolutely inconsistent for a man to have a love affair and be married," he said smilingly. "There are men, you know, who are in love with their own wives. I happen to be one of these. When you said love affairs, I assumed you meant——"

"There are men," interrupted The Thinking Machine, "who because of being married dare not admit any other entanglements." The aggressive blue eyes were staring straight into Garland's.

After a moment the young man rose, with something like anger in his manner. "I don't happen to be one of them," he said sharply.

The Thinking Machine shrugged his shoulders. "Now, what is the name of the man who robbed you and cut those coats?" he asked.

"I don't know," retorted Garland.

"I know that is what you told the police," said the scientist, "but believe me, it would be best, and possibly save you trouble, for you to give me the name of that man."

"I don't know it," repeated Garland.

The Thinking Machine seemed satisfied on that point, but with his satisfaction came tiny, sinuous lines in his forehead. Hatch knew what that meant.

"You never saw the man before?" asked the scientist after a moment. The aggressiveness had gone from his voice now.

"No, I never saw him before," Garland replied.

"Nor a photograph of him?"

"No, never."

Almost imperceptibly the lines deepened in the brow of The Thinking Machine. His eyes were narrowed down to mere slits, and his thin lips set into a perfectly straight line. Garland studied the grotesque little figure with a curiosity backed by anger. For a long time there was silence, then:

"Mr. Garland, how long have you been married?"

"Four years."

The Thinking Machine shook his head and rose. "Please pardon me," he continued, "but what is your financial condition?"

"I am a salaried man; but it is a good salary, twelve thousand a year. Quite enough for my wife and myself."

"Your married life has been happy?"

"Perfectly."

Again The Thinking Machine shook his head.

Ten minutes later he and Hutchinson Hatch were in the street together.

"He has either lied, or else we have overlooked a unit," volunteered the scientist as they walked on. "Now, I can't believe that we missed anything—ergo, he lied, and yet I can't believe that."

"Well, that doesn't leave much," the reporter suggested.

"The next step," the scientist went on, "will be to establish beyond all doubt that he told the truth. I leave that to you. Get his record for the last five years, and inquire particularly about his family life, his club life, and always bear in mind the possibility of another woman in the case. There is a woman—some woman—because she was in the automobile. Of course, the case is inconsequential, since the money has been returned; but I happen to be interested in it, because the return of the money bears out my hypothesis, and other things tend to upset it."

Hatch covered the affair thoroughly. Garland had told the truth, as far as investigation could develop. Hatch so informed the scientist.

"It is singular, very singular," remarked The Thinking Machine, in deep abstraction. "By the inexorable rule of logic, we reach a point where we must believe that Garland slit the lining of the coats himself, and had the money sent to him from Denver. When we attempt to find a motive for that—we plunge into absurdities. Two and two always make four, Mr. Hatch, not *some*times, but *all* the time. No problem in arithmetic can be correctly solved, if one figure is missing. There is one figure missing. I'll find it. In your investigation of Garland's career you found out something about his father?"

"Yes. He died several years ago. His name, by the way, was also Carroll Garland."

The Thinking Machine turned suddenly and squinted at the reporter. "Here is our missing unit, Mr. Hatch," he said. "Do you happen to know if there were ever any other Carroll Garlands in the family?"

"Years ago, yes. The great-grandfather of the present one was also a Carroll Garland."

The little scientist rose suddenly, paced back and forth half a dozen times, then passed into an adjoining room. Five minutes later he reentered, with his hat and coat. Accompanied by the reporter, he went straight to one of the fashionable clubs, and sent in a card. After a few minutes' wait, a young man appeared.

"My name is Van Dusen," began The Thinking Machine. "I came here to see you about a personal matter. Could we go to some place where we shall not be disturbed for a minute?"

The young man led the way into a private parlor and closed the door.

"It's about that compromising letter which you carry there," and The Thinking Machine touched the young man on the breast with one long, slender finger.

"Did she send you?"

"No."

"Well, what business is it of yours, then?"

"I do not think that a man of honor, a man of your social position—would care to carry about with him a paper which would not only imperil but might wreck the reputation of a woman who is now another man's wife."

That The Thinking Machine had spoken correctly Hatch could not doubt from the expression on the other's face.

"Another man's wife," repeated the young man in astonishment. "Since when?"

"A week or so ago. She is now in the West with her husband. He knows of the existence of this document, therefore whatever vengeful spirit you may have had in preserving it is wasted. I would advise you to destroy it."

For a minute or more the young man stared straight into the squinted eyes. "If the lady in question should have made such a request of me in person, I should have destroyed it," said the young man; "otherwise I——"

"She makes that request now, through me," the scientist lied glibly.

"Did she ask you to come to me?"

"She makes that request now, through me," repeated the scientist.

Again the young man was silent. Finally he slowly removed his overcoat and laid it across the table. Then from a pocket in the lining, the opening of which was concealed in a seam where the sleeve joined the coat, he removed a letter. A strange expression played about his face, reminiscent, thoughtful, even tender as he offered it to The Thinking Machine. Instead of accepting it, the scientist struck a match and touched it to the corner. In silence the three men watched it burn.

"It is obvious to the dullest intelligence," said The Thinking Machine to Hutchinson Hatch, "that the man who entered Garland's room at the hotel was not a thief. He went there to open the lining of Garland's overcoat. Why? To find something which he had reason to believe was concealed therein. True, he took some money, but we can readily imagine that he happened to need a large sum at the minute, and took it, intending to return it, as he did.

"When we know that he was not a thief, we know that the thing he sought was in the lining of the coat. It just happened that this particular coat was not Garland's. The thief did not know that when he cut it, but he had been so certain of finding what he sought that he took pains to see it was Garland's coat. Instead of Garland's name, he found on a tailor's tab inside the pocket the name of Dickson. If we give him credit for intelligence at all, we must give him credit for imagining how another man's coat came into Garland's possession. Therefore, he went to Dickson's room, found Garland's coat, ripped that as he had the first. Still nothing. Naturally, then, he went to Garland's home and ripped open the third coat.

"All this was obvious. Now we come to the less obvious. What was he after? Money? No, he left money behind him. Jewelry? Possibly, but not probably, for his was not a mercenary pursuit. Then what? The remainder: some document or letter which was of such importance that he practically risked his life for it. Now, was this letter or document of value to him or to some one else?

"At this point logic met an obstacle in the veiled woman who waited in the automobile. Would the man permit the woman to take the chance she was taking with him if the document had been of value only to himself? It seems unlikely. On the other hand, if the document was of value to her, might she not insist on accompanying him?

"What paper was he after? A will or deed? Perhaps, but would not that have gone into a court of law? A letter? More likely. So what did we have? A man risking his life, prison at least, to recover a letter for a woman near and dear to him. She, perhaps, informed him that the letter was concealed in the lining of Carroll Garland's overcoat. How she knew this does not appear. We can even imagine the woman confessing the existence of a letter by which her character was menaced before she consented to become his wife. In that event, everything else is accounted for; no other hypothesis would fit all the circumstances, therefore it would seem that there could be no mistake. I failed to see at the moment that there might be another Carroll Garland. When I saw that, I telephoned to Garland, and he informed me that he had a cousin of the same name who occasionally visited this city and always stayed at the club where we called. You know what happened when we saw this second Carroll Garland. In searching for a Carroll Garland the stranger came across the wrong man and held him up. That is all, I think."

There was a long silence.

"By the way," Hatch inquired, suddenly. "What is the name of the strange man and the woman?"

"Why, I don't know," responded The Thinking Machine in surprise.

THE PROBLEM OF THE HIDDEN MILLION

The gray hand of death had already left its ashen mark on the wrinkled, venomous face of the old man who lay huddled up in bed. Save for the feverishly brilliant eyes—cunning, vindictive, hateful—there seemed to be no spark of life in the aged form. The withered lips were mute, and the thin, yellow, clawlike hands lay helplessly outstretched on the white sheets. All physical power was gone; only the brain remained doggedly alive. Two men and two women stood beside the death bed. Upon each in turn the glittering eyes rested with the merciless, unreasoning hatred of age. Crouched on the floor was a huge St. Bernard dog, and on a perch across the room was a parrot which screeched abominably.

The gloom of the wretched little room was suddenly relieved by a ruddy sunbeam, which shot athwart the bed and lighted the scene fantastically. The old man noted it, and his lips curled into a hideous smile.

"That's the last sun I'll ever see," he piped feebly. "I'm dying—dying! Do you hear? And you're all glad of it, every one of you. Yes, you are! You are glad of it because you want my money. You came here to make me believe you were paying a last tribute of respect to your old grandfather. But that isn't it. It's the money you want—the money! But I've got a surprise for you. You'll never get the money. It's hidden safely—you'll never get it. You all hate me, you have hated me for years, and after that sun dies, you'll all hate me worse. But not more than I hated you. You'll all hate me worse then, because I'll be gone and you'll never know where the money is hidden. It will lie there safely where I put it, rotting and crumbling away; but you shall never warm your fingers with it! It's hidden—hidden—hidden!"

There was rasping in the shrunken throat, a deeply drawn breath, then the figure stiffened, and a distorted soul passed out upon the Eternal Way.

Martha held a card within the blinding light of the reflector, and Professor Augustus S. F. X. Van Dusen, with his hands immersed to the elbows in some chemical mess, squinted at it.

"Dr. Walter Ballard," he read. "Show him in."

After a moment Dr. Ballard entered. The scientist was still absorbed in his labors, but paused long enough to jerk his head toward a chair. Dr. Ballard accepted this as an invitation, and sat down, staring curiously at the singular, childlike figure of this eminent man of science, at the mop of tangled, straw-yellow hair, the enormous brow, and the peering blue eyes.

"Well?" demanded the scientist abruptly.

"I beg your pardon," began Dr. Ballard with a little start. "Your name was mentioned to me some time ago by a newspaper reporter, Hutchinson Hatch, whom I chanced to meet in his professional capacity. He suggested then that I come and see you, but I thought it useless. Now the affair in which we were both interested at that time seems hopelessly beyond solution, so I come to you for aid.

"We want to find one million dollars in gold and United States bonds, which were hidden by my grandfather, John Walter Ballard, some time before his death just a month ago. The circumstances are altogether out of the ordinary."

The Thinking Machine abandoned his labors, and dried his hands carefully, after which he took a seat facing Dr. Ballard. "Tell me about it," he commanded.

"Well," began Dr. Ballard reminiscently, as he settled back in his chair, "the old man—my grandfather—died, as I said, a month ago. He was nearly eighty-six, and the last five or six years of his life he spent as a recluse in a little house twenty-five miles from the city, a place some distance from any other house. He had a spot of ground there, half an acre or so, and lived like a pauper, despite the fact that he was worth at least a million dollars. Previous to the time he went there to live, there had been an estrangement with my family, his sole heirs. My family consists of myself, wife, son, and daughter.

"My grandfather lived in the house with me for ten years before he went out to this hut, and why he left us then is not clear to any member of my family, unless," and he shrugged his shoulders, "he was mentally unbalanced. Anyway, he went. He would neither come to see us, nor would he permit us to go to see him. As far as we know, he owned no real property of any sort, except this miserable little place, worth altogether—furnishing and all—not more than a thousand or twelve hundred dollars.

"Well, about a month ago, some one stopped at the house for

something, and found he was ill. I was notified, and with my wife, son and daughter, went to see what we could do. He took occasion on his death bed to heap vituperation upon us, and incidentally to state that something like a million dollars was left behind, but hidden.

"For the sake of my son and daughter, I undertook to recover this money. I consulted attorneys, private detectives, and in fact exhausted every possibility. I ascertained beyond question that the money was not in a bank anywhere, and hardly think he would have left it there, because, of course, if he had, even with a will disinheriting us, the law would have turned it over to us. He had no safe deposit vault as far as one month of close searching could reveal, and the money was not hidden in the house or grounds. He stated on his death bed that it was in bonds and gold, and that we should never find it. He was just vindictive enough not to destroy it, but to leave it somewhere, believing we should never find it. Where did he hide it?"

The Thinking Machine sat silently for several minutes, with his enormous yellow head tilted back, and slender fingers pressed together. "The house and grounds were searched?" he asked.

"The house was searched from cellar to garret," was the reply. "Workmen, under my direction, practically wrecked the building. Floors, ceilings, walls, chimney, stairs, everything—little cubby holes in the roof, the foundation of the chimney, the pillars, even the flagstones leading from the gate to the door, everything was examined. The posts were sounded to see if they were solid, and a dozen of them were cut through. The posts on the veranda were cut to pieces, and every stick of furniture was dissected—mattresses, beds, chairs, tables, bureaus—all of it. Outside in the grounds the search was just as thorough. Not one square inch but what was overturned. We dug it all up to a depth of ten feet. Still nothing."

"Of course," said the scientist, at last, "the search of the house and grounds was useless. The old man was shrewd enough to know that they would be searched. Also it would appear that the search of banks and safety deposit vaults was equally useless. He was shrewd enough to foresee that, too. We shall for the present assume that he did not destroy the money or give it away; so it is hidden. If the brain of man is clever enough to conceal a thing, the brain of man is clever enough to find it. It's a little problem in subtraction, Dr. Ballard." He was silent for a moment. "Who was your grandfather's attending physician?"

"I was. I was present at his death. Nothing could be done. It was merely the collapse consequent upon old age. I issued the burial certificate."

"Were any special directions left as to the place or manner of burial?"

"No."

"Have all his papers been examined for a clue as to the possible hiding place?"

"Everything. There were no papers to amount to anything."

"Have you those papers now?"

Dr. Ballard silently produced a packet and handed it to the scientist."

"I shall examine these at my leisure," said The Thinking Machine. "It may be a day or so before I communicate with you."

Dr. Ballard went his way. For a dozen hours The Thinking Machine sat with the papers spread out before him, and the keen, squinting, blue eyes dissected them, every paragraph, every sentence, every word. At the end he rose and bundled up the papers impatiently.

"Dear me! Dear me!" he exclaimed irritably. "There's no cipher—that's certain. Then what?"

Devastating hands had wrought the wreck of the little house where the old man died. Standing in the midst of its litter, The Thinking Machine regarded it closely and dispassionately for a long time. The work of destruction had been well done.

"Can you suggest anything?" asked Dr. Ballard impatiently.

"One mind may read another mind," said The Thinking Machine, "when there is some external thing upon which one can concentrate as a unit. In other words, when we have a given number, the logical brain can construct either backward or forward. There are so many thousands of ways in which your grandfather could have disposed of this money that the task becomes tremendous in view of the fact that we have no starting point. It is a case for patience, rather than any other quality; therefore, for greater speed, we must proceed psychologically. The question then becomes, not one of where the money is hidden, but one of where that sort of man would hide it.

"Now what sort of man was your grandfather?" the scientist continued. "He was crabbed, eccentric, and possibly not mentally sound. The cunning of a diseased mind is greater than the cunning of a normal one. He boasted to you that the money was in existence, and his last words were intended to arouse your curiosity; to hang over you all the rest of your life, and torment you. You can imagine the vindictive, petty brain like that putting a thing safely beyond your reach—but just beyond it—near enough to tantalize, and yet far enough to remain undiscovered. This seems to me to be the mental attitude in this case. Your grandfather knew that you would do just what you have done here; that is, search the house and lot. He knew, too, that you would search banks and safety deposit vaults, and with a million at stake he knew it would be done thoroughly. Knowing this, naturally he would not put the money in any of those places.

"Then what? He doesn't own any other property, as far as we know, and we shall assume that he did not buy property in the name of some other person; therefore, what have we left? Obviously, if the money is still in existence, it is hidden on somebody else's property. And the minute we say that, we have the whole wide world to search. But again, doesn't the deviltry and maliciousness of the old man narrow that down? Wouldn't he have liked to remember as a dying thought that the money was always just within your reach, and yet safely beyond it? Wouldn't it have been a keener revenge to have you dig over the whole place, while the money was hidden just six feet outside in a spot where you would never dig? It might be sixty or six hundred or six thousand. But there we have the law of probability to narrow these limits; so——"

Professor Van Dusen turned suddenly and strolled across the uneven ground to the property line. Walking slowly and scrutinizing the ground as he went, he circled the lot, returning to the starting point. Dr. Ballard had followed along behind him.

"Are all your grandfather's belongings still in the house?" asked the scientist.

"Yes, everything just as he left it, that is, except his dog and a parrot. They are temporarily in charge of a widow down the road here."

The scientist looked at Dr. Ballard quickly. "What sort of dog is it?" he inquired.

"A St. Bernard, I think," replied Dr. Ballard wonderingly.

"Do you happen to have a glove or something that you know your grandfather wore?"

"I have a glove, yes."

From the debris which littered the floor of the house, a well-worn glove was recovered.

"Now the dog, please," commanded the scientist.

A short walk along the country road brought them to a house, and here they stopped. The St. Bernard, a shaggy, handsome, boisterous old chap with wise eyes was led out in leash. The Thinking Machine thrust the glove forward, and the dog sniffed at it. After a moment he sank down on his haunches, and with head thrust forward and upward, whined softly. It was the call to its master.

The Thinking Machine patted the heavy-coated head, and with the glove still in his hand made as if to go away. Again came the whine, but the dog sank down on the floor, with his head between his forepaws, regarding him intently. For ten minutes the scientist sought to coax the animal to follow him, but he lay motionless.

"I don't mind keepin' that dog here, but that parrot is powerful noisy," said the woman after a moment. She had been standing by, watching the scientist curiously. "There ain't no peace in the house."

"Noisy—how?" asked Dr. Ballard.

"He swears, and sings and whistles, and does 'rithmetic all day long," the woman explained. "It nearly drives me distracted."

"Does arithmetic?" inquired The Thinking Machine.

"Yes," replied the woman, "and he swears just terrible. It's almost like havin' a man about the house. There he goes now."

From another room came a sudden, squawking burst of profanity, followed instantly by a whistle, which caused the dog on the floor to prick up his ears.

"Does the parrot talk well?" asked the scientist.

"Just like a human bein'," replied the woman, "an' just about as sensible as some I've seen. I don't mind his whistling, if only he wouldn't swear so, and do all his figgering out loud."

For a minute or more the scientist stood, staring down at the dog in deep thought. Gradually there came some subtle change in his expression. Dr. Ballard was watching him closely.

"I think perhaps it would be a good idea for me to keep the parrot for a few days," suggested the scientist finally. He turned to the woman. "Just what sort of arithmetic does the bird do?"

"All kinds," she answered promptly. "He does all the multiplication table. But he ain't very good in subtraction."

"I shouldn't be surprised," commented The Thinking Machine. "I'll take the bird for a few days, doctor, if you don't mind."

And so it came to pass that when The Thinking Machine returned to his apartment he was accompanied by as noisy and vociferous a companion as anyone would care to have.

Martha, the aged servant, viewed him with horror as he entered. "The professor must be getting old," she muttered. "I suppose there'll be a cat next."

Two days later Dr. Ballard was called to the telephone. The Thinking Machine was at the other end of the wire.

"Take two men whom you can trust and go down to your grandfather's place," instructed the scientist curtly. "Take picks, shovels, a compass, and a long tape line. Stand on the front steps facing east. To your right will be an apple tree some distance off that lot on the adjoining property. Go to that apple tree. A boulder is at its foot. Measure from the edge of that stone twenty-six feet due north by the compass, and from that point fourteen feet due west. You will find your money there. Then please have some one come and take this bird away. If you don't, I'll wring its neck. It's the most obnoxious creature I've ever heard. Good by."

Dr. Ballard slipped the catch on the suitcase and turned it upside down on the laboratory table. It was packed—literally packed—with United States bonds. The Thinking Machine fingered them idly.

"And there is this, too," said Dr. Ballard.

He lifted a stout sack from the floor, cut the string, and spilled out its contents beside the bonds. It was gold, thousands and thousands of dollars. Dr. Ballard was frankly excited about it. The Thinking Machine accepted it as he accepted all material things.

"How much is there of it?" he asked quietly.

"I don't know," replied Dr. Ballard.

"And how did you find it?"

"As you directed—twenty-six feet north from the boulder, and fourteen feet west from that point."

"I knew that, of course," snapped The Thinking Machine. "But how was it hidden?"

"It's rather peculiar," explained Dr. Ballard. "Fourteen feet brought the man who had measured it to the edge of an old dried-up well, twelve or fifteen feet deep, not expecting any such thing, he tumbled into it. In his efforts to get out, he stepped upon a stone which protruded from one side. That fell out and revealed the wooden box, which contained all this."

"In other words," said the scientist, "the money was hidden in such a manner that it would in time have come to be buried twelve or fifteen feet below the surface, because the well, being dry, would ultimately, of course, have been filled in."

Dr. Ballard had been listening only hazily. His hands had been playing in and out of the heap of gold. The Thinking Machine regarded him with something like contempt about his thin-lipped mouth.

"How—how did you ever do it?" asked Dr. Ballard.

"I am surprised that you want to know," remarked The Thinking Machine cuttingly. "You know how I reached the conclusion that the money was not hidden either in the house or lot. The plain logic of the thing told me that, even before the search you made demonstrated it. You saw how logic narrowed down the search, and you saw my experiment with the dog. That was purely an experiment. I wanted to see the instinct of the animal. Would it lead him anywhere?—perhaps the spot where the money had been hidden? It did not.

"But the parrot? That was another matter. It just happens that once before I had an interesting experience with a bird—a cockatoo which figured in a sleepwalking case—and naturally was interested in this bird. Now, what were the circumstances in this case? Here was a bird that talked exceptionally well, yet that bird had been living for five years alone with an old man. It is a fact that no matter how well a parrot may talk, it will forget in the course of time, unless there is someone around who talks. This old man was the only person near this bird. Therefore from the fact that the bird talks, we know that the old man talked; from the fact that the bird repeated the multiplication table, we know that the old man repeated it. From the fact that the bird whistles, we know that the old man whistled, perhaps to the dog. And in the course of five years of these circumstances, a bird would have come to that point where it would repeat only those words or sounds that the old man used.

"All this shows, too, that the old man talked to himself. Most people who live alone a great deal do that. Then came a question as to whether at any time the old man had ever repeated the secret of the hiding place within the hearing of the bird—not once, but many times, because it takes a parrot a long time to learn phrases. When we know the vindictiveness which lay behind the old man's actions in hiding the money, when we know how the thing preyed on his mind, coupled with the fact that he talked to himself, and was not wholly sound mentally, we can imagine him doddering about the place alone, repeating the very thing of which he had made so great a secret. Thus, the bird learned it, but learned it disjointedly, not connectedly, so when I brought the parrot here, my idea was to know by personal observation what the bird said that didn't connect—that is, that had no obvious meaning. I hoped to get a clue which would result, just as the clue I did get, did result.

"The bird's trick of repeating the multiplication table means nothing except it shows the strange workings of an unbalanced mind. And yet, there is one exception to this. In a disjointed way, the bird knows all the multiplication tables to ten, except one. For instance—listen."

The Thinking Machine crept stealthily to a door and opened it softly a few inches. From somewhere out there came the screeching of the parrot. For several minutes they listened in silence. There was a flood of profanity, a shrill whistle or two, then the squawking voice ran off into a monotone.

"Six times one are six, six time two are twelve, six times three are eighteen, six times four are twenty-four—and add two——"

"That's it," explained the scientist, as he closed the door. "Six times four are twenty-four—add two. That's the one table the bird does not know. The thing is incoherent, except as applied to a peculiar method of remembering a number. That number is twenty-six. On one occasion I heard the bird repeat a dozen times, 'Twenty-six feet to the polar star.' That could mean nothing except the direction of the twenty-six feet—due north. One of the first things I noticed the bird saying was something about fourteen feet to the setting sun—or due west. When set down with twenty-six, I could readily see that I had something to go on.

"But where was the starting point? Again, logic. There was no tree or stone inside the lot, except the apple tree which your workmen cut down, and that was more than twenty-six feet from the boundary of the lot in all directions. There was one tree in the adjoining lot, an apple tree with a boulder at its foot. I knew that by observation. And there was no other tree, I knew also, within several hundred feet; therefore, that tree or boulder, rather, was a starting point—not the tree so much as the boulder, because the tree might be cut down, or would in time decay. The chances are the stone would have been allowed to remain there indefinitely. Naturally your grandfather would measure from a prominent point—the boulder. That is all. I gave you the figures. You know the rest."

For a minute or more, Dr. Ballard stared at him blankly. "How was it you knew," he asked, "that the directions should have been first twenty-six feet north, then fourteen feet west, instead of first fourteen west, and then twenty-six feet north."

The Thinking Machine looked at him with scorn. "What difference would it have made?" he said peevishly. "Try it on a piece of paper, if you cannot do it mentally."

Half an hour later Dr. Ballard went away carrying the money and the parrot in its cage. The bird cursed The Thinking Machine roundly, as Dr. Ballard went down the steps.

THE PROBLEM OF THE BROKEN BRACELET

The girl in the green mask leaned against the foot of the bed and idly fingered a revolver which lay in the palm of her daintily gloved hand. The dim glow of the night lamp enveloped her softly, and added a sinister glint to the bright steel of the weapon. Cowering in the bed was another figure, the figure of a woman. Sheets and blankets were drawn up tightly to her chin, and startled eyes peered anxiously, as if fascinated at the revolver.

"Now please don't scream!" warned the masked girl. Her voice was quite casual, the tone in which one might have discussed an affair of far removed personal interest. "It would be perfectly useless, and besides, dangerous."

"Who are you?" gasped the woman in the bed, staring horror-stricken at the inscrutable mask of her visitor. "What do you want?"

A faint flicker of amusement lay in the shadowy eyes of the masked girl, and her red lips twitched slightly. "I don't think I can be mistaken," she said inquiringly. "This is Miss Isabel Leigh Harding?"

"Y-yes," was the chattering reply.

"Originally of Virginia?"

"Yes."

"Great-granddaughter of William Tremaine Harding, an officer in the Continental Army about 1775?"

The inflection of the questioning voice had risen almost imperceptibly; but the tone remained coldly, exquisitely courteous. At the last question the masked girl leaned forward a little expectantly.

"Yes," faltered Miss Harding faintly.

"Good, very good," commented the masked girl and there was a note of repressed triumph in her voice. "I congratulate you, Miss Harding, on your self-possession. Under the same circumstances most women would have begun by screaming. I should have myself."

"But who are you?" demanded Miss Harding again. "How did you get in here? What do you want?"

She sat bolt upright in bed, with less of fear now than curiosity in her manner, and her luxuriant hair tumbled about her semibare shoulders in profuse dishevelment.

At the sudden movement the masked girl took a firmer grip on the revolver, and moved it forward a little threateningly. "Now please don't make any mistake!" she advised Miss Harding pleasantly. "You will notice that I have drawn the bell rope up beyond your reach and knotted it. The servants are on the floor above in the extreme rear, and I doubt if they could hear a scream. Your companion is away for the night, and besides there is this." She tapped her weapon significantly. "Furthermore, you may notice that the lamp is beyond your reach; so that you cannot extinguish it as long as you remain in bed."

Miss Harding noticed all these things, and was convinced.

"Now as to your question," continued the masked girl quietly. "My identity is of absolutely no concern or importance to you. You would not even recognize my name if I gave it to you. How did I get here? By opening an unfastened window in the drawing room on the first floor and walking in. I shall leave it unlatched when I go; so perhaps you had better have some one fasten it, otherwise thieves may enter." She smiled a little at the astonishment in Miss Harding's face. "Now as to why I am here and what I want."

She sat down on the foot of the bed, drew her cloak more closely about her, and folded her hands in her lap. Miss Harding placed a pillow and lounged against it comfortably, watching her visitor in astonishment. Except for the mask and the revolver, it might have been a cosy chat in any woman's boudoir.

"I came here to borrow from you—borrow, understand," the masked girl went on, "the least valuable article in your jewel box."

"My jewel box!" gasped Miss Harding suddenly. She had just thought of it, and glanced around at the table where it lay open.

"Don't alarm yourself," the masked girl remarked reassuringly. "I have removed nothing from it."

The light of the lamp fell full upon the open casket whence radiated multicolored flashes of gems. Miss Harding craned her neck a little to see, and seeing sank back against her pillow with a sigh of relief.

"As I said, I came to borrow one thing," the masked girl continued evenly. "If I cannot borrow it, I shall take it."

Miss Harding sat for a moment in mute contemplation of her visitor. She was searching her mind for some tangible explanation of this nightmarish thing. After a while she shook her head, meaning thereby that even conjecture was futile. "What particular article do you want?" she asked finally.

"Specifically by letter, from the prison in which he was executed by order of the British commander, your great-grandfather, William Tremaine Harding, left a gold bracelet, a plain band, to your grandfather," the masked girl explained. "Your grandfather, at that time a child, received the bracelet, when twenty-one years old, from the persons who held it in trust for him, and on his death, March 25, 1853, left it to your father. Your father died intestate in April, 1898, and the bracelet passed into your mother's keeping, there being no son. Your mother died within the last year. Therefore, the bracelet is now, or should be, in your possession. You see," she concluded, "I have taken some pains to acquaint myself with your family history."

"You have," Miss Harding assented. "And may I ask why you want this bracelet?"

"I should answer that it was no concern of yours."

"You said borrow it, I believe?"

"Either I will borrow it or take it."

"Is there any certainty that it will ever be returned? And if so, when?"

"You will have to take my word for that, of course," replied the masked girl. "I shall return it within a few days."

Miss Harding glanced at her jewel box. "Have you looked there?" she inquired.

"Yes," replied the masked girl. "It isn't there."

"Not there?" repeated Miss Harding.

"If it had been there, I should have taken it and gone away without disturbing you," the masked girl went on. "Its absence is what caused me to wake you."

"Not there!" said Miss Harding again wonderingly, and she moved as if to get up.

"Don't do that, please!" warned the masked girl quickly. "I shall hand you the box if you like."

She rose and passed the casket to Miss Harding, who spilled out its contents on her lap.

"Why, it is gone!" she exclaimed.

"Yes, from there," said the other a little grimly. "Now please tell me immediately where it is. It will save trouble."

"I don't know," replied Miss Harding hopelessly.

The masked girl stared at her coldly for a moment, then drew back the hammer of the revolver until it clicked.

Miss Harding stared in sudden terror.

"All this is merely time wasted," said the masked girl sternly, coldly. "Either the bracelet or this!" Again she tapped the revolver.

"If it is not here, I don't know where it is," Miss Harding rushed on desperately. "I placed it here at ten o'clock last night—here in this box—when I undressed. I don't know—I can't imagine——"

The masked girl tapped the revolver again several times with one gloved finger. "The bracelet!" she demanded impatiently.

Fear was in Miss Harding's eyes now, and she made a helpless, pleading gesture with both white hands. "You wouldn't kill me—murder me!" she gasped. "I don't know. I—Here, take the other jewels. I can't tell you."

"The other jewels are of absolutely no use to me," said the girl coldly. "I want only the bracelet."

"On my honor," faltered Miss Harding, "I don't know where it is. I can't imagine what has happened to it. I— I——" she stopped helplessly.

The masked girl raised the weapon threateningly, and Miss Harding stared in terror.

"Please, please, I don't know!" she pleaded hysterically.

For a little while the masked girl was thoughtfully silent. One shoe tapped the floor rhythmically; the eyes were contracted. "I believe you," she said slowly at last. She rose suddenly and drew her coat closely about her. "Good night," she added as she started toward the door. There she turned back. "It would not be wise for you to give an alarm for at least half an hour. Then you had better have some one latch the window in the drawing room. I shall leave it unfastened. Good night."

And she was gone.

Hutchinson Hatch, reporter, had just finished relating the story to The Thinking Machine, incident by incident, as it had been reported to Chief of Detectives Mallory, when the eminent scientist's aged servant, Martha, tapped on the door of the reception room and entered with a card.

"A lady to see you, sir," she announced.

The scientist extended one slender white hand, took the card, and glanced at it.

"Your story is merely what Miss Harding told the police?" he inquired of the reporter. "You didn't get it from Miss Harding herself?"

"No, I didn't see her."

"Show the lady in, Martha," directed The Thinking Machine. She turned and went out, and he passed the card to the reporter.

"By George! It's Miss Harding herself," Hatch exclaimed. "Now we can get it all straight!"

There was a little pause, and Martha ushered a young woman into the room. She was girlish, slender, daintily yet immaculately attired, with deep brown eyes, firmly molded chin and mouth, and wavy hair. Hatch's expression of curiosity gave way to one of frank admiration as he regarded her. There was only the most impersonal sort of interest in the watery blue eyes of The Thinking Machine. She stood for a moment with gaze alternating between the distinguished man of science and the reporter.

"I am Mr. Van Dusen," explained The Thinking Machine. "Allow me, Miss Harding—Mr. Hatch."

The girl smiled and offered a gloved hand cordially to each of the two men. The Thinking Machine merely touched it respectfully; Hatch shook it warmly. The eyes were veiled demurely for an instant, then the lids were lifted suddenly, and she favored the newspaper man with a gaze that sent the blood to his cheeks.

"Be seated, Miss Harding," the scientist invited.

"I hardly know just what I came to say, and just how to say it," she began uncertainly, and smiled a little. "And anyway I had hoped that you were alone; so——"

"You may speak with perfect freedom before Mr. Hatch," interrupted The Thinking Machine. "Perhaps I shall be able to help you; but first will you repeat the history of the bracelet as nearly as you can in the words of the masked woman who called upon you so—so unconventionally."

The girl's brows were lifted inquiringly, with a sort of start.

"We were discussing the case when your card was brought in," continued The Thinking Machine tersely. "We shall continue from that point, if you will be so good."

The young woman recited the history of the bracelet slowly and carefully.

"And that statement of the case is correct?" queried the scientist.

"Absolutely, so far as I know," was the reply.

"And as I understand it, you were in the house alone; that is, alone except for the servants?"

"Yes. I live there alone, except for a companion and two servants. The servants were not within the sound of my voice, even if I had screamed, and Miss Tablott, my companion, it happened, was out for the night."

The Thinking Machine had dropped back into his chair, with squint eyes turned upward, and long white fingers pressed tip to tip. He sat thus silently for a long time. The girl at last broke the silence.

"Naturally I was a little surprised," she remarked falteringly, "that I should have appeared just in time to interrupt a discussion of the singular happenings in my home last night, but really——"

"This bracelet," interrupted the little scientist again. "It was of oval form, perhaps, with no stones set in it, or anything of that sort, merely a band that fastened with an invisible hinge. That's right, I believe?"

"Quite right, yes," replied the girl readily.

It occurred to Hatch suddenly that he himself did not know—in fact, had not inquired—the shape of the bracelet. He knew only that it was gold and of no great value. Knowing nothing about what it looked like, he had not described it to The Thinking Machine, therefore he raised his eyes inquiringly now. The drawn face of the scientist was inscrutable.

"As I started to say," the girl went on, "the bracelet and the events of last night have no direct connection with the purpose of my visit here."

"Indeed?" commented the scientist.

"No. I came to see if you would assist me in another way. For instance," and she fumbled in her pocket book. "I happened to know, Professor Van Dusen, of some of the remarkable things you have accomplished, and I should like to ask if you can throw any light on this for me."

She drew from the pocketbook a crumpled, yellow sheet of paper—a strip perhaps an inch wide, thin as tissue, glazed, and extraordinarily wrinkled. The Thinking Machine squinted at its manifold irregularities for an instant curiously, nodded, sniffed at it, then slowly began to unfold it, smoothing it out carefully as he went. Hatch leaned forward eagerly and stared. He was a little more than astonished at the end to find that the sheet was blank. The Thinking Machine examined both sides of the paper thoughtfully.

"And where did you find the bracelet at last?" he inquired casually.

"I have reason to believe," the girl rushed on suddenly, regardless of the question, "that this strip of paper has been substituted for one of real value—I may say one of great value—and I don't know how to proceed, unless——"

"Where did you find the bracelet?" demanded The Thinking Machine again, impatiently.

Hatch would have hesitated a long time before he would have said the girl was disconcerted at the question, or that there had been any real change in the expression of her pretty face. And yet——

"After the masked woman had gone," she went on calmly. "I summoned the servants and we made a search. We found the bracelet at last. I thought I had tossed it into my jewel box when I removed it last night; but it seems I was careless enough to let it fall down behind my dressing table, and it was there all the time the—— masked woman was in my room."

"And when did you make this discovery?" asked The Thinking Machine.

"Within a few minutes after she went out."

"In making your search, you were guided, perhaps, by a belief that in the natural course of events the bracelet could not have disappeared from your jewel box unless some one had entered the room before the masked woman entered; and further that if anyone had entered you would have been awakened?"

"Precisely." There was another pause. "And now please," she went on, "what does this blank strip of paper mean?"

"You had expected something with writing on it, of course?"

"That's just what I had expected," and she laughed nervously. "You may rest assured I was considerably surprised at finding that."

"I can imagine you were," remarked the scientist dryly.

The conversation had reached a point where Hatch was hopelessly lost. The young woman and the scientist were talking with mutual understanding of things that seemed to have no connection with anything that had gone before. What was the paper anyway? Where did it come from? What connection did it have with the affairs of the previous night? How did——

"Mr. Hatch, a match, please," requested The Thinking Machine.

Wonderingly the reporter produced one and handed it over. The imperturbable man of science lighted it and thrust the mysterious paper into the blaze. The girl rose with a sudden, startled cry, and snatched at the paper desperately, extinguishing the match as she did so. The Thinking Machine turned disapproving eyes on her.

"I thought you were going to burn it!" she gasped.

"There is not the slightest danger of that, Miss Harding," declared The Thinking Machine coldly. He examined the blank sheet again. "This way, please."

He rose and led the way into his tiny laboratory across the narrow hall, with the girl following. Hatch trailed behind, wondering vaguely what it was all about. A small brazier flashed into flame as The Thinking Machine applied a match, and curious eyes peered over his shoulders as he held the blank strip, now smoothed out, so that the rising heat would strike it.

For a long time three pairs of eyes were fastened on the mysterious paper, all with understanding now; but nothing appeared. Hatch glanced round at the young woman. Her face wore an expression of tense excitement. The red lips were slightly parted in anticipation, the eyes sparkling, and the cheeks flushed deeply. In staring at her the reporter forgot for the instant everything else, until suddenly:

"There! There! Do you see?"

The exclamation burst from her triumphantly, as faint, scrawly lines grew on the strip suspended over the brazier. Totally oblivious of their presence apparently, The Thinking Machine was squinting steadily at the paper, which was slowly crinkling up into wavy lines under the influence of the heat. Gradually the edges were charring, and the odor of scorched paper filled the room. Still the scientist held the paper over the fire. Just as it seemed inevitable that it would burst into flame, he withdrew it and turned to the girl.

"There was no substitution," he remarked tersely. "It is sympathetic ink."

"What does it say?" demanded the young woman abruptly. "What does it mean?"

The Thinking Machine spread the scorched strip of paper on the table before them carefully, and for a long time studied it minutely.

"Really, my dear young woman, I don't know," he said crabbedly at last. "It may take days to find out what it means."

"But something is written there! Read it!" the girl insisted.

"Read it for yourself," said the scientist impatiently. "I am frank to say it's beyond me as it is now. No, don't touch it. It will crumble to pieces."

Faintly, yet decipherable under a magnifying glass, the three were able to make out this on the paper:

Stonehedge—idim-serpa'l ed serueh soirt a tnaeG ed eteT al rap eetej erbmo'l ed etniop al srevart a sroU'd rehcoR ud eueuq al ed dron ua sdeip tnec.

"What does it mean? What does it mean?" demanded the young woman impatiently. "What does it mean?"

The sudden hardening of her tone caused both Hatch and The Thinking Machine to turn and stare at her. Some strange change had come over her face. There was chagrin, perhaps, and there was more than that—a merciless glitter in the brown eyes, a grim expression about the chin and mouth, a greedy closing and unclosing of the small, well-shaped hands.

"I presume it's a cipher of some sort," remarked The Thinking Machine curtly. "It may take time to read it and to learn definitely just where the treasure is hidden, and you may have to wait for——"

"Treasure!" exclaimed the girl. "Did you say treasure? There is treasure, then?"

The Thinking Machine shrugged his shoulders. "What else?" he asked. "Now, please, let me see the bracelet."

"The bracelet!" the girl repeated, and again Hatch noted that quick change of expression on her pretty face. "I—er—must you see it? I—er——" And she stopped.

"It is absolutely necessary, if I make anything of this," and the scientist indicated the charred paper. "You have it in your pocketbook, of course."

The girl stepped forward suddenly and leaned over the laboratory table, intently studying the mysterious strip of paper. At last she raised her head as if she had reached a decision.

"I have only a—a part of the bracelet," she announced, "only half. It was unavoidably broken, and——"

"Only half?" interrupted The Thinking Machine and he squinted coldly into the young woman's eyes.

"Here it is," she said at last, desperately almost. "I don't know where the other half is; it would be useless to ask me."

She drew an aged, badly scratched half circlet of gold from her pocketbook, handed it to the scientist, then went and looked out the window. The Thinking Machine examined it—the delicate decorative tracings, then the invisible hinge where the bracelet had been rudely torn apart. Twice he raised his squint eyes and stared at the girl as she stood silhouetted against the light of the window. When he spoke again, there was a deeper note in his voice—a singular softening, an unusual deference.

"I shall read the cipher, of course, Miss Harding," he said slowly. "It may take an hour, or it may take a week, I don't know." Again he scrutinized the charred paper. "Do you speak French?" he inquired suddenly.

"Enough to understand and to make myself understood," replied the girl. "Why?"

The Thinking Machine scribbled off a copy of the cipher and handed it to her.

"I'll communicate with you when I reach a conclusion," he remarked. "Please leave your address on your card here," and he handed her the card and pencil.

"You know my home address," she said. "Perhaps it would be better for me to call this afternoon late, or tomorrow."

"I'd prefer to have your address," said the scientist. "As I say, I don't know when I shall be able to speak definitely."

The girl paused for a moment and tapped the blunt end of the pencil against her white teeth thoughtfully with her left hand. "As a matter of fact," she said at last, "I am not returning home now. The events of last night have shaken me considerably, and I am now on my way to Blank Rock, a little seashore town where I shall remain for a few days. My address there will be the High Towers."

"Write it down, please!" directed The Thinking Machine tersely. The girl stared at him strangely, with a challenge in her eyes, then leaned over the table to write. Before the pencil had touched the card, however, she changed her mind and handed both to Hatch, with a smile.

"Please write it for me," she requested. "I write a wretched hand, anyway, and besides I have on my gloves." She turned again to the little scientist, who stood squinting over her head. "Thank you so much for your trouble," she said in conclusion. "You can reach me at this address, either by wire or letter, for the next fortnight."

And a few minutes later she was gone. For a while The Thinking Machine was silent as he again studied the faint writing on the strip of paper.

"The cipher," he remarked to Hatch at last, "is no cipher at all; it's so simple. But there are some other things I shall have to find out first, and—suppose you drop by early tomorrow to see me."

Half an hour later The Thinking Machine went to the telephone, and after running through the book, called a number.

"Is Miss Harding home yet?" he demanded, when an answer came.

"No, sir," was the reply, in a woman's voice.

"Would you mind telling me, please, if she is left-handed?"

"Why, no, sir. She's right-handed. Who is this?"

"I knew it, of course. Good by."

The Thinking Machine was squinting into the inquiring eyes of Hutchinson Hatch.

"The reason why the police are so frequently unsuccessful in explaining the mysteries of crime," he remarked, "is not through lack of natural intelligence, or through lack of a birthgiven aptitude for the work, but through the lack of an absolutely accurate knowledge which is wide enough to enable them to proceed. Now here is a case in point. It starts with a cipher, goes into an intricate astronomical calculation, and from that into simple geometry. The difficulty with the detectives is not that they could not work out each of these as it was presented, perhaps with the aid of some outsider, but that they would not recognize the existence of the three phases of the problem in the first place.

"You have heard me say frequently, Mr. Hatch, that logic is inevitable—as inevitable as that two and two make four not *some*times, but *all* the time. That is true; but it must have an indisputable starting point—the one unit which is unassailable. In this case unit produces unit in order, and the proper array of these units gives a coherent answer. Let me demonstrate briefly just what I mean.

"A masked woman, employing the methods at least of a thief, demands a certain bracelet of this Miss Harding. She doesn't want jewels; she wants that bracelet. Whatever other conjectures may be advanced, the one dominant fact is that that bracelet, itself of little comparative value, is worth more than all the rest to her—the masked woman, I mean—and she has endangered her liberty and perhaps life to get it. Why? The history of the bracelet as she herself stated it to Miss Harding gives the answer. A man in prison, under sentence of death, had that bracelet at one time. We can conjecture immediately, therefore, that the masked woman knew that the fact of its having been in this man's possession gave him an opportunity at least of so marking the bracelet—or of confiding in it, I may say, a valuable secret. One's first thought, therefore, is of treasure—hidden treasure. We shall go further and say treasure hidden by a Continental officer to prevent its falling into other hands as loot. This officer under sentence of death, and therefore cut off from all communication with the outside, took a desperate means of communicating the location of the treasure to his heirs. That is clear, isn't it?"

The reporter nodded.

"I described the bracelet—you heard me—and yet I had never seen it, nor had I a description of it. That description was merely a forward step, a preliminary test of the truth of the first assumptions. I reasoned that the bracelet must be of a type which could be employed to carry a message safely past prying eyes; and there is really only one sort which is feasible, and that is the one I described. These bracelets are always hollow, the invisible hinges hold them together on one side, and they lock in the other. It would be perfectly possible, therefore, to write the message the prisoner wanted to send out on a strip of tissue paper, or any other thin paper, and cram it into the bracelet at the back end. In that event it would certainly pass inspection; the only difficulty would be for the outside person to find it. That was a chance; but it was all a chance anyway.

"When the young woman came here and produced a strip of thin paper, apparently blank, with the multitude of wrinkles in it, I immediately saw that that paper had been recovered from the bracelet. It was old, yellow and worn. Therefore, blank or not, that was the message which the prisoner had sent out. You saw me hold it over the brazier, and saw the characters appear. It was sympathetic ink, of course.

"Hard to make in prison, you say? Not at all. Writing either with lemon juice or milk, once dry, is perfectly invisible on paper; but when exposed to heat at any time afterward, it will appear. That is a chemical truth.

"Now the thing that appeared was a cipher—an absurd one, still a cipher. Extraordinary precaution of the prisoner who was about to die! This cipher—let me see exactly," and the scientist spelled it out:

Stonehedge—idim-serpa'l ed serueh soirt a tnaeG ed eteT al rap eetej erbmo'l ed etniop al srevart a sroU'd rehcoR ud eueuq al ed dron ua sdeip tnec.

"If you know anything of languages, Mr. Hatch," he continued, "you know that French is the only common language where the apostrophe and the accent marks play a very important part. A moment's study of this particular cipher therefore convinced me that it was in French. I tried the simple expedient of reading it backward, with this result

> Stonehedge. Hundred feet due north from the tail of Bear Rock through apex (or point) of shadow cast by Giant's Head. Three P.M.

"I had read the cipher and knew the English clear version before I gave a copy of it to the young woman who was here. I specifically asked her if she knew French, to give her a clue by which she might interpret the cipher herself. And thus I blazed the way within a few minutes to the point where astronomical and geometrical calculations were next. Please bear in mind that this message from the dead was not dated.

"Now, about the young woman herself," continued the scientist after a moment. "The statement of how she came to find the bracelet was obviously untrue; particularly are we convinced of this when she cannot, or will not, explain how it was broken. Therefore, another field is open for scrutiny. The bracelet was broken. If we assume that it is *the* bracelet, and there is no reason to doubt it, and we know that it is in her possession, we know also that more than one person had been searching for it. We know positively that that other person—not the masked girl, but the girl who had preceded her to Miss Harding's room on the same night—got the bracelet from Miss Harding, and we are safe in assuming that it passed out of that other person's hand by force. The bracelet had been literally torn apart at the hinge. In other words, there had been a physical contest, and one piece of the circlet, the piece with the message, passed out of the hands of the person who had preceded the masked woman and stolen the bracelet.

"But this is by the way. Stonehedge is the name of the old Tremaine Harding estate, about twenty miles out, and there the Tremaine Harding family valuables were hidden by William Tremaine Harding, who died by bullet, a martyr to the cause of freedom. We shall get the treasure this afternoon after I have settled one or two dates and made the astronomical and geometrical calculations which are necessary."

There was silence for a minute or more, broken at last by the impatient "Honk, honk!" of an automobile outside.

"We'll go now," announced The Thinking Machine as he rose. "There is a car for us."

He led the way out, Hatch following. A heavy touring car, with three seats, driven by a young woman, was waiting at the door. The woman was a stranger to the reporter, but there was no introduction.

"Did you get the date of Captain Harding's imprisonment?" asked The Thinking Machine.

"Yes," was the reply. "June 3, 1776."

The Thinking Machine clambered in, Hatch following silently, and the car rushed away. It paused in a suburb long enough to pick up two workmen with picks and shovels, who took their places in the back seat, and then the automobile with its strange company—a pretty woman, a newspaper reporter, a distinguished scientist, and two laborers—proceeded on its way. Hatch, alone in the second seat, heard only one remark by the scientist, and this was:

"Of course she was clever enough to read the cipher, after I gave her the hint that it was in French; so we shall find that the place has been dug over, but there is only one chance in three hundred and sixty-five that the treasure was found. I give her credit for extraordinary cleverness, but not enough to make the necessary astronomical calculations."

A run of an hour and a half brought them to Stonehedge, a huge old estate with ramshackle dwelling and acres of rock-ridden ground. Away off in the northwest corner were two large stones—Bear Rock and Giant's Head—rising fifteen or twenty feet above the ground. The car was driven over a rough road and stopped near them.

"You see, she did read the cipher," remarked the scientist placidly. "Workmen have already been here."

Straight ahead of them was an excavation ten feet or more square. Hatch peered into it, while The Thinking Machine busied himself by plunging a stake at the so-called tail of Bear Rock. Then he glanced at his watch—it was half past two o'clock—and sat down with the young woman in the shadow of Giant's Head. Hatch lounged on the ground near them, and the workmen made themselves comfortable in their own way.

"We can't do anything till three o'clock," remarked The Thinking Machine.

"And just what shall we do then?" inquired the young woman expectantly. It was the first time she had spoken since they started.

"It is rather difficult to explain," said The Thinking Machine. "The hole over there proves that the young woman read the cipher, of course. Now here briefly is why the treasure was not found. Today is September 17. A measurement was made, according to instructions, from the tail of Bear Rock through the apex of the shadow of Giant's Head precisely at three o'clock yesterday one hundred feet due north, or as near north as possible. The hole shows the end of the hundred-foot line. Now we know that Captain Harding was imprisoned on June 3, 1776. We know he buried the treasure before that date; we have a right to assume it was only shortly before. On June 3 of any year the apex of the shadow will be in a totally different place from September 17, because of the movement of the earth about the sun and the relative changes in the sun's position. What we must do now is to find precisely where the shadow falls at three o'clock today, then make our calculations to show where it will fall say one week before June 3. Do you follow me? In other words, a difference of half a foot in the location of the apex of the shadow will make a difference of many feet at the end of one hundred feet when we follow the cipher."

At precisely three o'clock The Thinking Machine noted the position of the shadow, and then began a calculation which covered two sheets of blank paper which Hatch had had in his pocket.

"This is correct," said The Thinking Machine at last as he rose and planted another stake in the ground. "There is a chance, of course, that we miss fire the first time because of a change in the surface of the ground, or a few days' error in the assumed date, but this is mathematically correct."

Then, with the assistance of the newspaper man and the young woman, he drew his hundred foot line, and planted a third stake.

"Dig here!" he told the workmen.

One hour later the long-lost family plate and jewels of the ancient Harding family had been unearthed. The Thinking Machine and the others stooped over the rotting box which had been brought to the surface and noted the contents. Roughly the value was above two hundred thousand dollars.

"And I think that is all, Miss Harding," said the scientist at last. "It is yours. Load it into your car there, and drive home."

"Miss Harding!" Hatch repeated quickly, with a glance at the young woman. "Miss Harding!"

The Thinking Machine turned and squinted at the reporter for a moment. "Didn't you know that the young woman who called on me was not Miss Harding?" he demanded. "It was evident in her every act—in her failing to explain the broken bracelet, and in the fact that she was left-handed. You must have noticed that. Well, this is Miss Harding, and she is right-handed."

The girl smiled at Hatch's astonishment.

"Then the other woman merely impersonated Miss Harding?" he asked at last.

"That is all, and cleverly," replied The Thinking Machine. "She merely wanted me to read the cipher for her. I put her on the track of reading it herself purposely, and she and the persons associated with her are responsible for the excavation over there."

"But who is the other young woman?"

"She is the one who visited Miss Harding, wearing a mask."

"But what is her name? And who is the third woman? And how did this all come about now?"

"I'm sure I haven't the faintest idea," responded the little scientist shortly. "We have the masked woman to thank, however, for placing the solution of the affair into our hands. Who she is, and what she is, is of no real consequence now, particularly as Miss Harding has this."

The scientist indicated the box with one small foot, and then turned and clambered into the waiting automobile.

THE PROBLEM OF THE CROSS MARK

It was an unsolved mystery, apparently a riddle without an answer, in which Watson Richards, the distinguished character actor, happened to play a principal part. The story was told at the Mummers Club one dull afternoon. Richards' listeners were three other actors, a celebrated poet, and a newspaper reporter named Hutchinson Hatch.

"You know there are few men in the profession today who really amount to anything, who haven't had their hard knocks. Well, my hard times came early, and lasted a long time. So it was just about three years ago to a day that a real crisis came in my affairs. It seemed the end. I had gone one day without food, had bunked in the park that night, and here it was two o'clock in the afternoon of another day. It was dismal enough.

"I was standing on a corner, gazing moodily across the street at the display window of a restaurant, rapidly approaching the don't care stage. Some one came up behind and touched me on the shoulder. I turned listlessly enough, and found myself facing a stranger—a clean-cut, well groomed man of some forty years.

"'Is this Mr. Watson Richards, the character actor?' he asked.

"'Yes,' I replied.

"'I have been looking for you everywhere,' he explained briefly. 'I want to engage you to do a part for one performance. Are you at liberty?'

"You chaps know what that meant to me just at that moment. Certainly the words dispelled some unpleasant possibilities I had been considering.

"'I am at liberty—yes,' I replied, 'Be glad to do it. What sort of part is it?'

"'An old man,' he informed me. 'Just one performance, you know. Perhaps you'd better come up town with me and see Mr. Hallman right now.'

"I agreed with a readiness which approached eagerness, and he called a passing cab. Hallman was perhaps the manager, or stage manager, I thought. We had driven on for a block in the general direction of up town, my companion chatting pleasantly. Finally he offered me a cigar. I accepted it. I know now that the cigar was drugged, because I had hardly taken more than two or three puffs from it when I lost myself completely.

"The next thing I remember distinctly was of stepping out of the cab—I think the stranger assisted me—and going into a house. I don't know where it was—I didn't know then—didn't know even the street. I was dizzy, giddy. And suddenly I stood before a tall, keen-faced, clean-shaven man. He was Hallman. The stranger introduced me and then left the room. Hallman regarded me keenly for several minutes, and somehow under that scrutiny my dormant faculties were aroused. I had thrown away the cigar at the door.

"'You play character parts?' Hallman began.

"'Yes, all the usual things,' I told him. 'I'm rather obscure, but——'

"'I know,' he interrupted, 'but I have seen your work, and like it. I have been told too that you are remarkably clever at make-up.'

"I think I blushed—I hope I did, anyway—I know I nodded. He paused to stare at me for a long time.

"'For instance,' he went on finally, 'you would have no difficult at all in making up as a man of seventy-five years?'

"'Not the slightest,'" I answered. 'I have played such parts.'

"'Yes, yes, I know,' and he seemed a little impatient. 'Well, your make-up is the matter which is most important here. I want you for only one performance; but the make-up must be perfect, you understand." Again he stopped and stared at me. 'The pay will be one hundred dollars for the one performance.'

"He drew out a drawer of a desk and produced a photograph. He looked at it, then at me, several times, and finally placed it in my hands.

"'Can you make-up to look precisely like that?' he asked quietly.

"I studied the photograph closely. It was that of a man about seventy-five years old, of rather a long cast of features, not unlike the general shape of my own face. He had white hair, and was clean-shaven. It was simple enough, with the proper wig, a make-up box, and a mirror.

"'I can,' I told Hallman.

"'Would you mind putting on the make-up here now for my inspection?' he inquired.

"'Certainly not,' I replied. It did not strike me at the moment as unusual. 'But I'll need the wig and paints.'

"'Here they are,' said Hallman abruptly and produced them. 'There's a mirror in front of you. Go ahead.'

"I examined the wig and compared it with the photograph. It was as near perfect as I had ever seen. The make-up box was new and the most complete I ever saw. It didn't occur to me until a long time afterward that it had never been used before. So I went to work. Hallman paced up and down nervously behind me. At the end of twenty minutes I turned upon him a face which was so much like the photograph that I might have posed for it. He stared at me in amazement.

"'By George,' he exclaimed. 'That's it! It's marvelous!' Then he turned and opened the door. 'Come in Frank,' he called, and the man who had conducted me there entered. Hallman indicated me with a wave of his hand . . .

"'How is it?' he asked.

"Frank, whoever he was, also seemed astonished. Then that passed and a queer expression appeared on his face. You may imagine that I awaited their verdict anxiously.

"'Perfect—absolutely perfect,' said Frank at last.

"'Perhaps the only thing,' Hallman mused critically 'is that it isn't quite pale enough.'

"'Easily remedied,' I replied and turned again to the make-up box. A moment later I turned back to the two men. Simple enough, you know—it was one of those pallid, pasty faced make-ups—the old man on the verge of the grave, and all that sort of thing—good deal of pearl powder.

"'That's it!' exclaimed the two men.

"The man Frank looked at Hallman inquiringly.

"'Go ahead,' said Hallman, and Frank left the room.

"Hallman went over, closed and locked the door, after which he came back and sat down in front of me, staring at me for a long time in silence. At length he opened an upper drawer of the desk and glanced in. A revolver lay there, right under his hand. I know now he intended that I should see it.

"'Now, Mr. Richards,' he said at last very slowly, 'what we want you to do is very simple, and as I said there's a hundred dollars in it. I know your circumstances perfectly—you need the hundred dollars.' He offered me a cigar, and foolishly enough I accepted it. 'The part you are to play is that of an old man, who is ill in bed, speechless, utterly helpless. You are dying, and you are to play the part. Use your eyes all you want; but don't speak!'

"Gradually the dizziness I had felt before was coming upon me again. As I said, I know now it was the cigar; but I kept on smoking.

"'There will be no rehearsal,' Hallman went on, and now I knew he was fingering the revolver I had seen in the desk, but it made no particular impression on me. 'If I ask you questions, you may nod an affirmative, but don't speak! Do only what I say, and nothing else!'

"Full realization was upon me now; but everything was growing hazy again. I remember I fought the feeling for a moment; then it seemed to overwhelm me, and I was utterly helpless under the dominating power of that man.

"'When am I to play the part?' I remember asking.

"'Now!' said Hallman suddenly, and he rose. 'I'm afraid you don't fully understand me yet, Mr. Richards. If you play the part properly, you get the hundred dollars; if you don't, this!'

"He meant the revolver. I stared at it dumbly, overcome by a helpless terror, and tried to stand up. Then there came a blank, for how long I don't know. The next thing I remember I was lying in bed propped up against several pillows. I opened my eyes feebly enough, and there wasn't any acting about it either, because whoever drugged those cigars knew his business.

"There in front of me was Hallman, with a grief-stricken expression on his face which made all my art seem amateurish. There was another man there (not Frank) and a woman who seemed to be about forty years old. I couldn't see their faces—I wouldn't even be able to suggest a description of them, because the room was almost dark. Just the faintest flicker of light came through in low tones—sickroom voices—but I couldn't hear and doubt if I could have followed their conversation if I had heard.

"Finally the door opened and a girl entered. I have seen many women, but—well she was peculiarly fascinating. She gave one little cry, rushed toward the bed impulsively, dropped on her knees beside it, and buried her face in the sheets. She was shaking with sobs.

"Then I knew—intuitively, perhaps, but I knew—that in some way I was being used to injure that girl. A sudden feeling of fearful anger seized upon me, but I couldn't move to save my soul. Hallman must have caught the blaze in my eyes, for he came forward on the other side of the bed, and, under cover of a handkerchief which he had been using rather ostentatiously, pressed the revolver against my side.

"But I wouldn't be made a tool of. In my dazed condition I know I was seized with a desperate desire to fight it out—to make him kill me if he had to, but I would not deceive the girl. I knew if I could jerk my head down on the pillow it would disarrange the wig, and perhaps she would see. I couldn't. I might pass my hands across my make-up and smear it. But I couldn't lift my hands. I was struggling to speak, and couldn't.

"Then somehow I lost myself again. Hazily I remember that somebody placed a paper in front of me on a book—a legal-looking document—and guided my hand across it; but that isn't clear. I was helpless, inert, so much clay in the hands of this man Hallman. Then everything faded—slowly, slowly. My impression was that I was actually dying; my eyelids closed of themselves and the last thing I saw was the shining gold of that girl's hair as she sobbed there beside me.

"That's all of it. When I became fully conscious again a policeman was shaking me. I was sitting on a bench in the park. He swore at me volubly, and I got up and moved slowly along the path with my hands in my pockets. Something was clenched in one hand. I drew it out and looked at it. It was a hundred-dollar bill. I remember I got something to eat; and I woke up in a hospital.

"Well, that's the story. Make what you like of it. It can never be solved, of course. It was three years ago. You fellows know what I have done in that time. Well, I'd give it all, every bit of it, to meet that girl again (I should know her), tell her what I know, and make her believe that it was no fault of mine."

Hutchinson Hatch related the circumstances casually one afternoon a day or so later to Professor Augustus S. F. X. Van Dusen—The Thinking Machine.

That eminent man of science listened petulantly, as he listened to all things. "It happened in this city?" he inquired at the end.

"Yes."

"But Richards has no idea what part of the city?"

"Not the slightest. I imagine that the drugged cigar and a naturally weakened condition made him lose his bearings while in the cab."

"I dare say," commented the scientist. "And of course he has never seen Hallman again?"

"No—he would have mentioned it if he had."

"Does Richards remember the exact date of the affair?"

"I dare say he does, though he didn't mention it," replied the reporter.

"Suppose you see Richards and get the date—exactly, if possible," remarked The Thinking Machine. "You might telephone it to me. Perhaps——" and he shrugged his slender shoulders.

"You think there is a possibility of solving the riddle?" demanded the reporter eagerly.

"Certainly," snapped The Thinking Machine. "It requires no solution. It is ridiculously simple—obvious, I might say—and yet I dare say the girl Richards referred to has been the victim of some huge plot. It's worth looking into for her sake."

"Remember, it happened three years ago," Hatch suggested tentatively.

"It wouldn't matter particularly if it happened thirty years ago," declared the scientist. "Logic, Mr. Hatch, remains the same through all the ages—from Adam and Eve to us. Two and two made four in the

Garden of Eden just as they do now in a counting house. Therefore, the solution, I say, is absurdly simple. The only problem is to discover the identity of the principals in the affair—and a child could do that."

Later that afternoon Hatch telephoned to The Thinking Machine from the Mummers Club.

"That date you asked for was May 19, three years ago," said the reporter.

"Very well," commented The Thinking Machine. "Drop by tomorrow afternoon. Perhaps we can solve the riddle for Richards."

Hatch called late the following afternoon, as directed, but The Thinking Machine was not in.

"He went out about nine o'clock and hasn't returned yet," the scientist's aged servant, Martha, informed him.

That night about ten o'clock Hatch used the telephone in a second attempt to reach The Thinking Machine.

"He hasn't come in yet," Martha told him over the wire. "He said he would be back for luncheon; but he isn't here yet."

Hatch replaced the receiver thoughtfully on the hook. Early the next morning he again used the telephone, and there was a note of anxiety in Martha's voice when she answered.

"He hasn't come yet, sir," she explained. "Please, what ought I to do? I'm afraid something has happened to him."

"Don't do anything yet," replied Hatch. "I dare say he'll return today."

Again at noon, at six o'clock, and at eleven that night Hatch called Martha on the telephone. Still the scientist had not appeared. Hatch, too, was worried now; yet how should he proceed? He didn't know, and he hesitated to think of the possibilities. On the morrow, however, something must be done—he would take the matter to Detective Mallory at police headquarters if necessary.

But this was made unnecessary unexpectedly by the arrival next morning of a letter from The Thinking Machine. As he read, an expression of bewilderment spread over Hatch's face. Tersely, the letter was like this:

> Employ an expert burglar, a careful, clever man. At two o'clock of the night following the receipt of this letter, go with him to the alley which runs behind No. 810 Blank St. Enter this house with him from the rear, go up two flights of stairs, and let him pick the lock of the third door on the left from the head of the stairs. Silence above everything. Don't shoot if possible to avoid it.
>
> VAN DUSEN
>
> P.S. Put some ham sandwiches in your pocket.

Hatch stared at the note in blank bewilderment for a long time, but he obeyed orders. Thus it came to pass that at ten minutes of two o'clock that night he boosted the notorious Blindy Bates—a man of rare accomplishments in his profession, who at the moment happened to be out of prison—to the top of the rear fence of No. 810 Blank St. Bates hauled up the reporter and they leaped down lightly inside the yard.

The back door was simplicity itself to the gifted Bates, and yielded in less than sixty seconds from the moment he laid his hand on it. Then came a sneaking, noiseless advance along the lower hall, to the accompaniment of innumerable thrills up and down Hatch's spinal column; up the first flight safely, with Blindy Bates leading the way; then along the hall and up the second flight. There was absolutely not a sound in the house—they moved like ghosts.

At the top of the second flight Bates shot a gleam of light from his dark lantern along the hall. The third door it was. And a moment later he was concentrating every faculty on the three locks of this door. Still there had been not the slightest sound. The one spot in the darkness was the bull's eye of the lantern as it illuminated the lock. The first lock was unfastened, then the second, and finally the third. Bates didn't open the door—he merely stepped back—and the door opened as of its own volition. Involuntarily Hatch's hand closed fiercely on his revolver, and Bates's ready weapon glittered a little in the darkness.

"Thanks," came after a moment, in the quiet, querulous voice of The Thinking Machine. "Mr. Hatch, did you bring those sandwiches?"

Half an hour later The Thinking Machine and Hatch appeared at police headquarters. Being naturally of a retiring, unostentatious disposition, Bates did not accompany them. Instead, he went his way fingering a bill of moderately large denomination.

Detective Mallory was at home in bed; but Detective Cunningham, another shining light, received his distinguished visitor and Hatch.

"There's a man named Howard Guerin now asleep in his state room aboard the steamer *Austriana*, which sails at five o'clock this morning—just an hour and a half from now—for Hamburg," began The Thinking Machine without any preface. "Please have him arrested immediately."

"What charge?" asked the detective.

"Really, it's of no consequence," replied The Thinking Machine. "Attempted murder, conspiracy, embezzlement, fraud—whatever you like. I can prove any or all of them."

"I'll go after him myself," said the detective.

"And there is also a young woman aboard," continued The Thinking Machine, "a Miss Hilda Fanshawe. Please have her detained, not arrested, and keep a close guard on her—not to prevent escape, but to protect her."

"Tell us some of the particulars of it," asked the detective.

"I haven't slept in more than forty-eight hours," replied The Thinking Machine. "I'll explain it all this afternoon, after I've rested a while."

The Thinking Machine, for the benefit of Detective Mallory and his satellites, recited briefly the salient points of the story told by the actor, Watson Richards. His listeners were Howard Guerin, tall, keen-faced, and clean-shaven; Miss Hilda Fanshawe, whose pretty face reflected her every thought; Hutchinson Hatch, and three or four headquarters men. Every eye was upon the drawn face of the diminutive scientist, as he sat far back in his chair, with squint eyes turned upward, and fingertips pressed together.

"From the facts as he stated them, we know beyond all question, in the very beginning, that Mr. Richards was used as a tool to further some conspiracy or fraud," explained The Thinking Machine. "That was obvious. So the first thing to do was to learn the identity of those persons who played the principal parts in it. From Mr. Richards' story we apparently had nothing, yet it gave us practically the names and addresses of the persons at the bottom of the thing.

"How? To find how, we'll have to consider the purpose of the conspiracy. An actor—an artist in facial impersonation, we might say—is picked up in the street and compelled to go through the mummery of a death bed scene while stupefied with drugs. Obviously this was arranged for the benefit of some person who must be convinced that he or she had witnessed a dissolution and the signature of a will, perhaps—and a will signed under the eyes of that person for whose benefit the farce was acted.

"So we assume a will was signed. We know, within reason, that the mummery was arranged for the benefit of a young woman—Miss Fanshawe here. From the intricacy and daring of the plot, it was pretty safe to assume that a large sum of money was involved. As a matter of fact, there was—more than a million. Now, here is where we take an abstract problem and establish the identity of the actors in it. That will was signed by compulsory forgery, if I may use the phrase, by an utter stranger—a man who could not have known the handwriting of the man whose name he signed, and who was in a condition that makes it preposterous to imagine that he even attempted to sign that name. Yet the will was signed, and the conspirators had to have a signature that would bear inspection. Now, what have we left?

"When a person is incapable of signing his or her name, physically or by reason of no education, the law accepts a cross mark as a signature, when properly witnessed. We know Mr. Richards couldn't have known or imitated the signature of the old man he impersonated; but he did sign—therefore a cross mark, which could have been established beyond question in a court of law. Now, you see how I established the identity of the persons in this fraud. I got the date of the incident from Mr. Richards, then a trip to the surrogate's office told me all I wanted to know. What will had been filed for probate about that date which bore the cross mark as a signature? The records answered the question instantly—John Wallace Lawrence.

"I glanced over the will. It specifically allowed Miss Hilda Fanshawe a trivial thousand dollars a year, and yet she was Lawrence's adopted daughter. See how the joints began to fit together? Further, the will left the bulk of the property to Howard Guerin, a Mrs. Francis—since deceased, by the way—and one Frank Hughes. The men were his nephews, the woman his niece. The joints continued to fit nicely, therefore the problem was solved. It was an easy matter to find these people, once I knew their names. I found Guerin—Mr. Richards knew him as Hallman—and asked him about the matter. From the fact that he locked me up in a room of his house and kept me prisoner for two days, I was convinced that he was the principal conspirator. And so it proves."

Again there was silence. Detective Mallory took three long breaths, and asked a question. "But where was John Wallace Lawrence when this thing happened?"

"Miss Fanshawe had been in Europe, and was rushing home, knowing that her adopted father was dying," The Thinking Machine explained. "As a matter of fact, when she returned, Mr. Lawrence was dead—he died the day before the farce which had been arranged for her benefit, and at the moment his body lay in an upstairs room. He was buried two days later—a day after the imposture—and she attended his funeral. You see, there was no reason why she should have suspected anything. I don't happen to know the provisions of Lawrence's real will, but I dare say it left practically everything to her. The thousand-dollar allowance by the conspirators was a sop to stop possible legal action."

The door of the room opened, and a uniformed man thrust his head in. "Mr. Richards wants to see Professor Van Dusen," he announced.

Immediately behind him came the actor. He stopped in the door and stared at Guerin for a moment.

"Why, hello Hallman!" he remarked pleasantly. Then his eyes fell upon the girl, and a flash of recognition lighted them.

"Miss Fanshawe, permit me, Mr. Richards," said The Thinking Machine. "You have met before. This is the gentleman you saw die."

"And where is Frank Hughes?" asked Detective Mallory.

"In South Africa," replied the scientist. "I learned a great deal while I was a prisoner."

A deeply troubled expression suddenly appeared on Hutchinson

Hatch's face that night when he was writing the story for his newspaper, and he went to the telephone and called The Thinking Machine.

"If you were guarded so closely as a prisoner in that room, how on earth did you mail that letter to me?" he inquired.

"Guerin came in to say some unpleasant things," came the reply, "and placed several letters he intended to post on the table for a moment. The letter for you was already written and stamped, and I was seeking a way to mail it, so I put it with his letters and he mailed it for me."

Hatch burst out laughing.

THE PROBLEM OF THE SOUVENIR CARDS

There were three of the post cards. The first one was a vividly colored picture of the Capitol at Washington. It was postmarked, "Philadelphia, November 12, 2:20 P.M." Below the picture in a small copperplate hand, were these figures and symbols: "I-28-38-4 x 47-30-2 x 21-10-8 x 65-5 x 29-32-11 x 40-2-9x."

The second post card was a picture of Park Square, Boston, with the majestic figures of Lincoln and the slave in the foreground. This, too, was postmarked Philadelphia, but the date was November 13. The symbols and figures were unquestionably written by the same hand as those on the first: "II-155-19-9 x 205-2-8 x agree x 228-31-2x present tense x 235-13-4."

The third card was a colored reproduction of an idyllic bayou near New Orleans. Again the postmark was Philadelphia, but the date was November 14. This card contained only: "III-11-1-9 x 181-15-10 x press."

Professor Augustus S. F. X. Van Dusen—The Thinking Machine—turned and twisted the post cards in his slender fingers while he studied them through squinting, watery, blue eyes. At last he laid them on a table beside him, and sank back in his chair, with long white fingers pressed tip to tip. He was in a receptive mood.

"Well?" he demanded abruptly.

The bearded stranger who had offered two cards for his scrutiny was gazing at the diminutive figure and the drawn petulant face of the scientist, seemingly in mingled wonder and amusement. It was difficult for him to associate this crabbed little man with those achievements which had placed his name so high in the sciences. After a moment the visitor's gaze wavered a little and dropped.

"My name is William C. Colgate," he began. "Sometime since—four weeks and three days to be exact—a diamond was stolen from my house in this city, and no trace of it has ever been found. It was one I bought uncut in South Africa five years ago, and its weight is about thirty carats. When cut, I imagine it will be eighteen to twenty carats, and it is, as it stands now, worth about forty thousand dollars. You may have read something of the theft in the newspapers?"

"I never read the newspapers," remarked The Thinking Machine.

"Well, in that event," and Colgate smiled, "I can briefly state the facts in the case. For several years I have had in my employment a secretary, Charles Travers. He is about twenty-five years old. Within the last four or five months I have noticed a change in his manner. Where formerly he had been quiet and unassuming, he has, through evil associations I dare say, grown to be a little wild, and, I believe, has lived beyond his means. I took occasion twice to remonstrate with him. The first time he seemed contrite and repentant; the second time he grew angry, and the following day disappeared. The diamond went with him."

"Do you know that?" demanded The Thinking Machine.

"I know it as well as one may know anything," replied Colgate positively. "I doubt if anyone except Travers knew where I kept the jewel. Certainly my servants did not, and certainly my wife and daughters did not. Besides my wife and two daughters have been in Europe for months. The police seem to be unable to learn anything, so I came to you."

"Just where did you keep the jewel?"

"In a drawer of my desk," was the reply. "Ultimately I had intended to have it cut and present it to my oldest daughter, possibly on the occasion of her marriage. Now——" Colgate waved his hand.

The Thinking Machine sat silent for several minutes. His squint eyes were turned steadily upward and several tiny lines appeared in the domelike brow. "The problem then seems to be merely one of finding your secretary," he stated at last. "The diamond is of course so large that it would be absurd to attempt to dispose of it in its present shape. Travers is an intelligent man; we shall give him credit for realizing this about the diamond. And yet if it should be cut up into smaller stones, its value would dwindle to a tenth part of what it is now. Under those circumstances, would he have it cut up?"

"That is one of the questions which I should like to have answered."

For the second time The Thinking Machine picked up and examined the three post cards. "And what have these to do with it?" he demanded.

"That's another question I should like to have answered," said Colgate. "I can only believe that in some way they bear on the mystery surrounding the disappearance of the gem. Perhaps they give a clue to where it is now."

"This is Travers's handwriting?"

"Yes."

"The cards obviously constitute a cipher of some sort," declared the scientist. "Were you and Travers accustomed to communicate in cipher?"

"Not at all."

"Then why is this in cipher?" demanded The Thinking Machine belligerently. He glared at Colgate much as if he held him to blame.

Colgate shrugged his shoulders.

"Of course," continued the scientist, "I can find out what it means. It is elementary in character, and yet I doubt if, after we know what is in it, it will be particularly illuminating. Still, giving Travers credit for intelligence, I should imagine this to be an offer to return the diamond, probably for a consideration. But why in cipher?"

Colgate did not seem to be able to add to what he had already said, and after a few minutes took his leave, with instructions from The Thinking Machine to return on the following day, after the scientist had had an opportunity to study the post cards. He called at the appointed hour.

Have you a three-volume book of any sort that you read or refer to frequently?"

For some reason Colgate seemed a little startled. It was only momentary, however. "I suppose I have several books of three volumes."

"No particular one that your secretary would know that you read frequently?" insisted the scientist.

Again some strange impalpable expression shifted across Colgate's face. "No," he said after a moment.

The Thinking Machine rose "It will be necessary then," he said, "for me to go over your library and see if I can't find the book to which this cipher refers."

"Book?" asked Colgate curiously. "If the cipher has no relation to the diamond, I don't see that——"

"Of course you don't see," snapped the scientist. "Come along and let me see."

Colgate seemed a little perturbed by the suggestion. He folded his immaculate gloves over and over as he stared at the inscrutable face before him. "it would be impossible," he said at last, "to find anything in my library just now. As I said, my wife and daughter are abroad, and during their absence I have taken occasion to have my library and one or two other rooms redecorated and refinished. All my books meanwhile are packed away helterskelter."

The Thinking Machine sat down again and stared at him

inquiringly. "Then when your library is in order again, you may call," he said tersely. "I can do nothing until I see the books."

"But—but——" stammered Colgate.

"Good day," said The Thinking Machine curtly.

Colgate went away. It was not till three days later that he reappeared. If one might have judged by his manner, he had achieved something in his absence; yet when he spoke, it was in the same exquisitely modulated tone of the first visit.

"The work of redecorating has been completed," he said to The Thinking Machine. "My library is again in order, and you may examine it at your leisure. If you care to go now, my carriage is at the door."

The Thinking Machine stared at him for a moment, then picked up his hat. At the door of the Colgate mansion Colgate and the scientist were met by a graven-faced footman, who received their hats and coats in silence. Colgate conducted his guest straight into the library. It was a magnificently appointed place, reflecting in its every detail the splendid purchasing power of money. To this sheer luxury, however, The Thinking Machine was oblivious. His undivided attention was on the book shelves.

From one end of the long room to the other he walked, time after time, reading the titles of the books as he passed. There were Dickens, Balzac, Kipling, Stevenson, Thackeray, Zola—all of them. Three or four times he paused to draw out a volume and examine it. Each time he replaced it without a word and continued his search. Colgate stood by, watching him curiously.

The Thinking Machine had just paused to draw out one of the Dumas books when the stolid faced footman appeared in the door with a telegram.

"Is this for you, sir?" he asked of Colgate.

"Yes," replied Colgate.

He drew out the yellow sheet and permitted the envelope to fall to the floor. The Thinking Machine picked it up with something like eagerness in his manner. It was directed to "William C. Colgate." The scientist looked almost astonished as he turned again to the book shelves.

It was ten minutes later that The Thinking Machine took out three volumes together. These comprised the famous old English novel, *Ten Thousand a Year,* a rare and valuable first edition. The leaves of volume one fluttered through his fingers until he came to page 28. After a moment he said, "Ah!" Then he went on to page 47. He studied that for a moment or more, after which he said, "Ah!" once again.

"What is it?" inquired Colgate quickly.

The Thinking Machine turned his cold squint eyes up into the eager face above him. "It is the key to the cipher," he said.

"What is it? Read it!" commanded Colgate. His clear, alert eyes were fastened on the, to him, meaningless page. He sought vainly there for something to account for the scientist's exclamation. But he saw only words—a page of words with no apparent meaning beyond the text of the story. "What is it?" he demanded again, and there was a little glitter in his eye. "Does it say where the diamond is?"

"Considering the fact that I have seen only words of a possible twenty or thirty, I don't know what it says," declared The Thinking Machine aggressively. "The best I can say now is that with the aid of these books I shall find the diamond."

For half an hour or more the scientist was busy running through the book in an aimless sort of way. Finally he closed the third volume with a snap, and stood up.

"Travers says that he will return the gem for ten thousand dollars," he announced.

"Oh, he does, does he?" Colgate's tone was a sneer. Again in his face The Thinking Machine read some subtle quality which brought a slight wrinkle of perplexity to his brow.

"You don't have to pay it, you know," he explained tartly. "I can get it without the ten thousand dollars, of course."

"Well, get it, then!" said Colgate a little impatiently. "I want the diamond, and it is absurd to suppose that I shall pay ten thousand dollars for my own property. Come on! Let's do what is to be done immediately."

"I'll do what is to be done immediately; but I will do it without your assistance," remarked The Thinking Machine. "I shall send for you tomorrow. When you come, the diamond will be in my possession. Good day."

Colgate stared after him blankly as he went out.

The Thinking Machine was talking over the telephone with Hutchinson Hatch, reporter.

"Do you know William C. Colgate by sight?" he demanded.

"Very well," Hatch replied.

"Is he red-headed?"

"No."

"Good by."

On the following morning a short advertisement appeared in all the city newspapers. It was simply:

Will give ten thousand dollars. Matter is not in hands of police. To insure your safety, telephone 1103 Bay and arrange details.

It was only a few minutes past nine o'clock that morning when The Thinking Machine was called to the telephone. For some reason he had difficulty in understanding, possibly due to the spluttering of the receiver. Then he did understand, and sat down for some time, apparently to consider what he had heard. Later he telephoned to Hutchinson Hatch.

"It's about this theft of the Colgate diamond," he explained. "The secretary, Travers, who is wanted for the theft, is now somewhere in the North End, either drunk or drugged, and possibly disguised. I imagine his photograph has been in all the newspapers. I have been talking to him over the telephone, and he is to call me again about eleven o'clock. Go down to the North End near the corner of Hanover and Blank Streets, hire a telephone for the morning, and call me. Remain at the phone from half-past ten until I call you. You are to get Travers. When you get him, bring him here. Don't notify the police."

"But will I get him?" asked the reporter.

"If you don't, you are stupid," retorted The Thinking Machine.

At five minutes of eleven o'clock the scientist's telephone rang. He was sitting staring at it at the moment, but instead of answering, stepped to the door and called Martha, his aged servant.

"Answer the telephone," he directed, "and tell whoever is there that I am not here. Tell them I shall return in ten minutes and to be sure to call me again."

Martha followed the instructions and hung up the receiver. Instantly The Thinking Machine went to the telephone.

"Can you tell me, please, the number of the telephone which just called me?" he asked quickly. "No, I don't want a connection. Number 34710 North? Where is that? In a café at Hanover and Blank Streets?" he said. "Thanks."

A minute later he had Hatch on the wire again. "Travers will call me in five minutes from 34710 North, in a café at Hanover and Blank Streets," he said. "Get him and bring him here as quickly as you can. Good by."

So it came about that within less than an hour a cab rushed up to the door, and Hutchinson Hatch, accompanied by a young man, entered. The man was Travers. A week's scrubby beard was on his chin, his face was perfectly pallid; the fever of drink and fear glittered in his eyes. Hatch had to support him to a chair, in which he dropped back limply. The Thinking Machine scowled down into the young man's face, and was met by a fishy, imbecilic stare in return.

"Are you Mr. Travers?" inquired The Thinking Machine.

"That's all right—that's all right," muttered the young man, and overcome by the exertion of speech, his head dropped back and in a moment he was sound asleep.

Without apparent compunction The Thinking Machine went through his pockets. After a moment he found what seemed to be a rough rock crystal. He squinted at it closely as he turned and twisted it back and forth in his hand, then passed it to Hatch for inspection.

"That's worth forty thousand dollars," he remarked casually.

"Is this the——"

"It's the Colgate diamond," interrupted The Thinking Machine. "I surmised that he would have it somewhere about him, because he would have no place to hide it—and now for the second man—the brains of the theft. First I shall telephone for Colgate. Look at him when he enters, for I think you will be greatly surprised. And above all, remember to be careful."

Looking deeply into the quiet, squint eyes of the scientist, Hatch read a warning. He understood and nodded. Travers, stupefied, was removed to an adjoining room.

A few minutes later there was a rattle of carriage wheels, the door bell rang, and Colgate entered. Hatch glanced at him, then turned quietly to look out of a window.

"You have the diamond?" burst out Colgate suddenly.

"I said I would have it when you came," retorted The Thinking Machine. "Now for these post cards," and the scientist produced the three cards that had been handed to him at first. "Perhaps you would be interested to know what was really on them?"

"I haven't the slightest curiosity," said Colgate impatiently. "All I want is the diamond. If you will give me that, I think perhaps that will terminate this affair, and there will be no necessity of taking up more of your time."

"Of course, you have no desire to prosecute Travers?" asked The Thinking Machine enigmatically. "But as to these post cards. They constitute what is known as the book cipher. For your information I may state that it is always possible to know a book cipher by the fact that a small number, rarely above twelve or fourteen, always precedes the X; the X merely divides the words. For instance, on the first card we have I-28-38-4; in other words, volume one, page 28, line 38 and the fourth word of that line. Unless one knows or can learn the name of the book which is the basis of the cipher, it is perhaps the most difficult of all. Any ordinary cipher may be solved precisely as Poe solved his cipher in 'The Gold Bug.'"

"But I am not at all interested——" protested Colgate.

"So really all that was necessary for me to do was to find out what book was the basis of this particular cipher," continued The Thinking Machine to Hatch, without heeding his visitor's remark. "I knew of course it was some book in Mr. Colgate's home. The clue to what book was given, either wittingly or unwittingly, by the single I, the two I's and the three I's on the first, second, and third cards. Did these represent volumes? I found a dozen three-volume books in Mr. Colgate's library, but in each instance there was no connection in the first three or four words which I found in accordance with the number given; that is, until I came to *Ten Thousand a Year*. The first word I found in that was 'will,' the second, page 47, line 30, second word was 'return,' the third was 'diamond.' So I knew that was the book I wanted. Here is the full meaning of the cipher as it appears on the three cards, as I have transcribed it."

He handed Colgate a slip of paper, on which was written:

> Will return diamond for ten thousand. If you agree, informed (present tense—i.e., inform) me in daily press.

"This all seems very clever and very curious indeed," commented Colgate, "but really I do not think——"

"The book of Mr. Colgate's is a first edition—there is also a first edition in the public library," the scientist went on placidly, "so Travers had no difficulty on that score. We shall admit that the cards were mailed in Philadelphia; perhaps he went there and later returned to this city. The manner in which I got possession of the diamond—by first discovering Travers through an advertisement and the keeping him at the telephone until he was inveigled here, by my assistant—is possibly of no interest; it was all very easily done by a prearranged plan with the telephone exchange; so now, Mr.—Mr.——"

"Colgate," his visitor supplied, as if surprised at the hesitancy.

"I mean your real name," said the scientist quietly.

There was a sudden tense silence. Hatch had come a little closer, and was staring at the stranger with keen, inquiring eyes.

"This is not the Mr. William C. Colgate you know, Mr. Hatch?"

"No."

"Do you happen to have an idea who he is?"

"If I am not mistaken," Hatch replied calmly, "this is a gentleman I have met before on an exceedingly interesting occasion—Mr. Bradlee Cunnyngham Leighton."

At the name the erstwhile Colgate turned upon the reporter with a snarl. There was a quick movement of his right hand, and Hatch found himself blinking down the barrel of a revolver as Leighton slowly moved backward toward the door.

The Thinking Machine moved around behind the aggressor. "Mr. Leighton," he said almost pleasantly, "if you don't lower that revolver, I shall blow your brains out." For one instant Leighton hesitated, then glanced back quickly toward the scientist. That diminutive man stood calmly, with his hands in his pockets. Instantly Hatch leaped. There was a quick, sharp struggle, a few muttered curses, and then the discomfited Leighton, in his turn, was gazing down the revolver barrel.

"Won't you gentlemen sit down?" suggested The Thinking Machine.

They were all sitting down when Detective Mallory rushed up from police headquarters. Leighton was farthest from the door. The Thinking Machine sat staring at him with the revolver held in position for quick use.

"Ah, Mr. Mallory," he said without turning his head or glancing back. "This is Mr. Bradlee Cunnyngham Leighton. You may have heard of him before?"

"Do you mean the Englishman who brought the Varron necklace to this country?" blurted out the detective.

"The same man of the carrier pigeon case," said Hatch grimly.

"I should like particularly to call your attention to Mr. Leighton," continued The Thinking Machine. "He is a man of accomplishments. We know how he distinguished himself by the simple expedient of using carrier pigeons in the Varron necklace affair. In this case he has risen to greater heights. First, I am assuming something—he plotted with young Travers to steal the Colgate diamond. In some manner, which is not essential here, Travers got the diamond and sought to profit by the theft alone by negotiating its return for ten thousand dollars. Travers wrote a cipher to Mr. Colgate, making the proposition—it is probable he knew Mr. Colgate would understand his cipher. I shall give Leighton credit for anticipating just this possibility and intercepting the post cards. They meant nothing to him, so—please note this—he came to me as Colgate, knowing that Mr. Colgate was in Europe with his family, and sought my assistance in recovering the gem from his fellow conspirator. The sublime audacity of all these conceptions marks Mr. Leighton as little short of a genius in his particular profession.

"Only once was Mr. Leighton embarrassed. That was when I told him I should have to visit his library. But he even rose to this necessity brilliantly. He delayed my visit for a day or so, and in some manner, possibly by forgery, secured an entrance to Mr. Colgate's home, perhaps as a cousin of the same name. There he received me. Two or three things had happened to arouse doubt in my mind as to whether he was the true Mr. Colgate.

"First was his hesitancy in connection with my visit to the library; then while I was in the house, a telegram came for Mr. William C. Colgate. The servant asked Mr. Leighton in my presence if the telegram was for him. That question would never have been asked if he had been the real William C. Colgate. Then finally I asked Mr. Hatch over the phone if William C. Colgate was red-headed. William C. Colgate is not red-headed. This gentleman is not Mr. Colgate. I now knew this much. Hatch recognized him as Leighton. He saw him at the time you were interested in his escape from a Scotland Yard man—Conway, who wanted him for stealing a necklace. That is all, I think."

"But the diamond and Travers?" asked the detective.

"Here is the diamond," said The Thinking Machine, and he produced it from one of his pockets. "Travers is lying on a bed in the next room in a drunken stupor."

THE PROBLEM OF THE VANISHING MAN

There was a feverish restlessness in the merciless gray eyes, an unpleasant frown on his brow, as Charles Duer Carroll paused on the curb in front of a tall downtown office building and stared moodily across the busy street into nothingness. Carroll was a remarkable-looking young man in many ways. He was young—only thirty—and physically every line of his body expressed power, sturdiness rather than youth, force rather than grace. He was blessed too with an indomitable, uncompromising jaw, the jaw of a fighting man. The chin was square, the lips thin, avaricious perhaps, the nose slightly hooked, the cheek bones high. In general his appearance was that of a keenly alert man who is never surprised: who chooses his way and pursues it aggressively without haste, without mercy, and without mistakes.

Despite his youth—it may have been because of it—Carroll was president and active head of the great brokerage concern, the Carroll-Swayne-McPartland Company, with general offices on the fourth floor of this huge building behind him. He held that responsible position by right of being the grandson of its founder, old Nick Carroll. Upon his retirement from active business a year previously the old man, a wrinkled, venomous image of the young, had banged his desk with lusty fist and so declared it—Charlie Carroll was to be his successor. There had been heartburnings, objections, violent protest even: but the old man owned five thousand of the ten thousand shares of the company, and—Charles Duer Carroll was president.

Financially the young man was interested in the company only to the extent of owning twenty-five shares, this being a gift from old Nick and a necessary qualification for an office holder. Beyond this rather meager possession—meager at least in comparison with the holdings of other officers and stockholders of the company—young Carroll had only his salary of twenty thousand dollars a year—nothing else, for he had been exalted to this from a salary of eighteen hundred and a clerk's desk in the general office. Here for six years, old Nick Carroll had drilled the business into him, warp and woof; then had come the exaltation.

Thus it came about that a pauper, from the viewpoint of financial circles, directed the affairs of a company whose business ran into millions and tens of millions annually. If young Carroll felt that he needed advice, he did not hesitate to disregard his fellows and go straight to the fountainhead, old Carroll. And when he asked for that advice he regarded it scrupulously, minutely. At other times—in fact, as a general thing—young Carroll sailed on his own course—took the bit in his teeth and did as he pleased—leaving accrued profits to inform the various stockholders of his actions. At such times old Nick was wont to rub his skinny hands together and smile.

For months after young Carroll assumed the reins of government there had been fear of a misstep and consequent wreck in the conservative hearts of officers and stockholders, except in the case of old Carroll; then this apprehension was dissipated, leaving a residue of rankling envy. Not one man in authority would have said it was not for the best that old Nick had thrust this infusion of aggressive young blood into the staid old company; but half a dozen persons at interest could have enumerated a thousand reasons why a youth of thirty should not hold the position of president, when some older man—one of themselves—knew the business better and had been in the office longer.

Be that as it may, Charles Duer Carroll, the pauper, was president of the company. When he stepped into that position he brought with him new vigor and virility and curt, merciless methods which had enabled him to achieve things. This was the young man—this Charles Duer Carroll—who stood on the curb one morning staring, glaring, across the busy street. At last he dropped a half-smoked cigar, ground it to shreds on the pavement beneath a vigorous heel, and turning stared up at the building. There was a window of his office in the corner straight above him, and there was work that called. But Carroll wasn't thinking of that particularly; he was thinking of——

He snapped his fingers impatiently and entered the building. An elevator whirled him up to the fourth floor, and he entered the large outer office of the company. The forbidding frown was still on his brow, the steeliness in his gray eyes. Several clerks nodded respectfully as he entered; but there was no greeting in return, not even a curt time of day. He strode straight across the room to his private office without a glance either to right or left, banging the door behind him.

Over in a corner of the outer office Gordon Swayne, secretary and treasurer, was dictating letters. He glanced round with an expression of annoyance on his face at the sudden noise. "Who did that?" he demanded of his stenographer.

"It was Mr. Carroll, sir."

"Oh!" and he resumed his dictation.

For an hour or more he continued dictating; then a letter which required the attention of President Carroll came to hand and he went into the private office. He came out after a moment and spoke to his stenographer again.

"Did Mr. Carroll go into his office this morning?"

"Yes, sir."

Swayne turned and glanced round the outer office inquiringly. "Did you see him come out?" he inquired.

"No, sir."

That was all. Swayne laid the letter aside for the moment and continued with other correspondence. From time to time he glanced impatiently at the clock, thence to the door from the hall. At ten minutes past eleven the stenographer returned to her own desk, and with a worried countenance Swayne went over and spoke to a bookkeeper near the door.

"Did you see Mr. Carroll go out?" he asked. "Or do you know where he went?"

"He hasn't gone out, sir," replied the bookkeeper. "I saw him go into his office a couple of hours ago."

Swayne went straight toward the private office with the evident intention of leaving the letter on the president's desk. The door of the room was still closed. He was reaching out his hand to open it, when it was opened from within and Carroll started out. Swayne stared at him a moment in a manner nearly approaching amazement.

"Well, what is it?" demanded Carroll curtly.

"I—er—here's something I wanted to ask you about," Swayne explained haltingly.

Carroll glanced over the extended letter. His brows contracted and he quickly looked up at the clock.

"Did this come in the morning mail?" he demanded impatiently.

"Yes, I knew——"

"You should have called it to my attention two hours ago," said Carroll sharply. "Answer by wire that we'll accept the proposition."

Swayne's face flamed suddenly at the tone and manner. "I tried to call it to your attention two hours ago," he explained; "but you were not in your office, nor were you out here."

"I've been in my office right along," said Carroll sharply, and he glared straight into Swayne's eyes. "Wire immediately that we'll accept the proposition."

The two men stood thus face to face, eyes challenging eyes, for an instant, then simultaneously turned away. Swayne's countenance showed not only anger but bewilderment; whatever Carroll felt was not evident. Perhaps there was more color in his face than was usually there; but it had been that way when he came out of the private office, therefore it was not due to any feeling aroused by the scene with Swayne.

That afternoon Carroll caused a neat placard to be placed on the door of his private office. It said briefly:

> Do not enter this room without knocking. If Mr. Carroll does not answer a knock, it is to be understood that he is not to be disturbed under any circumstances.

Swayne read it and wondered, feeling somehow that it was a direct rebuke to him; a dozen or more clerks read it and wondered, and commented upon it varyingly; two office boys read it and added their opinions. On the following day the incident was repeated with slight variations. Swayne saw Carroll enter the front door, pass through the main office, and go into the private office, closing the door behind him. Half an hour later Swayne spoke to the bookkeeper Black, to whom he had spoken the day before.

"Please hand that to Mr. Carroll in his private office," he directed.

The bookkeeper took the slip of paper which the secretary offered, crossed the office, and rapped on Carroll's door. After a minute he returned to Swayne, who was apparently adding a column of figures.

"Mr. Carroll doesn't answer, sir," explained the bookkeeper.

"You know he's in there, don't you?" asked Swayne blandly.

"I saw him go in a few minutes ago, yes, sir; but I didn't intrude because of the notice on the door."

"Oh, that's of no consequence," exclaimed Swayne impatiently. "This is a matter of importance. Take it in to him anyway, whether he answers or not."

Again the bookkeeper went away, and again he returned. "Mr. Carroll wasn't in there, sir," he explained; "and I had to leave the paper on his desk."

"I thought you said you saw him go in?" demanded Swayne.

"I did, sir."

"Well, he must be in there; he hasn't come out," insisted Swayne. "Are you sure he isn't there?"

"Why, positive, yes, sir," replied the bewildered bookkeeper.

Swayne was bending over the high desk intently studying the figures before him. The bookkeeper stood for a little while as if awaiting another order, then resumed his work.

"We'll go in there together and see if he isn't to be found," said Swayne at last in a most matter of fact tone.

"But I just——" the bookkeeper began.

"Never mind, come along," directed Swayne, "and don't talk too loud," he added in a lower tone.

Wonderingly the bookkeeper followed the secretary, Swayne himself rapped on the door. There was no answer, and finally he pushed the door open quietly. Carroll was sitting at his desk going over the morning mail. He apparently was not aware that the door had been opened, and Swayne started to close it as he and the bookkeeper withdrew.

"You were mistaken, Black," Swayne remarked casually.

"Come in, Mr. Swayne, you and Black," called Carroll just as the door was closing.

Swayne warned the bookkeeper to silence with one quick, comprehensive glance, then reopened the door, and they entered the private office, closing the door behind them. Swayne faced his superior calmly, defiantly, almost; the bookkeeper twiddled his fingers nervously.

"Since when is it customary for employees here to disobey my orders?" demanded Carroll coldly.

"Mr. Black told me you were not here, and I came to see myself," replied Swayne with a singular emphasis on every word.

"You see that he was mistaken, then?" demanded Carroll. "Mr. Black, we will not require your services any longer. Mr. Swayne will give you a check immediately for what is due you. And you, Mr. Swayne, understand that if my orders are not obeyed to the letter in this office I shall be compelled to make other changes. From this time forward the door will be locked when I am in my office. That's all."

"But I was obeying orders when——" Black began in trepidation.

"I put my order on the door for you to obey," interrupted Carroll. "Go write him a check, Mr. Swayne."

Swayne and Black went out and Swayne closed the door. Carroll had been seated as they went out; but no sooner closed now than they heard the lock click sharply inside.

"What does it mean, Black?" Swayne inquired quietly.

"I don't know, sir," replied the astonished bookkeeper. "He certainly was not in that room when I was in there. And for discharging me——"

"You are not discharged," Swayne said impatiently, with a new note in his voice. "You are going to take a vacation of a couple of weeks, though, on full salary. Meanwhile have luncheon with me today."

Professor Augustus S. F. X. Van Dusen—The Thinking Machine—straightened up in his chair suddenly and turned his squinting belligerent eyes full upon his two visitors.

"Never mind your personal opinion or prejudices, Mr. Swayne," he rebuked sharply. "If you want my assistance in this matter, I must insist that you relate the facts, and only the facts, freed of all coloring which may have been infused into them by your ill feeling toward Mr. Carroll. I understand readily enough the cause of this—this ill feeling. You are his senior in the office, and he was promoted over your head to be the president of the company, while you remain secretary and treasurer. Now give me the remainder of the facts, please."

There was a considerable pause. A flush had slowly mounted Swayne's face, and it was only with an obvious effort that he controlled himself. Once he looked toward Black, who had been a silent witness of the interview.

"Well, after those first two incidents." Swayne went on at last, "the door of Mr. Carroll's private office was always locked on the inside the moment he was left alone: Now I am not a fool, Professor Van Dusen. In my mind it stands to reason that if Mr. Carroll disappeared from that room twice when the door was left unlocked, he is gone from it practically all the time when the door is locked; therefore——"

"Opinion again," interrupted The Thinking Machine curtly. "Facts, Mr. Swayne, facts!"

"If he isn't gone, why does he keep the door locked?"

"Perhaps," and the crabbed little scientist regarded him coldly—"perhaps it's really because he is busy and doesn't want to be interrupted. That is always possible, you know. I'm that way myself sometimes."

"And where does he go? How does he go?"

"If I had to diagnose this case," remarked The Thinking Machine almost pleasantly, "I should say it was a severe attack of idle curiosity, complicated with prejudice and suspicion." Suddenly his whole tone, his whole manner, changed. "Has the conduct of the business of the company been all it should have been since Mr. Carroll has been in charge?" he demanded.

"Well, yes," admitted Swayne.

"Has he made money for the company?"

"Yes."

"Perhaps increased its earnings, if anything?"

Swayne nodded reluctantly.

"Nothing is stolen?" the scientist demanded. "Nothing is missing? Nothing has gone wrong?"

Three times Swayne shook his head.

The Thinking Machine rose impatiently. "If there had been anything wrong, of course you would have gone to the police," The Thinking Machine went on. "There being nothing wrong, you came to me. I don't mind giving what assistance I can in instances where it works for good; but my time is valuable to the world of science, Mr. Swayne, and really I can't be disturbed by such a trivial affair as this. If anything goes wrong, if anything does happen, you are at liberty to call again. Good day."

The two men rose, stood staring blankly at each other for a moment, then turned to go out. Swayne's face was crimson with anger, chagrin, at his abrupt dismissal. But at the door he turned back for one final question.

"Would you mind informing us how Mr. Carroll disappeared from his office on the two occasions when we know he did disappear, before he locked his door against us?"

"You saw him go in one door; he went out another, I suppose," replied The Thinking Machine.

"There is only one other door," retorted Swayne with something like triumph in his voice. "That is blocked in his office by his desk, and also blocked in the stockholders' meeting room, to which it leads, by a long couch. The offices are fifty feet from the ground; so he couldn't jump a window. He didn't go through the stockholders' room either, because that has only one door, and that opens into the outer office within two or three feet of the door to his private office. There are no fire escapes at either of his windows, I may add. Now, how did he get out—if he got out?"

The face was flushed and angry again, the voice raised stridently. The Thinking Machine stared for half a minute, then opened the door to the street.

"I don't know if you know it," he said calmly at last; "but you are almost convincing me that there is something wrong there, and that you are responsible for it. Good day."

The steel gray eyes of Charles Duer Carroll were blazing as he flung open the outside door of the offices of Carroll-Swayne-McPartland Company and entered the large general office. Was it anger? Not one of the dozen clerks who raised half-timid eyes as he appeared could have answered the question. Was it excitement? Still there would have been no answer. He went straight to his private office, without a look or word for his subordinates, then wheeled suddenly on his heel there and called "Mr. Swayne!"

The secretary and treasurer started a little at the imperative command, and Carroll motioned for him to approach. Then he led the way into his office, Swayne following, and the clerks outside heard the lock click. Swayne, inside, stood waiting the president's pleasure. A vague sense of physical danger oppressed him.

"Sit down," commanded Carroll. The secretary obeyed. "You are the secretary and treasurer of this company, are you not?" demanded Carroll brutally.

"Certainly. Why?"

"Then you know, or are supposed to know, exactly what securities this company holds in trust for its customers to protect margins, don't you?" Carroll went on. His eyes were blazing as the secretary met them.

"Certainly I know," Swayne responded after a moment.

"You know that in the three million dollars worth of securities in our vaults and safety deposit vaults over the city, there is one lot of four hundred thousand dollars' worth of United States gold bonds, and that these include the numbers 0043917 to 0044120?"

Swayne disregarded the urgent demand for an immediate answer which lay behind the tone, and stopped to consider the matter carefully. Was it a trap of some sort? He couldn't tell.

"Do you or do you not know that this consignment of bonds includes those numbers?" demanded Carroll hotly.

"Yes" was the reply, "I know that those numbers are included in the Mason-Hackett trust. Further I know that I locked them myself in the vault in the office here!"

Carroll's eyes were contracted to pin points, and all the latent power of a man seemed aroused as he turned savagely in his chair.

"If you know that to be true, then what does that mean?" and he flung down a sheet of paper violently under the eyes of the secretary and treasurer.

Swayne, with a vague sense of terror which he could not fathom at the moment, picked up the paper and glanced over it. It was an affidavit signed by E. C. Morgan & Co., brokers, and dated the day before. It was in the usual form, and attested, with innumerable reiterations, that United States Government gold bonds, numbers 0043917 to 0043940 inclusive, were in the possession of E. C. Morgan & Co., having been bought in the open market three days previously.

Swayne stared unbelievingly at the affidavit, and slowly, slowly, the color deserted his face until it was chalk white. Twice he raised his eyes from the affidavit to the strangely working face of Carroll, and twice he lowered them under the baleful glare they met. When he raised them the third time there was mystification, wonder, utter helplessness, in them.

"Well?" blazed out Carroll. "Well?" he repeated.

Swayne started to his feet.

"Just a moment Mr. Swayne," warned the president in a voice which had become suddenly and strangely quiet. "You had better remain here for a few minutes until we look into this." He rose and went to the door, and spoke to some one outside.

"Please bring me all the securities of all kinds in our vaults," he directed, "and send messengers to bring those which are in safety deposit vaults elsewhere. Bring them all to me personally—not to Mr. Swayne."

He closed the door and turned back toward the secretary. The color came back into Swayne's face with a rush under the impetus of some powerful emotion, and he stood swaying, closing and unclosing his hands spasmodically. At length he found tongue, and now his voice was as steady and quiet as was the other's.

"Do I understand you accuse me of—of stealing those bonds?" he demanded.

"The bonds are missing," was the reply. "They were in your care. It really is of no concern whether they were misappropriated or lost. The result is the same. Bonds were intrusted to us to protect our customers. We are responsible for them; you are responsible for us."

Swayne dropped back into a chair with his head in his hands. Utterly at a loss for words, he sat there until there came a respectful rap on the door. Carroll opened it, and a clerk entered with a package of the securities.

"Is this all of them?" inquired Carroll.

"All except about six hundred thousand dollars worth which were in a safety deposit vault farther up town," was the reply. "A messenger is on his way with them now."

Carroll dismissed him with a curt nod and spilled the securities on the table before him. Then he spoke to Swayne again. There was a singular softening of his tone—Swayne chose to read it as mocking.

"Really I'm very sorry, Mr. Swayne," the president said soothingly. "I had trusted you to the utmost: indeed, I dare say every stockholder in the company did, and whether you are at fault or not now remains to be seen. We know if those bonds are missing, as the affidavit asserts, there may be others missing, and the entire amount will have to be verified. I shall do that personally."

Still Swayne didn't speak. There seemed to be nothing to say. Once he glanced up into the steady gaze which was directed toward him, and relapsed immediately into his former position, with his head resting in his hands.

"Don't misunderstand me, please," said Carroll. "You are not a prisoner. This is a matter that will not go to the police—as yet anyway. It would not be safe for our office force to know what has happened. It might precipitate disaster. Meanwhile go on about your duties as if nothing has happened."

"My God, Charlie! you don't believe I stole them do you?" Swayne burst out at last piteously as he rose to his feet.

"That's the first time you have called me by that name since I have been president of this company," Carroll remarked irrelevantly. "I want to like you—I've always wanted to like you—but of late you have wilfully antagonized me. Now, my first duty is here," and he indicated the heap of securities on his desk. "I must not be interrupted until I have finished. It is as necessary to you as to me; so go on about your work. Afterward we'll see what we can do."

For an hour, perhaps, Swayne sat at his desk gazing dreamily across the office. Half a dozen questions were asked; he didn't answer. But slowly some strong determination seized upon him, and at last it brought him to his feet, with staring eyes. For only an instant he hesitated over this idea which had come to him, and then spoke to the girl in charge of the office telephone exchange.

"Connect booth 3 with Central," he commanded sharply, "then leave the exchange there and don't answer a ring under any circumstances."

Within less than a minute Swayne was talking to The Thinking Machine over the wire.

"This is Gordon Swayne," he began abruptly. "Something happened. I don't know what. You told me I might call on you if something did happen. Can you come to the office at once?"

"What happened?" demanded The Thinking Machine irritably.

"I'm afraid it's a huge defalcation," was the instant response. "Carroll has locked himself in the room from which he had disappeared previously, with millions of dollars in securities which came into his possession by a trick, and I believe as firmly as I believe I'm living that he has run away with them. It's the only thing to account for his strange actions. He went into the room an hour ago—I'd wager my life he isn't there now."

"Why don't you rap on the door and ask for him?" came an imperturbable question.

"Can you come at once?" demanded Swayne abruptly.

"I'll be there in fifteen minutes," was the reply. "Don't do anything absurd until I get there; and don't call the police, because you are probably only suffering from another manifestation of that complaint with which I found you suffering from before. Good by."

Swayne forced himself to calmness again and after a few minutes' wait rapped quietly on the door of the private office. There was no response from inside. He tried the door. It was locked. It was just then that the door from the hall opened, and The Thinking Machine entered, peering about his curiously. Swayne related the incidents of the morning in detail.

"I believe—I know—Carroll has stolen those securities!" Swayne burst out at last. "What shall I do?"

For a minute or more The Thinking Machine sat silently squinting upward with white fingers at rest tip to tip, then he rose and readjusted his glasses.

"I believe," he said quietly, "I'd smash in the door. It might be something worse than you think."

Swayne called to two of the clerks as he went, and the four men paused for an instant at the entrance to the private office.

"Well, do it!" commanded The Thinking Machine irritably.

Swayne and the clerks placed their shoulders against the door; then from inside there came a sharp click. It was the key turning in the lock. They drew back and waited. The door swung open, and Carroll in person appeared before them, with both hands behind his back. There was an instant's pause, then in the strained, harsh voice of Swayne came the question—an accusation:

"Where are those securities?"

"Here," responded Carroll, and he produced them from behind his back. "Swayne you are a childish idiot," he added sharply.

The Thinking Machine nearly smiled.

The explanation of the problem of the vanishing man, as The Thinking Machine stated it, was ludicrously simple. After Carroll had so mercilessly smashed Swayne's hypothesis of a defalcation, by appearing in person with the bonds and other securities, the secretary had stalked out moodily, and now he was in The Thinking Machine's small reception room, staring gloomily at the floor.

"My first diagnosis fits the case," remarked the diminutive scientist. "Idle curiosity with complications. You see, Mr. Swayne, you business men are too practical, if I may say so. You in this instance could not or would not see beyond the obvious. A little imagination would have aided you—imagination coupled with a knowledge of the rudimentary rules of logic. Logic doesn't make mistakes—it is as certainly infallible as that two and two make four, not *some*times but *all* the time.

"Briefly I knew from your first statement of the case that Mr. Carroll was comparatively poor, despite the fact that he is the head of this great company. In ninety-nine cases out of a hundred every man wants to get rich. Mr. Carroll had increased the earnings of his company; but he had not increased his own, therefore let us credit him with a desire to get rich. If he did not have such a desire, he would not be in the position he now holds. The moment we allow for this, and also allow for the fact that the securities were returned intact, we have the solution of the entire affair. I am admitting that not only did Mr. Carroll disappear from his private office at the times you specify, but that he was also gone from that office practically all the time he kept the door locked.

"In the stock markets (I have just enough acquaintance with them to know that money begets money) it is possible to make or lose millions in an hour. Therefore, if Mr. Carroll could get all the securities of the company into his possession for an hour, and cared to do so, he could work wonders in the open market. This is precisely what he did. By a trick, we'll say, he got them together in a way which could not arouse even your suspicions, and used them on the market. The inference is that he made money by the use of those securities for that hour—the fact that he brought them back shows that he did not lose money, or he would not have had them. So, that's all of it: Mr. Carroll used the firm's money to make money for himself. Technically he has committed a crime; but——"

"It is a crime then?" demanded Swayne. "He was a criminal then, when he accused me of—of stealing the United States bonds?"

"By accusing you of appropriating or misplacing those bonds he did the necessary thing," replied The Thinking Machine, "that is, distracted your attention and gave himself, in your eyes, the best possible excuse for getting all the securities together without even a glimmer of light as to his purpose when he got them. Mr. Carroll is a very remarkable and very able man; he knows how to get it. In other words, he is tremendously resourceful."

"But how—how did he leave that private office to use the securities, say in a market transaction?" Swayne insisted.

"Simply enough," was the reply. "I don't know, but I dare say through a window. It is a simple matter to stand on a window sill and swing yourself to the sill of the next window, particularly when a man has the steady nerve and strength of this man. If perchance the next room was unoccupied, you see how simple it would have been for Mr. Carroll to leave his office and remain away for hours, with the door of his private office locked behind him. There is really no mystery about the affair at all. It is simply a question of how much the transaction netted Mr. Carroll."

An hour later the board of directors of the Carroll-Swayne-McPartland Company met in the room adjoining Carroll's private office. The call had been issued by Swayne without consulting President Carroll. The secretary stated the case pithily, violently even. Carroll listened to the end.

"I am very glad that the directors have met," he said then as he rose. "I have committed a crime technically, as Mr. Swayne says. By that crime I have made a little more than two million dollars. The tremendous power which the millions of securities of this company gave me allowed me to turn the market upside down, to manipulate it at will, then to withdraw. This company is old; it's conservative. If this thing becomes known outside, it will hurt. But this company has its securities again, intact. I have made a fortune. If the company chooses to accept one-half of what I made, I to hold the other half, it is agreeable to me. I had intended to make this proposition anyway."

There was a long argument, a great many words, and finally acquiescence.

"And now shall I resign?" inquired Carroll finally.

"No," returned old Nick Carroll. "You young scoundrel, if you even think about resigning, why—why, confound it, we'll fire you! A man who can do such a thing as that—why, Charlie, you're a wonder! You'll stay! Do you understand?"

He rose and glared defiantly about the room. There was not even a head shake—nothing.

"You stay on the job, Charlie," said the old man. "That's all."

THE PROBLEM OF THE AUTO CAB

Hutchinson Hatch gathered up his overcoat and took the steps coming down two at a time. There was no car in sight, nothing on wheels—in fact, until—yes, here was an automobile turning the corner, an automobile cab drifting along apparently without purpose. Hatch hailed it.

"Get me out to Commonwealth Avenue and Arden Street in a hurry!" he instructed. "Take a chance with the speed law, and I'll make it worth while. It's important."

He yanked open the door, stepped in, and closed it with a slam. The chauffeur gave a twist to his lever, turned the car almost within its length, and went scuttling off up the street.

Safely inside, Hatch became suddenly aware that he had a fellow passenger. Through the gloom he felt, rather than saw, two inquisitive eyes staring out at him, and there was the faintest odor of violets.

"Hello!" Hatch demanded. "Am I in your way?"

"Not in the slightest," came the voice of a woman. "Am I in yours?"

"Why—I beg your pardon," Hatch stammered. "I thought I had the cab alone—didn't know there was a passenger. Perhaps I'd better get out?"

"No, no!" protested the woman quickly. "Don't think of it."

Then from outside came the bellowing voice of a policeman. "Hey there! I'll report you!"

Glancing back, Hatch saw him standing in the middle of the street jotting down something in a note book. The chauffeur made a few uncomplimentary remarks about bluecoats in general, swished round a corner, and sped on. With a half smile of appreciation on his lips, Hatch turned back to his unknown companion.

"If you will tell me where you are going," he suggested, "I'll have the chauffeur set you down."

"It's of no consequence," replied the woman a little wearily. "I am going no place particularly—just riding about to collect my thoughts."

A woman unattended, riding about in an automobile at fifteen minutes of eleven o'clock at night to collect her thoughts! And the chauffeur didn't know he had a passenger! The reporter sat oblivious of the bumping, grinding, of the automobile, trying to consider this unexpected incident calmly.

"You are a reporter?" inquired the woman.

"Yes" Hatch replied. "How did you guess it?"

"From seeing you rush out of a newspaper office in such a hurry at this time of night," she replied. "Something important, I dare say?"

"Well, yes," Hatch agreed. "A jewel robbery at a ball. Don't know much about it yet. Just got a police bulletin stating that Mrs. Windsor Dillingham had been robbed of a necklace worth thirty-thousand dollars at a big affair she is giving to-night."

The inside of the cab was lighted brilliantly by the electric arc outside, and Hatch had an opportunity of seeing the woman face to face at close range. She was pretty: she was young, and she was well dressed. From her shoulders she was enveloped in some loose cloak of dark material, but it was not drawn together at her throat, and her bare neck gleamed.

There being nothing whatever to say, Hatch sat silently staring out of the window as the automobile whirled into Commonwealth Avenue, and slowed up as it approached Arden Street.

"Will you do me one favor, please?" asked the woman.

"Yes, if I can," was the reporter's reply.

"Allow me, please, to get out of the automobile on the side away from the curb, and be good enough to attract the attention of the chauffeur to yourself while I am doing it. Here is a bill," and she pressed something into Hatch's hand. "You may pay the chauffeur a tip for the passenger he didn't know he had."

Hatch agreed in a dazed sort of way, and the automobile came to a stop. He stepped out on the curb, and slammed the door as the chauffeur leaped down from his seat. From the other side came the answering door slam, as if an echo.

Five minutes later Hatch joined Detective Mallory inside. At just that moment the detective was listening to the story of Mrs. Dillingham's maid.

"There's nothing missing but the necklace," she explained; "so far, at least, as we have been able to find out. Mrs. Dillingham began dressing at about half-past eight o'clock, and I assisted her as usual. I suppose it was half-past nine when she finished. All that time the necklace was in the jewel box on her dressing table. It was the only article of jewelry in the box.

"Well, the butler came up about half-past nine o'clock for his final instructions, and Mrs. Dillingham went into the adjoining room to talk to him. It was not more than a minute later when she sent me down to the conservatory for a rose for her hair. She was still talking to him when I returned five minutes later. I put the rose in her hair, and she sent me into her dressing room for her necklace. When I looked into the jewel box, the necklace was gone. I told Mrs. Dillingham. The butler heard me. That's all I know of it, except that Mrs. Dillingham went into hysterics and fainted, and I telephoned for a doctor."

Detective Mallory regarded the girl coldly. Hatch knew perfectly what was coming. "You are quite sure," asked the detective, "that you did not take the necklace with you when you went down to the conservatory, and pass it to a confederate on the outside."

The sudden pallor of the girl, her abject, cringing fright, answered the question to Hatch's satisfaction even before she opened her lips with a denial. Hatch himself was about to ask a question, when a footman entered.

"Mrs. Dillingham will see you in her boudoir," he announced.

From the lips of Mrs. Dillingham they heard identically the same story the maid had told. Mrs. Dillingham did not suspect anyone of her household.

For half an hour the detective interrogated her; then there came a rap at the door, and a woman entered.

"Why, Dora!" exclaimed Mrs. Dillingham.

The young woman went straight to her, put her arms about her shoulders protectingly, then turned to glare defiantly at Detective Mallory and Hutchinson Hatch. The reporter gasped—it was the mysterious woman of the automobile. An exclamation was on his lips, but something in her eyes warned him, and he was silent.

When, on the following day, Hutchinson Hatch related the circumstances of the theft of Mrs. Dillingham's necklace to Professor Augustus S. F. X. Van Dusen—The Thinking Machine—he did not mention the mysterious woman in the automobile. However curious those incidents in which he and she had figured were, they were inconsequential, and there was nothing to connect them in any way with the problem in hand. The strange woman's meeting with Mrs. Dillingham in the reporter's presence had convinced him that she was an intimate friend.

"Just what time was the theft discovered?" inquired The Thinking Machine.

"Within a few minutes of half-past nine.

"At what time did most of the guests arrive?"

"Between half-past nine and ten o'clock."

"Then at half-past nine," continued the scientist, "there could have been many persons there?"

"Perhaps a dozen," returned the reporter.

"And who were they?"

"Their names, you mean? I don't know."

"Well, find out," directed The Thinking Machine crustily. "If the servants are removed from the case, and there were a dozen other persons in the house, common sense tells us to find out who and what they were. Suppose, Mr. Hatch, you had attended that ball and stolen that necklace; what would have been your natural inclination afterward?"

Hatch stared at him blankly for a minute, then smiled whimsically. "You mean how would I have tried to get away with it?" he asked.

"Yes. When would you have left the place?"

"That's rather hard to say," Hatch declared thoughtfully. "But I think I should either have gone before anybody else did, through fear of discovery, or else I should have been one of the last, through excess of caution."

"Then proceed along those lines," instructed The Thinking Machine. "You might almost put that down as a law of criminology. It will enable you in the beginning, therefore, to narrow down the dozen or so guests to the first and last who left."

Deeply pondering this little interjection of psychology into a very material affair, Hatch went his way. In the course of events he saw Mrs. Dillingham, who, out of consideration for her guests, flatly refused to give their names.

Luckily for Hatch, the butler didn't feel that way about it at all. This was due partly to the fact that Detective Mallory had given him a miserable half-hour, and partly, perhaps, to the fact that the reporter oiled his greedy palm with a bill of two figures.

"To begin with," said the reporter, "I want to know the names of the first dozen or so persons who arrived here that evening—I mean those who were here when you sent to speak with Mrs. Dillingham."

"I might find out, sir. Their cards were laid on the silver as they arrived, and that silver, I think has remained undisturbed. Therefore, the first dozen cards on it would give you the names you want."

"Now, that's something like it," commented the reporter enthusiastically. "And do you remember any person who left the house rather early that evening?"

"No, sir," was the reply. Then suddenly there came a flash of remembrance across the stoical face. "But I remember that one gentleman arrived here twice. It was this way. Mr. Hawes Campbell came in about eleven o'clock, and passed by without handing me a card.

Then I remembered that he had been here earlier and that I had his card. But I don't recall that anyone went out, and I was at the door all evening except when I was up stairs talking to Mrs. Dillingham."

On a bare chance, Hatch went to find Campbell. Inquiry at his two clubs failed to find him, and finally Hatch called at his home.

At the end of five minutes, perhaps, Hatch caught the swish of skirts in the hallway, then the portiers were thrust aside and—again he was face to face with the mysterious woman of the automobile.

"My brother isn't here," she said calmly, without the slightest sign of any recognition; "Can I do anything for you?"

Her brother! Then she was Miss Campbell, and Mrs. Dillingham had called her Dora—Dora Campbell!

"Well—er——" Hatch faltered a little, "it was a personal matter I wanted to see him about."

"I don't know when he will return," Miss Campbell announced.

Hatch stared at her for a moment; he was making up his mind. At last, he took the bit in his teeth. "We understand, Miss Campbell," he said at last slowly and emphatically, "that your brother, Hawes Campbell has some information which might be of value in unraveling the mystery surrounding the theft of Mrs. Dillingham's necklace."

Miss Campbell dropped into a chair, and unconsciously Hatch assumed the defensive. "Mrs. Dillingham is very much annoyed, as you must know," Miss Campbell said, "about the publicity given to this affair; particularly as she is confident that the necklace will be returned within a short time. Her only annoyance, beyond the wide publicity, as I said, is that it has not already been returned."

"Returned?" gasped Hatch.

Miss Campbell shrugged her shoulders. "She knows," she continued, "that the necklace is now in safe hands, that there is no danger of its being lost to her, but the situation is such that she cannot demand its return."

"Mrs. Dillingham knows where the necklace is, then?" he asked.

"Yes," replied Miss Campbell.

"Perhaps you know?"

"Perhaps I do," she responded readily. "I can assure you that Mrs. Dillingham is going to take the affair out of the hands of the police, because she knows her property is safe—as safe as if it was in your hands, for instance. It is only a question of time, when it will be returned."

"Where is the necklace?" Hatch demanded suddenly.

Again Miss Campbell shrugged her shoulders.

"And what does your brother know about the affair?"

"I can't answer that question, of course," was the response.

"Well, why did he go to Mrs. Dillingham's early in the evening, then go away, and return about eleven o'clock?" insisted the reporter bluntly.

For the first time there came a change in Miss Campbell's manner, a subtle, indefinable something which the reporter readily saw, but to which he could attach no meaning.

"I can't say more than I have said," she replied after a moment. "Believe me," and there was a note of earnestness in her voice, "it would be far better for you to drop the matter, because otherwise you may be placed in—a ridiculous position."

And that was all—a threat, delicately veiled it is true, but a threat nevertheless. She rose and led the way to the door.

Hatch didn't realize the significance of that remark, then, nor, did it occur to him that the mysterious affair in the automobile had not been mentioned between them: for here was material, knotty, incoherent, inexplicable material, for The Thinking Machine, and there he took it. Again he told the story; but this time all of it—every incident from the moment he hailed the automobile in front of his office on the night of the robbery until Miss Campbell closed the door.

"Why didn't you tell me all of it before?" demanded The Thinking Machine irritably.

"I couldn't see that the affair in the automobile had any connection with the robbery," explained the reporter.

"Couldn't see!" stormed the eminent man of science. "Couldn't see! Every trivial happening on this whole round earth bears on every other happening, no matter how vast or how disconnected it may seem; the correlation of facts makes a perpetually unbroken chain. In other words, if Mrs. Leary hadn't kept a cow, Chicago would not have been destroyed by fire. Couldn't see!"

For an instant The Thinking Machine glared at him, and the change from petulant annoyance to deep abstraction, as that singular brain turned to the problem at hand, was almost visible. It was uncanny. Then the scientist dropped back into his chair with eyes turned upward and long slender fingers pressed tip to tip. Ten minutes passed, twenty, thirty, and he turned suddenly to the reporter.

"What was the number of that automobile?" he demanded.

Hatch grinned in sheer triumph. Of all the questions he could have anticipated this was the most unlikely, and yet he had the number set down in his note book where it would ultimately become a voucher in his expense account. He consulted the book.

"Number 869019," he replied.

"Now find that automobile," directed The Thinking Machine. "It is important that you do so at once."

"You mean that the necklace——" Hatch began breathlessly.

"When you bring the automobile here, I will produce the necklace," declared The Thinking Machine emphatically.

Hatch returned half a dozen hours later with troubled lines in his face. "Automobile No. 869019 has disappeared, evaporated into air," he declared with some heat. "There was one that night, because I was in it, and the highway commission's records show a private cab license granted to John Kilrain under the number, but it has disappeared."

"Where is Kilrain?" inquired The Thinking Machine.

"I didn't see him; but I saw his wife," explained the reporter. "She didn't know anything about the automobile No. 869019, or said she didn't. She said his auto car was——"

"No. 610698," interrupted The Thinking Machine. It was not a question; it was the statement as of one who knew.

Hatch stared from the scientist to the note book where he had written down the number the woman gave him, and then he looked his utter astonishment.

"Of course, that is the number," continued The Thinking Machine, as if someone had disputed it. "It is past midnight now, and we won't try to find it; but I'll have it here to-morrow at noon. We shall see for ourselves how safely the necklace has been kept."

Detective Mallory entered and glanced about inquiringly. He saw only The Thinking Machine and Hutchinson Hatch.

"I sent for you," explained the scientist, because in half an hour or so I shall either place the Dillingham necklace in your hands, or turn over to you the man who knows where it is. You may use your own discretion as to whether or not you will prosecute. Under all the circumstances, I believe the case is one for a sanatarium, rather than prison. In other words, the person who took the necklace is not wholly responsible."

"Who is it?" demanded the detective.

"You don't happen to know all the facts in this case," continued The Thinking Machine without heeding the question. "I got them all, only after Mr. Hatch, at my suggestion, had located the thief. Originally I began where you left off. I believe you had eliminated the servants, and I presumed there was not a burglary. Ultimately this led to Hawes Campbell in a manner which is no interest to you. Then I got all the facts.

"When Mr. Hatch left his office to go to Mrs. Dillingham's, he took an automobile which happened to be passing," resumed the scientist. "It was a cab No. 869019. Inside that cab he found, much to his astonishment, a woman—a young woman in evening dress. She made the surprising statement that the chauffeur didn't know she was there, and that she was not going anywhere—was merely riding around to collect her thoughts. And this was, please remember, about eleven o'clock at night. On its face this incident had no connection with the jewel theft; but by a singular chain of coincidences subsequently developed, it seemed that Mr. Hatch had arrived at the solution of the mystery before he even knew the circumstances of the theft."

Detective Mallory nodded doubtfully. "But how does that connect with the——" he began.

"Subsequent developments establish a direct connection," interrupted The Thinking Machine. "We have the woman in the automobile. We shall presume that she must have had some strong motive for leaving a house at that time of night and doing the apparently purposeless things that she did do. We don't know this motive from these facts—we only know there was a motive.

"Now when you and Mr. Hatch were talking to Mrs. Dillingham, a woman entered the room. Mr. Hatch recognized her immediately as the woman in the automobile. Everything indicated that she was an intimate friend of Mrs. Dillingham's. So we pass on to the point where Mr. Hatch found that Hawes Campbell arrived at the ball early, went away again, and returned after eleven o'clock. Mr. Hatch wanted to know why he left, and went to his home to inquire. Campbell's sister met him there. She was the woman he had met in the automobile. So we have Campbell leaving the ball, immediately after the theft, say, and his sister between nine-thirty and eleven, and screening herself in an automobile.

"Why? I have said, Mr. Mallory, that imagination—the ability to bridge gaps temporarily—is the most essential part of the logical mind. Now, if we imagine that Campbell stole the necklace, that he went home, that his sister found it out, that there was some sort of scene which terminated in her flight with the necklace, we account for absolutely every incident preceeding and following Mr. Hatch's arrival at the Dillingham place.

"I have made inquiries. The Campbells are worth, not thousands, but millions. Therefore, the question. Why should Hawes Campbell steal a necklace. The answer, kleptomania. And again, it was known to the sister, who tried in her own manner to return the stolen property and avoid the scandal. When she was in the automobile, she was trying to collect her thoughts—trying to invent a way to return the necklace. It was the merest chance that Mr. Hatch happened to get into that particular vehicle.

"Now, we come to the most difficult part of the problem," and The Thinking Machine dropped still further back into the cavernous depths of his chair. "What would a frightened, perhaps hysterical woman do with that necklace? From the fact that it has not been returned, we know that she didn't venture into the house with it, and leave it casually in any one of a hundred places where it might have been discovered without danger to herself. Yet, everything indicates that she had it while she was in the cab, intending to regain possession of it later, and return it. Now, that cab number was 869019. Strangely enough, after Mr. Hatch left the cab, it seems to have disappeared. The chauffeur, John Kilrain, has another cab number now, 610698—that is, autocab No. 869019 was made to disappear by the simple act of turning over the number board upside down, giving us 610698."

"Well, by George!" exclaimed Detective Mallory. No mere words would convey the reporter's astonishment; he gasped.

"Now," continued The Thinking Machine after a moment, "there are two reasons, both good, why auto cab number 869019 should have disappeared. The vital one, it seems to me, is that Kilrain discovered the necklace inside and kept it; the other is that he was threatened with arrest by the policeman who took his number for speeding, and to avoid a fine, disguised the identity of his cab. There are one or two other possibilities; but if the necklace isn't found in the automobile, I should advise, not arrest, but a close watch on Kilrain, both at his home and in his intercourse with other chauffeurs at the various cab stands."

There was a rap at the door, and Martha appeared. "Did you want an automobile, sir?"

"We'll be right out," returned the scientist.

And so it came about that The Thinking Machine, Detective Mallory, and Hutchinson Hatch searched the very vitals of auto cab No. 869019, temporarily masquerading as No. 610698, while Kilrain stood by in perturbed amazement. At the end he was allowed to go.

"Remember, please, what I advised you to do," The Thinking Machine reminded Detective Mallory.

With eyes that were heavy with sleep Hutchinson Hatch crawled out of bed and answered the insistent ringing of his telephone. The crabbed voice of The Thinking Machine came over the wire in a question.

"If Miss Campbell was so anxious to return the necklace that night, she couldn't have done better than to have handed it to a reporter who was going to the house to investigate the robbery?"

"I don't think so," Hatch replied wonderingly.

"Did you have on your overcoat that night?"

"I had it with me."

"Suppose you go look in the pockets, and——"

Hatch dropped the receiver, already inspired by the suggestion, and dragged his overcoat out of the closet. In the left hand lower pocket was a small package. He opened it with trembling fingers. There before his eyes lay, the iridescent, gleaming bauble. It had been in his possession from an hour after it was stolen until this very instant. He rushed back to thc tclcphonc.

"I've got it!" he shouted.

"Silly of me not to have thought of it in the first place," came the querulous voice of The Thinking Machine. Good night."

THE ROSWELL TIARA

Had it not been for the personal interest of a fellow savant in the case, it is hardly likely that the problem of the Roswell tiara would ever have come to the attention of The Thinking Machine. And had the problem not come to his attention, it would inevitably have gone to the police. Then there would have been a scandal in high places, a disrupted home and everlasting unhappiness to at least four persons. Perhaps it was an inkling of this latter possibility that led The Thinking Machine—to take initial steps in the solution of a mystery which seemed to have only an obvious ending.

When he was first approached in the matter, The Thinking Machine was in his small laboratory, from which had gone forth truths that shocked and partially readjusted at least three of the exact sciences. His enormous head, with its long yellow hair, bobbed up and down over a little world of chemical apparatus, and the narrow, squint eyes peered with disagreeable satisfaction at a blue flame which spouted from a brazier. Martha, an aged woman who was the scientist's household staff, entered. She was not tall yet she towered commandingly above the slight figure of her eminent master. Professor Van Dusen turned to her impatiently.

"Well? Well?" he demanded shortly.

Martha handed him two cards. On one was the name Charles Wingate Field, and on the other Mrs. Richard Watson Roswell. Charles Wingate Field was a name to juggle with in astronomy—The Thinking Machine knew him well; the name of the woman was strange to him.

"The gentleman said it was very important," Martha explained, "and the poor lady was crying."

"What about?" snapped the scientist.

"Lord, sir, I didn't ask her," exclaimed Martha.

"I'll be there in a moment."

A few minutes later The Thinking Machine appeared at the door of the little reception room, which he regarded as a sort of useless glory, and the two persons there arose to meet him. One was a woman apparently of forty-five years, richly gowned, splendid of figure and with a distinct, matured beauty. Her eyes showed she had been weeping but now her tears were dried and she caught herself staring curiously at the pallid face, the keen blue eyes and the long slender hands of the scientist. The other person was Mr. Field.

There was an introduction and the scientist motioned them to seats. He himself dropped into a large cushioned chair, and looked from one to the other with a question in his eyes.

"I have been telling Mrs. Roswell some of the things you have done, Van Dusen," began Mr. Field. "I have brought her to you because this is a mystery, a problem, an abstruse problem, and it isn't the kind of thing one cares to take to the police. If you——"

"If Mrs. Roswell will tell me about it?" interrupted the scientist. He seemed to withdraw even further into the big chair. With head tilted back, eyes squinting steadily upward and white fingers pressed tip to tip he waited.

"Briefly," said Mrs. Roswell, "it has to do with the disappearance of a single small gem from a diamond tiara which I had locked in a vault—a vault of which no living person knew the combination except myself. Because of family reasons I could not go to the police, and——"

"Please begin at the beginning," requested The Thinking Machine. "Remember I know nothing whatever of you or your circumstances."

It was not unnatural that Mrs. Roswell should be surprised. Her social reign was supreme, her name was constantly to be seen in the newspapers, her entertainments were gorgeous, her social doings on an elaborate scale. She glanced at Mr. Field inquiringly, and he nodded.

"My first husband was Sidney Grantham, an Englishman," she explained. "Seven years ago he left me a widow with one child—a son Arthur—now twenty-two years old and just out of Harvard. Mr. Grantham died intestate and his whole fortune together with the family jewels, came to me and my son. The tiara was among these jewels.

"A year ago I was married to Mr. Roswell. He, too, is a man of wealth, with one daughter, Jeannette, now nineteen years old. We live on Commonwealth Avenue and while there are many servants I know it is impossible——"

"Nothing is impossible, Madam," interposed The Thinking Machine positively. "Don't say that please. It annoys me exceedingly."

Mrs. Roswell stared at him a moment then resumed:

"My bed room is on the second floor. Adjoining and connecting with it is the bed room of my step-daughter. This connecting door is always left unlocked because she is timid and nervous. I keep the door from my room into the hall bolted at night and Jeanette keeps the hall door of her room similarly fastened. The windows, too, are always secured at night in both rooms.

"My maid and my daughter's maid both sleep in the servant's quarters. I arranged for this because, as I was about to state, I keep about half a million dollars worth of jewels in my bed room, locked in a small vault built into the wall. This little vault opens with a combination. Not one person knows that combination except myself. It so happens that the man who set it is dead.

"Last night, Thursday, I attended a reception and wore the tiara. My daughter remained at home. At four o'clock this morning I returned. The maids had retired; Jeanette was sleeping soundly. I took off the tiara and placed it, with my other jewels, in the vault. I know that the small diamond now missing was in its setting at that time. I locked the vault, shot the bolt and turned the combination. Afterwards I tried the vault door to make certain it was fastened. It was then—then——"

For no apparent reason Mrs. Roswell suddenly burst into tears. The two men were silent and The Thinking Machine looked at her uneasily. He was not accustomed to women anyway, and women who wept were hopelessly beyond him.

"Well, well, what happened?" he asked brusquely at last.

"It was perhaps five o'clock when I fell asleep," Mrs. Roswell continued after a moment. "About twenty minutes later I was aroused by a scream of 'Jeanette, Jeanette, Jeanette.' Instantly I was fully awake. The screaming was that of a cockatoo which I have kept in my room for many years. It was in its usual place on a perch near the window, and seemed greatly disturbed.

"My first impression was that Jeanette had been in the room. I went into her room and even shook her gently. She was asleep so far as I could ascertain. I returned to my own room and then was amazed to see the vault door standing open. All the jewels and papers from the vault were scattered over the floor. My first thought was of burglars who had been frightened away by the cockatoo. I tried every door and every window in both Jeanette's room and mine. Everything was securely fastened.

"When I picked up the tiara, I found that a diamond was missing. It had evidently been torn out of the setting. I searched for it on the floor and inside the vault. I found nothing. Then of course I could only associate its disappearance with some act of—of my step-daughter's. I don't believe the cockatoo would have called her name if she had not been in my room. Certainly the bird could not have opened the vault. Therefore I—I——"

There was a fresh burst of tears and for a long time no one spoke.

"Do you burn a night lamp?" asked The Thinking Machine finally.

"Yes," replied Mrs. Roswell.

"Did the bird ever disturb you at any time previous to last night—that is, I mean, at night?"

"No."

"Has it any habit of speaking the word 'Jeanette.'"

"No. I don't think I ever heard it pronounce the word more than three or four times before. It is stupid and seems to dislike her."

The Thinking Machine took down a volume of an encyclopedia which he studied for a moment.

"Have you any record anywhere of that combination?" he inquired.

"Yes, but it would have been impossi——"

The scientist made a little impatient gesture with his hands.

"Where is this record?"

"The combination begins with the figure three," Mrs. Roswell hastened to explain. "I jotted it down in a French copy of *Les Miserables* which I keep in my room with a few other books. The first number, three, appears on Page 3, the second on Page 33, and the third on Page 333. The combination in full is 3-14-9. No person could possibly associate the numbers in the book with the combination even if he should notice them."

Again there was the quick, impatient gesture of the scientist's hands. Mr. Field interpreted it aright as annoyance.

"You say your daughter is nervous," The Thinking Machine said. "Is it serious? Is there any somnambulistic tendency that you know of?"

Mrs. Roswell flushed a little.

"She has a nervous disorder," she confessed at last. "But I know of no somnambulistic tendency. She has been treated by half a dozen specialists. Two or three times we feared—feared——"

She faltered and stopped. The Thinking Machine squinted at her oddly, then turned his eyes toward the ceiling again.

"I understand," he said. "You feared for her sanity. And she may have the sleep-walking habit without your knowledge?"

"Yes, she may have," faltered Mrs. Roswell.

"And now your son. Tell me something about him. He has an allowance, I suppose? Is he inclined to be studious or otherwise? Has he any love affair?"

Again Mrs. Roswell flushed. Her entire manner resented this connection of her son's name with the affair. She looked inquiringly at Mr. Field.

"I don't see——" Mr. Field began, remonstratingly.

"My son could have nothing——" Mrs. Roswell interrupted.

"Madam, you have presented an abstract problem," broke in The Thinking Machine impatiently. "I presumed you wanted a solution. Of course, if you do not——" and he made as if to arise.

"Please pardon me," said Mrs. Roswell quickly, almost tearfully. "My son has an allowance of ten thousand a year; my daughter has the same. My son is inclined to be studious along political lines, while my daughter is interested in charity. He has no love affair except—except a deep attachment for his step-sister. It is rather unfortunate——"

"I know, I know," interrupted the scientist again. "Naturally you object to any affection in that direction because of a fear for the girl's mental condition. May I ask if there is any further prejudice on your part to the girl?"

"Not the slightest," said Mrs. Roswell quickly. "I am deeply attached to her. It is only a fear for my son's happiness."

"I presume your son understands your attitude in the matter?"

"I have tried to intimate it to him without saying it openly," she explained. "I don't think he knows how serious her condition has been, and is, for that matter."

"Of your knowledge has either your son or the girl ever handled or looked into the book where the combination is written?"

"Not that I know of, or ever heard of."

"Or any of your servants?"

"No."

"Does it happen that you have this tiara with you?"

Mrs. Roswell produced it from her hand bag. It was a glittering, glistening thing, a triumph of the jeweler's art, intricate and marvelously delicate in conception yet wonderfully heavy with the dead weight of pure gold. A single splendid diamond of four or five carats blazed at its apex, and radiating from this were strings of smaller stones. One was missing from its setting. The prongs which had held it were almost straight from the force used to pry out the stone. The Thinking Machine studied the gorgeous ornament in silence.

"It is possible for you to clear up this matter without my active interference," he said at last. "You do not want it to become known outside your own family, therefore you must watch for this thief—yourself in person. Take no one into your confidence, least of all your son and step-daughter. Given the same circumstances, the A B C rules of logic—and logic is inevitable—indicate that another may disappear."

Mrs. Roswell was frankly startled, and Mr. Field leaned forward with eager interest.

"If you see how this second stone disappears," continued The Thinking Machine musingly, without heeding in the slightest the effect of his words on the others, "you will know what became of the first and will be able to recover both."

"If another attempt is to be made," exclaimed Mrs. Roswell

apprehensively, "would it not be better to send the jewels to a safe deposit? Would I not be in danger myself?"

"It is perfectly possible that if the jewels were removed, the vault would be opened just the same," said The Thinking Machine quietly, enigmatically while his visitors stared. "Leave the jewels where they are. You may be assured that you are in no personal danger whatever. If you learn what you seek, you need not communicate with me again. If you do not, I will personally investigate the matter. On no condition whatever interrupt or attempt to prevent anything that may happen."

Mr. Field arose; the interview seemed to be at an end. He had one last question.

"Have you any theory of what actually happened?" he asked. "How was the jewel taken?"

"If I told you, you wouldn't believe it," said The Thinking Machine, curtly. "Good day."

It was on the third day following that Mrs. Roswell hurriedly summoned The Thinking Machine to her home. When he arrived she was deeply agitated.

"Another of the small stones has been stolen from the tiara," she told him hurriedly. "The circumstances were identical with those of the first theft, even to the screaming of the cockatoo. I watched as you suggested, have been watching each night but last night was so weary that I fell asleep. The cockatoo awoke me. Why would Jeanette——"

"Let me see the apartments," suggested the scientist.

Thus he was ushered into the room which was the center of the mystery. Again he examined the tiara, then studied the door of the vault. Afterwards he casually picked up and verified the record of the combination, locked and unlocked the vault twice after which he examined the fastenings of the door and the windows. This done he went over and peered inquisitively at the cockatoo on its perch.

The bird was a giant of its species, pure white, with a yellow crest which drooped in exaggerated melancholy. The cockatoo resented the impertinence and had not The Thinking Machine moved quickly, would have torn off his spectacles.

A door from another room opened and a girl—Jeanette—entered. She was tall, slender and exquisitely proportioned with a great cloud of ruddy gold hair. Her face was white with the dead white of illness and infinite weariness was in her eyes. She was startled at sight of a stranger.

"I beg your pardon," she said. "I didn't know——" and started to retire.

Professor Van Dusen acknowledged an introduction to her by a glance and a nod then turned quickly and looked at the cockatoo which was quarreling volubly with crest upraised. Mrs. Roswell's attention, too, was attracted by the angry attitude of her pet. She grasped the scientist's arm quickly.

"The bird!" she exclaimed.

"Jeanette, Jeanette, Jeanette," screamed the cockatoo, shrilly.

Jeanette dropped wearily into a chair, heeding neither the tense attitude of her step-mother nor the quarrelings of the cockatoo.

"You don't sleep well, Miss Roswell?" asked The Thinking Machine.

"Oh, yes," the girl replied. "I seem to sleep enough, but I am always very tired. And I dream constantly, nearly always my dreams are of the cockatoo. I imagine he calls my name."

Mrs. Roswell looked quickly at Professor Van Dusen. He crossed to the girl and examined her pulse.

"Do you read much?" he asked. "Did you ever read this?" and he held up the copy of *Les Miserables.*

"I don't read French well enough," she replied. "I have read it in English."

The conversation was desultory for a time and finally The Thinking Machine arose. In the drawing room down stairs he gave Mrs. Roswell some instructions which amazed her exceedingly, and went his way.

Jeanette retired about eleven o'clock that night and in an hour was sleeping soundly. But Mrs. Roswell was up when the clock struck one. She had previously bolted the doors of the two rooms and fastened the windows. Now she arose from her seat, picked up a small jar from her table, and crept cautiously, even stealthily to the bed whereon Jeanette lay, pale almost as the sheets. The girl's hands were outstretched in an attitude of utter exhaustion. Mrs. Roswell bent low over them a moment, then stole back to her own room. Half an hour later she was asleep.

Early next morning Mrs. Roswell 'phoned to The Thinking Machine, and they talked for fifteen minutes. She was apparently explaining something and the scientist gave crisp, monosyllabic answers. When the wire was disconnected he called up two other persons on the 'phone. One of them was Dr. Henderson, noted alienist; the other was Dr. Forrester, a nerve specialist of international repute. To both he said:

"I want to show you the most extraordinary thing you have ever seen."

The dim light of the night lamp cast strange, unexpected shadows, half revealing yet half hiding, the various objects in Mrs. Roswell's room. The bed made a great white splotch in the shadows, and the only other conspicuous point was the bright silver dial of the jewel vault. From the utter darkness of Jeanette Roswell's room came the steady, regular breathing of a person asleep; the cockatoo was gone from his perch. Outside was the faint night-throb of a city at rest. In the distance a clock boomed four times.

Finally the stillness was broken by a faint creaking, the tread of a light foot and Jeanette, robed mystically in white, appeared in the door of her room. Her eyes were wide open, staring, her face was chalk-like, her hair tumbled in confusion about her head and here and there was flecked with the glint of the night-light.

The girl paused and from somewhere in the shadows came a quick gasp, instantly stifled. Then, unhearing, she moved slowly but without hesitation across the room to a table whereon lay several books. She stooped over this and when she straightened up again she held *Les Miserables* in her hand. Several times the leaves fluttered through her fingers, and thrice she held the book close to her eyes in the uncertain light, then nodded as if satisfied and carefully replaced it as she had found it.

From the table she went straight toward the silver dial which gleamed a reflection of light. As she went, another figure detached itself noiselessly from the shadows and crept toward her from behind. As the girl leaned forward to place her hand on the dial a steady ray of light from an electric bulb struck her full in the face. She did not flinch nor by the slightest sign show that she was aware of it. From her face the light traveled to each of her hands in turn.

The dial whirled in her fingers several times and then stopped with a click, the bolt snapped and the vault door opened. Conspicuously in front lay the tiara glittering mockingly. Again from the shadows there came a quick gasp as the girl lifted the regal toy and tumbled it on the floor. Again the gasp was stifled.

With quick-moving, nervous hands she dragged the jewels out, permitting them to fall. She seemed to be seeking something else, seeking vainly, apparently, for after awhile she rose with a sigh, staring into the vault hopelessly. She stood thus for a dozen heart beats, then the low, guarded voice of the second figure was heard—low yet singularly clear of enunciation.

"What is it you seek?"

"The letters," she replied dreamily yet distinctly. There was a pause and she turned suddenly as if to re-enter her room. As she did so the light again flashed in her glassy eyes, and the second figure laid a detaining hand on her arm. She started a little, staggered, her eyes closed suddenly to open again in abject terror as she stared into the face before her. She screamed wildly, piercingly, gazed a moment then sank down fainting.

"Dr. Forrester, she needs you now."

It was the calm, unexcited, impersonal voice of The Thinking Machine. He touched a button in the wall and the room was flooded with light. Drs. Forrester and Henderson, suddenly revealed with Mr. and Mrs. Roswell and Arthur Grantham, came forward and lifted the senseless body. Grantham, too, rushed to her with pained, horror-stricken face. Mrs. Roswell dropped limply into a chair; her husband stood beside her helplessly stroking her hair.

"It's all right," said The Thinking Machine. "It's only shock."

Grantham turned on him savagely, impetuously and danger lay in the boyish eyes.

"It's a lie!" he said fiercely. "She didn't steal those diamonds."

"How do you know?" asked The Thinking Machine coldly.

"Because—because I took them myself," the young man blurted. "If I had known there was to be any such trick as this, I should never have consented to it."

His mother stared up at him in open-eyed wonder.

"How did you remove the jewels from the setting?" asked The Thinking Machine, still quietly.

"I—I did it with my fingers."

"Take out one of these for me," and The Thinking Machine offered him the tiara.

Grantham snatched it from his hand and tugged at it frantically while the others stared, but each jewel remained in its setting. Finally he sank down on the bed beside the still figure of the girl he loved. His face was crimson.

"Your intentions are good, but you're a fool," commented The Thinking Machine tartly. "I know you did not take the jewels—you have proven it yourself—and I may add that Miss Roswell did not take them."

The stupefied look on Grantham's face was reflected in those of his mother and step-father. Drs. Forrester and Henderson were busy with the girl, heedless of the others.

"Then where are the jewels?" Mrs. Roswell demanded.

The Thinking Machine turned and squinted at her with a slight suggestion of irritable reproach in his manner.

"Safe and easily found," he replied impatiently. He lifted the unconscious girl's hand and allowed his fingers to rest on her pulse for a moment, then turned to the medical men. "Would you have believed that somnambulistic sub-consciousness would have taken just this form?" he asked curtly.

"Not unless I had seen it," replied Dr. Henderson, frankly.

"It's a remarkable mental condition—remarkable," commented

Dr. Forrester.

It was a weirdly simple recital of the facts as he had found them that The Thinking Machine told downstairs in the drawing room an hour later. Dawn was breaking over the city, and the faces of those who had waited and watched for just what had happened showed weariness. Yet they listened, listened with all their faculties as the eminent scientist talked. Young Grantham sat white-faced and nervous; Jeanette was sleeping quietly upstairs with her maid on watch.

"The problem in itself was not a difficult one," The Thinking Machine began as he lounged in a big chair with eyes upturned. "The unusual, not to say strange features, which seemed to make it more difficult served to simplify it as a matter of fact. When I had all the facts, I had the solution in the main. It was adding a fact to a fact to get a good result as one might add two and two to get four.

"In the first place burglars were instantly removed as a possibility. They would have taken everything, not one small stone. Then what? Mr. Grantham here? His mother assured me that he was quiet and studious of habit, and had an allowance of ten thousand a year. Then remember always that he no more than anyone else could have entered the rooms. The barred doors excluded the servants too.

"Then we had only you, Mrs. Roswell, and your step-daughter. There would have been no motive for you to remove the jewel unless your object was to throw suspicion on the girl. I didn't believe you capable of this. So there was left somnambulism or a wilful act of your step-daughter's. There was no motive for the last—your daughter has ten thousand a year. Then sleep-walking alone remained. Sleep-walking it was. I am speaking now of the opening of the vault."

Grantham leaned forward in his chair gripping its arms fiercely. The mother saw, and one of her white hands was laid gently on his. He glanced at her impatiently then turned to The Thinking Machine. Mr. Roswell, the alienist, and the specialist, followed the cold clear logic as if fascinated.

"If somnambulism, then who was the somnambulist?" The Thinking Machine resumed after a moment. "It did not seem to be you Mrs. Roswell. You are not of a nervous temperament; you are a normal healthy woman. If we accept as true your statement that you were aroused in bed by the cockatoo screaming 'Jeannette' we prove that you were not the somnambulist. Your step-daughter? She suffered from a nervous disorder so pronounced that you had fears for her mental condition. With everyone else removed, she was the somnambulist. Even the cockatoo said that.

"Now let us see how it would have been possible to open the vault. We admit that no one except yourself knew the combination. But a record of that combination did appear; therefore it was possible for some one else to learn it. Your step-daughter does not know that combination when she is in a normal condition. I won't say that she knows it when in the somnambulistic state, but I will say that when in that condition *she knows where there is a record of it*. How she learned this I don't know. It is not a legitimate part of the problem.

"Be that as it may she was firmly convinced that something she was seeking, something of deep concern to her, was in that vault. It might *not* have been in the vault but in her abnormal condition she thought it was. She was not after jewels—her every act even tonight showed that. What else? Letters. I knew it was a letter, or letters, before she said so herself. What was in these letters is of no consequence here. You, Mrs. Roswell considered it your duty to hide them—possibly destroy them."

Both husband and son turned on Mrs. Roswell inquiringly. She stared from one to the other helplessly, pleadingly.

"The letters contained——" she started to explain.

"Never mind that, it's none of our business," curtly interrupted The Thinking Machine. "If there is a family skeleton, it's yours.

"Even with the practical certain knowledge that Miss Roswell *did* open the vault," The Thinking Machine resumed placidly, "and that she opened it in precisely the manner you saw tonight, I took one more step to prove it. This was after the second stone had disappeared. I instructed Mrs. Roswell to place a little strawberry jam on her step-daughter's hands while she was sleeping. If this jam appeared on the book the next time the vault was found open, it proved finally and conclusively that Miss Roswell opened it. I chose strawberry jam because it was unusual. I dare say no one who might have a purpose in opening that vault would go around with strawberry jam on his hands. This jam did appear on the book, and then I summoned you, Dr. Forrester, and you, Dr. Henderson. You know the rest. I may add that Mr. Grantham in attempting to take the theft upon himself merely made a fool of himself. No person with bare fingers could have torn out one of the stones."

There was a long pause, and deep silence while the problem as seen by The Thinking Machine was considered in the minds of his hearers. Grantham at last broke the silence.

"Where are the two stones that are missing?"

"Oh yes," said The Thinking Machine easily, as if that trivial point had escaped him. "Mrs. Roswell will you please have the cockatoo brought in?" he asked, and then explained to the others: "I had the bird removed from the room tonight for fear it would interrupt at the wrong moment."

Mrs. Roswell arose and gave some instructions to a servant who was waiting outside. He went away and returned later with a startled expression on his graven face.

"The bird is dead, madam," he reported.

"Dead!" repeated Mrs. Roswell.

"Good!" said The Thinking Machine rubbing his hands briskly together. "Bring it in anyhow."

"Why, what could have killed it?" asked Mrs. Roswell, bewildered.

"Indigestion," replied the scientist. "Here is the thief."

He turned suddenly to the servant who had entered bearing the cockatoo in state on a silver tray.

"Who? I?" gasped the astonished servant.

"No, this fellow," replied The Thinking Machine as he picked up the dead bird. "He had the opportunity; he had the pointed instrument necessary to pry out a stone—note the sharp hooked bill; and he had the strength to do it. Besides all that he confessed a fondness for bright things when he tried to snatch my eyeglasses. He saw Miss Roswell drop the tiara on the floor; its brightness fascinated him. He pried out the stone and swallowed it. It pained him, and he screamed 'Jeannette.' This same thing happened on two occasions. Your encyclopedia will tell you that the cockatoo has more strength in that sharp beak than you could possibly exercise with two fingers unless you had a steel instrument."

Later that day The Thinking Machine sent to Mrs. Roswell the two missing diamonds, the glass head of a hat pin and a crystal shoe button which he had recovered from the dead bird. His diagnosis of the case was acute indigestion.

THE HAUNTED BELL

It was one of those things, trivial enough, yet so strangely mystifying in its happening that the mind hesitated to accept it as an actual occurrence, despite the indisputable evidence of the sense of hearing. As the seconds ticked on, Franklin Phillips was not at all certain that it had happened, and gradually the doubt began to assume the proportions of a conviction. Then, because his keenly attuned brain did not readily explain it, the matter was dismissed as an impossibility. Certainly it had not happened. Mr. Phillips smiled a little. Of course, it was—it must be—a trick of his nerves.

But even as the impossibility of the thing grew upon him, the musical clang still echoed vaguely in his memory, and his eyes were still fixed inquiringly on the Japanese gong whence it had come. The gong was of the usual type—six bronze discs or inverted bowls of graduated sizes, suspended one above the other with the largest at the top, and quaintly colored with the deep, florid tones of Japan's ancient decorative art. It hung motionless at the end of a silken cord which dropped down sheerly from the ceiling over a corner of his desk. It was certainly harmless enough in appearance, yet—yet——

As he looked, the bell sounded again. It was a clear, rich, vibrant note—a boom which rang forth suddenly as if of its own volition, quavered full-toned, then diminished until it was only a lingering sense of sound. Mr. Phillips started to his feet with an exclamation.

Now, in the money marts of the world Franklin Phillips was regarded as a living refutation of all theories as to the physical disasters consequent upon a long pursuit of the strenuous life—a human antithesis of nerves. He breathed fourteen times to the minute, and his heart-beat was always within a fraction of seventy-one. This was true whether there were millions at stake in a capricious market or whether he ordered a cigar. In this calm lay the strength which had enabled him to reach his fiftieth year in perfect mental and physical condition.

Behind this utter normality was a placid, inquiring mind; so now deliberately he took a pencil and tapped the bells of the gong one after another, beginning at the bottom. The shrill note of the first told him instantly that was not the one which had sounded; nor was the second, nor the third. At the fourth he hesitated, and struck a second time. Then he tapped the fifth. That was it. The gong trembled and swayed slightly from the blow, light as it was, and twice again he struck it. Then he was convinced.

For several minutes he stood staring, staring blankly. What had caused the bell to ring? His manner was calm, cold, quiet, inquisitive—indomitable common sense inspired the query.

"I guess it was nerves," he said after a moment. "But I was looking at it, and——"

Nerves as a possibility were suddenly brushed ruthlessly aside, and he systematically sought some tangible explanation of the affair. Had a flying insect struck the bell? No. He was positive, because he had been looking directly at it when it sounded the second time. He would have seen an insect. Had something dropped from the ceiling? No. He would have seen that, too. With alert, searching eyes he surveyed the small room. It was his own personal den—a sort of an office in his home. He was alone now; the door was closed; everything appeared as usual.

Perhaps a window! The one facing east was open to the lightly-stirring air of the first warm evening of spring. The wind had disturbed the gong! He jumped at the thought as an inspiration. It faded when he saw the window curtains hanging down limply; the movement of the air was too light to disturb even these. Perhaps something had been tossed through the window! The absurdity of that conjecture was proved instantly. There was a screen in the window of so fine a mesh that hardly more than a grain of sand could pass through it. And this screen was intact.

With bewilderment in his face Mr. Phillips sat down again. Then recurred to him one indisputable fact which precluded the possibility of all those things he had considered. There had been absolutely no movement—that is, perceptible movement—of the gong when the bell sounded. Yet the tone was loud as if a violent blow had been struck. He remembered that when he tapped the bell sharply with his pencil, it swayed and trembled visibly, but the pencil was so light that the tone sounded far away and faint. To convince himself he touched the bell again, ever so lightly. It swayed.

"Well, of all the extraordinary things I ever heard of!" he remarked.

After a while, he lighted a cigar, and for the first time in his life his hand shook. The sight brought a faint expression of amused surprise to his lips; then he snapped his fingers impatiently, and settled back in his chair. It was a struggle to bring his mind round to material things; it insisted on wandering, and wove fantastic, grotesque conjectures in the drifting tobacco smoke. But at last common sense triumphed under the sedative influence of an excellent cigar, and the incident of the bell floated off into chimerical nothingness. Business affairs—urgent, real, tangible business affairs—focussed his attention.

Then, suddenly, clangorously, with the insistent acclaim of a fire alarm, the bell sounded—once! twice! thrice! Mr. Phillips leaped to his feet. The tones chilled him and stirred his phlegmatic heart-nerves to quicker action. He took a long, deep breath, and with one glance around the little room strode out into the hall. He paused there a moment, glanced at his watch—it was four minutes to nine—then went on to his wife's apartments.

Mrs. Phillips was reclining in a chair, and listening with an amused smile to her son's recital of some commonplace college event which happened to be of interest to him. She was forty or forty-two, perhaps, and charming. Women never learn to be charming until they are forty—until then they are only pretty and amiable—sometimes. The son, Harvey Phillips, rose as his father entered. He was a stalwart young man of perhaps twenty, a prototype of that hard-headed, masterful financier, Franklin Phillips.

"Why, Frank, I thought you were so absorbed in business that ——" Mrs. Phillips began.

Mr. Phillips paused and looked blankly, unseeingly, as one suddenly aroused from sleep, at his wife and son—the two dearest of all earthly things to him. The son noted nothing unusual in his manner; the wife, with intuitive eyes, read some vague uneasiness.

"What is it?" she asked solicitously. "Has something gone wrong?"

Mr. Phillips laughed nervously, and sat down near her.

"Nothing, nothing," he assured her. "I feel unaccountably nervous, somehow, and I thought I should like to talk to you rather than—than——"

"Keep on going over and over those stupid figures?" she interrupted. "Thank you."

She leaned forward with a gesture of infinite grace, and took his hand. He clenched it spasmodically to stop its absurd trembling, and, with an effort all the greater because it was repressed so sternly, regained control of his panic-stricken nerves. Harvey Phillips excused himself, and left the room.

"Harvey has just been explaining the mysteries of football to me," said Mrs. Phillips. "He's going to play on the Harvard eleven."

Her husband stared at her without the slightest heed or comprehension of what she was saying.

"Can you tell me," he asked suddenly, "where you got that Japanese gong in my room?"

"Oh, that? I saw it in the window of a queer old curio shop I pass sometimes on my charity rounds. I looked at it two or three months ago and bought it. The place is in Benton Street. It is kept by an old German—Wagner, I think his name is. Why?"

"It looks as if it might be very old—a hundred years, perhaps," remarked Mr. Phillips.

"That's what I thought," responded his wife; "and the coloring is exquisite. I had never seen one exactly like it, so——"

"It doesn't happen to have any history, I suppose?" he interrupted.

"Not that I know of."

"Or any peculiar quality, or—or attribute out of the ordinary?"

Mrs. Phillips shook her head.

"I'm sure I don't know what you mean," she replied. "The only peculiar quality I noticed was the singular purity of the bells, and, as I said, the coloring."

Mr. Phillips coughed over his cigar.

"Yes, I noticed the bells myself," he explained lamely. "It just struck me that the thing was—was out of the ordinary, and I was a little curious about it." He was silent a moment. "It looks as if it might have been valuable once."

"I hardly think so," Mrs. Phillips responded. "I believe twenty-five dollars is what I paid for it—all that was asked."

That was all that was said about the matter at the time. But on the following morning an early visitor at Wagner's shop was Franklin Phillips. It was a typical place of its kind, half curio and half furniture shop, with a coat of dust over all. There had been a crude attempt to enhance the appearance of the place by an artistic arrangement of several musty antique pieces, but otherwise it was a chaos of all things. An aged German met Mr. Phillips as he entered.

"Are you Mr. Wagner?" inquired the financier.

Extreme caution, amounting almost to suspicion, seemed to be a part of the old German's business *régime*, for he looked at his visitor from head to foot with keen eyes, then evaded the question.

"What do you want?" he asked.

"I want to know if you are Mr. Wagner," said Mr. Phillips tersely. "Are you, or are you not?"

The old man met his frank stare for a moment, then his cunning, faded eyes wavered and dropped.

"I am Johann Wagner," he said humbly. "What do you want?"

"Some time ago—two or three months—you sold a Japanese gong——" Mr. Phillips began.

"I never sold it," interrupted Wagner vehemently. "I never had a Japanese gong in the place. I never sold it."

"Of course you sold it," insisted Mr. Phillips. "A Japanese gong—do you understand? Six bells on a silken cord."

"I never had such a thing in my life—never had such a thing in my shop," declared the German excitedly. "I never sold it, so help me. I never saw it."

Curiosity and incredulity were in Mr. Phillips' eyes as he steadily faced the old German.

"Do you happen to have any assistant?" he asked. "Or did you have three months ago?"

"No, I never had a clerk," exclaimed the German with a violence which Mr. Phillips did not understand. "There has never been anybody here but me. I never had a Japanese gong here—I never sold one. I never saw one here."

Mr. Phillips studied the aged, wrinkled face before him calmly for several seconds. He was trying vainly to account for an excitement—a vehemence which was as inexplicable as it was unnecessary.

"It's absurd to deny that you sold the bell," he said finally. "My wife bought it of you, here, in this place."

"I never sold it!" stormed the German. "I never had it. No woman ever came here. I don't want women here. I don't know anything about a Japanese gong. I never had one here."

Deeply puzzled and thoroughly impatient, Mr. Phillips decided to forego this attempt at a casual inquiry into the history of the gong. After a little while he went away. The old German watched him cautiously with cunning, avaricious eyes until he stepped on a trolley car.

As the cool, pleasant days of early spring passed on, the bell held its tongue. Only once, and that was immediately after his visit to the old German's shop, did Mr. Phillips refer to it again. Then he inquired casually of his wife if she had bought it of the old man in person, and she answered in the affirmative, describing him. Then the question came to him: Why had Wagner absolutely denied all knowledge of the bell, of its having been in his possession, and of having sold it?

But after a time this question was lost in vital business affairs which engrossed his attention. The gong still hung over his desk, and he occasionally glanced at it. At such times his curiosity was keen, poignant even, but he made no further effort to solve the mystery which seemed to enshroud it.

So, until one evening a wealthy young Japanese gentleman, Oku Matsumi by name, son of a distinguished nobleman in his country's diplomatic service, came to dinner at the Phillips' home as the guest of Harvey Phillips. They were college mates, and a friendship had grown up between them which was curious, perhaps, but explainable on the ground of a mutual interest in art.

After dinner, Mr. Matsumi expressed his admiration for several pictures which hung in the luxurious dining-room and so it followed naturally that Mr. Phillips exhibited some other rare works of art. One of these pictures hung in the little room where the gong was. With no thought of that at the moment, Mr. Phillips led the way in, and the Japanese followed.

Then a peculiar thing happened. At sight of the gong, Mr. Matsumi seemed amazed, incredulously startled, and taking one step toward it, he bent as if in obeisance. At the same time his right hand was thrust outward and upward, as if describing some symbol in the air.

. . . Utter silence! A suppliant throng, bowed in awed humility, with hands outstretched, palms downward, and yellow faces turned in mute prayer toward the light which fluttered up feebly from the sacred fire upon the stony, leering countenance of Buddha. The gigantic golden image rose cross-legged from its pedestal, and receded upward and backward into the gloom of the temple. The multitude shaded off from bold outlines within the glow of the fire to a shadowy, impalpable mass in the remotest corners; hushed of breath, immovably staring into the drooping eyes of their graven god.

Behind the image was a protecting veil of cloth of gold. Presently there came a murmur, and the supplicants, with one accord, prostrated themselves until their heads touched the bare, cold stones of the temple floor. The murmur grew into the weirdly beautiful chant of the priests of Buddha. The flickering light for an instant gave an appearance of life to the heavy-lidded, drooping eyes; then it steadied again, and they seemed fixed on the urn wherein the fire burned.

After a moment, the curtain of gold was thrust aside in three places simultaneously, and three silken-robed priests appeared. Each bore in his hand a golden sceptre. Together they approached the sacred fire, and together they thrust the sceptres into it. Instantly a blaze spouted up, illuminating the vast, high-roofed palace of worship, and a cloud of incense arose. The sweetly sickening odor spread out, fan-like, over the throng.

The three priests turned away from the urn, and each, with slow, solemn tread, made his way to an altar of incense with the flaming torch held aloft. They met again at the feet of Buddha, and prostrated themselves, at the same time extending the right hand and forming some symbol in the air. The chant from behind the golden veil softened to a murmur, and the murmur grew into silence. Then!

"Gautama!"

The name came from the three together—the tone was a prayer. It reverberated for an instant in the recesses of the great temple, then the multitude with one motion raised themselves, repeated the single word, and groveled again on their faces.

"Siddhartha, ye Beloved!"

Again the three priests spoke, and again the supplicants moved as one, repeating the words. The burning incense grew heavy, the sacred fire flickered, and shadows flitted elusively over the golden graven face of the Buddha.

"Sakyamuni, Son of Wonder!"

The moving of the multitude as it swayed and answered was in perfect accord. It was as if one heart, one soul, one thought had inspired the action.

"Oh, Buddha! Wise One! Enlightened One!" came the voices of the priests again. "Oh, Son of Kapilavastu! Great One! You who found Nirvana! Your unworthy people are at your feet. Oh, Great One! We seek your gracious counsel."

The voices in chorus had risen to a chant. When they ceased there was the chill of suspense; a little shiver ran through the temple; there was a hushed movement of terrified anxiety. Of all the throng only the priests dared raise their eyes to the cold, graven face of the image. For an instant the chilling silence, then boldly, vibrantly a bell sounded—once!

"Buddha has spoken!"

It was a murmurous whisper, almost a sigh, plaintive, awe-stricken. The note of the bell trembled on the incense-laden air, then was dissipated, welded into silence again. Priests and people were cowering on the bare stones; the lights flared up suddenly, then flickered, and the semi-gloom seemed to grow sensibly deeper. Behind the veil of gold the chant of the priests began again. But it was in a more solemn note—a despairing wail. For a short time it went on, then died away.

Again the sacred fire blazed up as if caught by a gust of wind, but the glow did not light the Buddha's face now—it was concentrated on a bronze gong which dropped down sheerly on a silken cord at Buddha's right hand. There were six discs, the largest at the top, silhouetted against the darkness of the golden veil beyond. From one of these bells the sound had come, but now they hung mute and motionless. Only the three priests raised reverential eyes to it, and one, the eldest of them, rose.

"Oh, Voice of Buddha!" he apostrophised in a moving, swinging chant, and the face of the graven god seemed swallowed up in the shadows. "We, your unworthy disciples, await! Each year at the eleventh festival we supplicate. But thrice only hast thou spoken in the half century, and thrice within the eleventh day of your speaking our

Emperor has passed into the arms of Death and Nirvana. Shall it again be so, Great One?"

The chant died away, and the multitude raised itself to its knees with supplicating hands thrust out into the darkness toward the dim-lit gong. It was an attitude of beseeching, of prayer, of entreaty.

And again, as it hung motionless, the bell sounded. The tone rolled out melodiously, clearly—once! twice! thrice! Those who gazed at the miracle lowered their eyes lest they be stricken blind. And the bell struck on—four! five! six! A plaintive, wailing cry was raised; the priests behind the veil of gold were chanting again. Seven! eight! nine! The people took up the rolling chant as they groveled, and it swelled until the ancient walls of the temple trembled. Ten! eleven!

Utter silence! A suppliant throng, bowed in awed humility, with hands outstretched, palms downward, and yellow faces turned in mute prayer toward the light which fluttered up feebly from the sacred fire upon the stony, leering countenance of Buddha! . . .

Mr. Matsumi straightened up suddenly to find his host staring at him in perturbed amazement.

"Why did you do that?" Mr. Phillips blurted uneasily.

"Pardon me, but you wouldn't understand if I told you," replied the Japanese with calm, inscrutable face. "May I examine it, please?" and he indicated the silent and motionless gong.

"Certainly," replied the financier, wonderingly.

Mr. Matsumi, with a certain eagerness which was not lost upon the Englishman, approached the gong, and touched the bells lightly one after another, evidently to get the tone. Then he stooped and examined them carefully—top and bottom. Inside the largest bell—that at the top—he found something which interested him. After a close scrutiny, he again straightened up, and in his eyes was an expression which Mr. Phillips would have liked to interpret.

"I presume you have seen it before?" ventured the financier.

"No, never," was the reply.

"But you recognized it."

Mr. Matsumi merely shrugged his shoulders.

"And what made you do that?" By "that" Mr. Phillips referred to Mr. Matsumi's strange act when he first saw the bell.

Again the Japanese shrugged his shoulders. An exquisite, innate courtesy which belonged to him was apparently forgotten now in contemplation of the gong. The financier gnawed at his mustache. He was beginning to feel nervous—the nervousness he had felt previously—and his imagination ran riot.

"You have not had the gong long?" remarked Mr. Matsumi, after a pause.

"Three or four months."

"Have you ever noticed anything peculiar about it?"

Mr. Phillips stared at him frankly.

"Well, rather," he said at last, in a tone which was perfectly convincing.

"It rings, you mean—the fifth bell?"

Mr. Phillips nodded. There was a tense eagerness in the manner of the Japanese.

"You have never heard the bell ring eleven times?"

Mr. Phillips shook his head. Mr. Matsumi drew a long breath—whether it was relief the other couldn't say. There was silence. Mr. Matsumi closed and unclosed his small hands several times.

"Pardon me for mentioning the matter under such circumstances," he said at last, in a tone which suggested that he feared giving offense, "but would you be willing to part with the gong?"

Mr. Phillips regarded him keenly. He was seeking in the other's manner some inkling to a solution of a mystery which with each moment seemed to grow more hopelessly beyond him.

"I shouldn't care to part with it," he replied casually. "It was given to me by my wife."

"Then no offer I might make would be considered?"

"No, certainly not," replied Mr. Phillips tartly. There was a pause. "This gong has interested me immensely. I should like to know its history. Perhaps it is within your power to enlighten me?"

With the imperturbability of his race Mr. Matsumi declined to give any information. But with a graceful return of his former exquisite courtesy, he sought more definite knowledge for himself.

"I will not ask you to part with the gong," he said; "but perhaps you can inform me where your wife bought it?" He paused for a moment. "Perhaps it would be possible to get another like it?"

"I happen to know there isn't another," replied Mr. Phillips. "It came from a little curio shop in Benton Street, kept by a German named Johann Wagner."

And that was all. This incident passed as the other had, the net result being only further to stimulate Mr. Phillips' curiosity. It seemed a futile curiosity, yet it was ever present.

On the next evening, a balmy, ideal night of spring, Mr. Phillips had occasion to go into the small room. This was just before dinner was announced. It was rather close there, so he opened the east window to a grateful breeze, and placed the screen in position, after which he stooped to pull out a drawer of his desk. As he stooped there came again the clangorous boom of the bell—One! Two! Three! Four! Five! Six! Seven!

At the first stroke he straightened up, at the second he leaned forward toward the gong, with his eyes riveted to the fifth disc. As it continued to ring, he grimly held on to jangling nerves and looked for the cause. Beneath the bells, on top, all around them, he sought. There was nothing! Nothing! The sounds simply burst out, one after another, as if from a heavy blow, and the bell did not move. For the seventh time it struck, and then, with white, ghastly face and chilled, stiff limbs, Mr. Phillips rushed out of the room. A dew of perspiration grew in the palms of his quavering hands.

It was a night of little rest and strange dreams for him. At breakfast on the following morning Mrs. Phillips poured out his coffee, and then glanced through the mail which had been placed beside her. Several wrinkles appeared in her forehead as she deciphered one of the letters.

"Do you particularly care for that gong in your room?" she inquired.

Mr. Phillips started a little. That particular object had enchained his attention for the last dozen hours, awake and asleep.

"Why?" he asked.

"You know I told you I bought it of a curio dealer," Mrs. Phillips explained. "His name is Johann Wagner, and he offers me five hundred dollars if I will sell it back to him. I presume he has found it is more valuable than he imagined, and the five hundred would make a comfortable addition to my charity fund."

Mr. Phillips was deeply thoughtful. Johann Wagner! What was this new twist? Why had Wagner denied all knowledge of the gong to him? Having denied, why should he now make an attempt to buy it back? In seeking answers to these questions he was silent.

"Well, dear?" inquired his wife, after a pause. "You didn't answer me."

"No, don't sell the gong," he exclaimed abruptly. "Don't sell it at any price. I—I want it. I'll give you a cheque for your charity."

There was something of uneasiness in her devoted eyes. Some strange, subtle, indefinable air which she could not fathom was in his manner. With a little sigh which breathed her unrest, she finished her breakfast.

On the following morning still another letter came from Johann Wagner. It was an appeal—an impassioned appeal—hurriedly scrawled and almost incoherent in form. He *must* have the gong! He would give five thousand dollars for it. Mrs. Phillips was frankly bewildered at the letter, and turned it over to her husband. He read it through twice, with grimly set teeth.

"No!" he exclaimed violently. "It shan't be sold for any price." Then his voice dropped as he recollected himself. "No, my dear," he continued; "it shall not be sold. It was a present from you to me. I want it, but," and he smiled whimsically, "if he keeps raising the price it will add a great deal to your charity fund, won't it?"

Twice again within thirty-six hours Mr. Phillips heard the bell—once on one occasion and four on the other. And now visibly, tangibly, a great change was upon him. The healthy glow went from his face. There was a constant twitching of his hands; a continual impatient snapping of his fingers. His eyes lost their steady gaze. They roved aimlessly, and one's impression always was that he was listening. The strength of the master spirit was being slowly destroyed, eaten up by a hideous gnawing thing by which he seemed hopelessly obsessed. He took no one into his confidence; it was his own private affair to work out to the end.

This condition was upon him at a time when the activity of the speculative centers of the world was abnormal, and when every faculty was needed in the great financial schemes of which he was the center. He, in person, held the strings which guided millions. The importance of his business affairs was so insistently and relentlessly thrust upon him that he was compelled to meet them. But the effort was a desperate one, and that night late, when a city slept around him, the bell sounded twice.

When he reached his Wall Street office next day an enormous amount of detail work lay before him, and he attacked it with a feverish exaltation which followed upon days and nights of restlessness. He had been at his desk only a few minutes when his private telephone clattered. With an exclamation he arose; comprehending, he sat down again.

Half a dozen times within the hour the bell rang, and each time he was startled. Finally, he rose in a passion, tore the desk telephone from its connecting wires, and flung it into the waste-paper basket. Deliberately he walked round to the side of his desk, and with a well-directed kick smashed the battery box. His secretary regarded him in amazement.

"Mr. Camp," directed the financier sharply, "please instruct the office operator not to ring another telephone bell in this office—ever."

The secretary went out, and he sat down to work again. Late that afternoon he called on his family physician, Dr. Perdue, a robust individual of whom it was said that his laugh cured more patients than his medicine. Be that as it may, he was a successful man, high in his profession. Dr. Perdue looked up with frank interest as Phillips entered.

"Hullo, Phillips," was his greeting. "What can I do for you?"

"Nerves," was the laconic answer.

"I thought it would come to that," remarked the physician, and he shook his head sagely. "Too much work, too much worry, and too many cigars. And, besides, you're not as young as you once were."

"It isn't work or cigars," Phillips replied impatiently. "It's worry—

worry because of some peculiar circumstances which—which——"

He paused with a certain childish feeling of shame, of cowardice. Dr. Perdue regarded him keenly, and felt his pulse.

"What peculiar circumstances?" he demanded.

"Well, I—I can hardly explain it myself," replied Mr. Phillips, between tightly clenched teeth. "It's intangible, unreal, ghostly—what you will. Perhaps I can best make you understand it by saying that I'm always—I always seem to be waiting for something."

Dr. Perdue laughed heartily; Mr. Phillips glared at him.

"Most of us are always waiting for something," said the physician. "If we got it, there wouldn't be any particular object in life. Just what sort of thing is it you're always waiting for?"

Mr. Phillips rose suddenly, and paced the length of the room twice. His under jaw was thrust out a little, his teeth crushed together, but in his eyes lay a haunting, furtive fear.

"I'm always waiting for a—for a bell," he blurted fiercely, and his face became scarlet. "I know it's absurd, but I awake in the night trembling, and lie for hours waiting, waiting, yet dreading the sound as no man ever dreaded anything in this world. At my desk I find myself straining every nerve, waiting, listening. When I talk to any one I'm always waiting, waiting, waiting. Now, this minute, I'm waiting, waiting for it. The thing is driving me mad, man; mad. Don't you understand?"

Dr. Perdue rose with grave face, and led the financier back to his seat.

"You are behaving like a child, Phillips," he said sharply. "Sit down and tell me about it."

"Now, look here, Perdue," and Mr. Phillips brought his fist down on the desk with a crash. "You must believe it—you've *got* to believe it. If you don't, I shall go mad."

"Tell me about it," urged the physician quietly.

Then, haltingly, hesitatingly, the financier related the incidents as they had happened. Incipient madness, fear, terror blazed in his eyes, and at times his pale lips quivered as a child's might. The physician listened attentively, and nodded several times.

"The bell must be—must be haunted," Mr. Phillips burst out in conclusion. "There's no reasonable way to account for it. My common sense tells me that it doesn't sound at all, and yet I know it does."

Dr. Perdue was silent for several minutes.

"You know, of course, that your wife did buy the bell of the old German?" he asked, after a while.

"Certainly I know it. It's proved absolutely by the letters he writes, trying to get it back."

"And your fear doesn't come from anything the Japanese said?"

"It isn't the denial of the German, it isn't the childish things Mr. Matsumi said and did, it's the actual sound of the bell that's driving me insane—it's the hopeless, everlasting, eternal groping for a reason. It's an inanimate thing, and it acts as if—it acts as if it were alive!"

The physician had been sitting with his fingers on Mr. Phillips' wrist. Now he rose and mixed a quieting potion which the other swallowed at a gulp. Soon after his patient went home, somewhat more self-possessed, and with rigid instructions as to the regularity of his life and habits.

"You need about six months abroad more than anything else," Dr. Perdue declared. "Take three weeks, shape up your business, and go. Meanwhile, if you won't sell the gong, or throw it away, keep out of its reach."

Next morning a man—a stranger—was found dead in the small room where the gong hung. A bullet through the heart showed the manner of death. The door leading from the room into the hall was locked on the outside; an open window, facing east, indicated how he had entered, and suggested a possible avenue of escape for his slayer.

Attracted by the commotion which followed the discovery of the body, Mr. and Mrs. Phillips went to investigate, and thus saw the dead man. The wife entered the room first, and for an instant stood speechless, staring into the white, upturned face. Then came an exclamation:

"Why, it's the man from whom I bought the gong!"

She turned to find her husband peering over her shoulder. His face was ashen to the lips, his eyes wide and staring.

"Johann Wagner!" he exclaimed.

Then, as if frenzied, he flung her aside, and rushed to where the gong hung silent and motionless. He seemed bent on destruction as he reached for it with gripping fingers. Suddenly he staggered, as if from a heavy blow in the face, and covered both eyes with his hands.

"Look!" he screamed.

There was a smudge of fresh red blood on the fifth bell. Mrs. Phillips glanced from the bell to him inquiringly. He stood for a moment with hands pressed to his eyes, then laughed mirthlessly.

Here a small brazier spouting a blue flame, there a retort partially filled with some purplish, foul-smelling liquid, yonder a sinuous copper coil winding off into the shadows, and, moving about like an alchemist of old, the slender, child-like figure of Professor Augustus S. F. X. Van Dusen, Ph.D., LL.D., F.R.S., M.D., etc., etc. A ray of light shot down blindingly from a reflector above, and brilliantly illuminated the laboratory table. The worker leaned forward to peer at some minute particle under the microscope, and for an instant his head and face were thrown out against the darkness of the room like some grotesque, disembodied thing.

It was a singular head and face—a head out of all proportion to the body, dome-like, enormous, with a wilderness of straw-yellow hair. The face was small, wizened, petulant even; the watery blue eyes, narrow almost to the disappearing point, squinted everlastingly through thick spectacles; the mouth drooped at the corners. The small, white hands, which twisted and turned the object glass into focus, were possessed of extraordinarily long, slender fingers.

This man of the large head and small body was the Court of Last Appeal in contemporaneous science. His was the sanest, coldest, clearest brain in scientific achievement. His word was the final one. Once upon a time a newspaper man, Hutchinson Hatch, had dubbed him The Thinking Machine, and so it came about that the world at large had heard of and knew him by that title. The reporter, a tall, slender young man, sat now watching him curiously and listening. The scientist spoke in a tone of perpetual annoyance; but a long acquaintance had taught the reporter that it was what the man said and not the manner in which he said it, that was to be heeded.

"Imagination, Mr. Hatch, is the single connecting link between man and the infinite," The Thinking Machine was saying. "It is the one quality which distinguishes us from what we are pleased to call the brute creation, for we have the same passions, the same appetites, and the same desires. It is the most valuable adjunct to the scientific mind because it is the basis of all scientific progress. It is the thing which temporarily bridges gaps and makes it possible to solve all material problems, not some, but all of them. We can achieve nothing until we imagine it. Just so far as the human brain can imagine it can comprehend. It fails only to comprehend the eternal purpose, the Omnipotent Will, because it can not imagine it. For imagination has a limit, Mr. Hatch, and beyond that we are not to go."

This wasn't at all what Hatch had come to hear, but he listened with a sort of fascination.

"The first intelligent being," the irritated voice went on, "had to imagine that when two were added to two there would be a result. He found it was four, he proved it was four, and instantly it became immutable—a point in logic, a thing by which we solve problems. Thus, two and two make four, not sometimes, but always."

"I had supposed that imagination was limitless," Hatch ventured after a moment, "that it knew no bounds."

The Thinking Machine squinted at him coldly.

"On the contrary," he declared, "it has a boundary beyond which the mind of man merely reels, staggers, collapses. I'll take you there." He spoke as if it were just round the corner. "By aid of a microscope of far less power than the one there, the atomic or molecular theory was formulated. You know that—it is that all matter is composed of atoms. Now imagination suggested and logic immutably demonstrates that the atoms themselves are composed of other atoms, and that those atoms in turn are composed of still others, *ad infinitum*. They are merely invisible, and imagination—I am not now stating a belief, but citing an example of what imagination can do—can make us see the possibility of each of those atoms, down to infinity, being inhabited, being in itself a world relatively as distant from its fellows as we are from the moon. We can even imagine what those inhabitants would look like."

He paused a minute; Hatch blinked several times.

"But the boundary lies the other way—through the telescope," continued the scientist. "The most powerful glass ever devised has brought no suggestion of the end of the universe. It only brings more millions of worlds, invisible to the naked eye, into sight. The stronger the glass the more hopeless the task of even conjecturing the end, and here, too, the imagination can apply the atomic theory and logic will support it. In other words, atoms make matter, matter makes the world which is an inconceivably tiny speck in our solar system, an atom; therefore, all the millions and millions of worlds are mere atoms, infinitesimal parts of some far greater scheme. What greater scheme? There is the end of imagination! There the mind stops."

The conception made Hatch gasp a little. He sat silent for a long time, awed, oppressed. Never before in his life had he felt of so little consequence.

"Now, Mr. Hatch, this little problem that is annoying you," continued The Thinking Machine, and the matter-of-fact tone was a great relief. "What I have said has had, of course, no bearing on it except in so far as it demonstrates that imagination is necessary to solve a problem, that all material problems may be solved, and that in meeting them logic is the lever. It is a fixed quantity; its simplest rules have enabled me to solve petty affairs for you in the past, so——"

The reporter came to himself with a start. Then he laid before this master brain the circumstances which cast so strange a mystery about the death by violence of Johann Wagner, curio dealer, in the home of Franklin Phillips, millionaire. But his information was only from the time the police came into the affair. Mr. Phillips, Dr. Perdue and Mr. Matsumi alone knew of the ringing of the bell.

"The blood spot on one of the bells," Hatch told the scientist in conclusion, "may be the mark of a hand, but its significance doesn't appear. Just now the police are working on two queer points which they developed. First, Detective Mallory recognized the dead man as 'Old Dutch' Wagner, long suspected of conducting a 'fence'—that is, receiving and disposing of stolen goods; and, second, one of the servants in the Phillips household, Giles Francis, has disappeared. He hasn't been seen since eleven o'clock on the night before the body was found, and then he was in bed, sound asleep. Every article of his clothing, except a pair of shoes, trousers, and pajamas, was left behind."

The Thinking Machine turned away from the laboratory table and sank into a chair. For a long time he sat with his enormous yellow head thrown back, and his slender, white fingers pressed tip to tip.

"If Wagner was shot through the heart," he said at last, "we know that death was instantaneous, therefore he could not have made the blood-mark on the bell." This seemed to be a statement of fact. "But why should there *be* such a blood-mark on the bell."

"Detective Mallory thinks that——" began the reporter.

"Oh, never mind what he thinks," interrupted the other testily. "What time was the body found?"

"About half-past nine yesterday morning."

"Anything stolen?"

"Nothing. The body was simply there, the window open, and the door locked, and there was the blood-mark on the bell."

There was a pause. Cobwebby lines appeared on the broad forehead of the scientist, and the squint eyes narrowed down to mere slits. Hatch was watching him curiously.

"What does Mr. Phillips say about it?" asked The Thinking Machine. He was still staring upward, and his thin lips were drawn into a straight line.

"He is ill; how ill we don't know," responded the newspaper man. "Dr. Perdue has, so far, not permitted the police to question him."

The scientist lowered his eyes quickly.

"What's the matter with him?" he demanded.

"I don't know. Dr. Perdue has declined to make any statement."

Half an hour later, The Thinking Machine and Hatch called at the Phillips' house. They met Dr. Perdue coming out. His face was grave and preoccupied; the professional air of jocundity was wholly absent. He shook hands with The Thinking Machine, whom he had met years before beside an operating table, and reentered the house with him. Together the three went to the little room—the scene of the tragedy. The Japanese gong had not been removed. It still swung over the desk. The crabbed little scientist went straight to it, and for five minutes devoted his undivided attention to a study of the splotch on the fifth bell. From the expression of his face Hatch could gather nothing. What the scientist saw might or might not have been illuminating.

Was the blood splotch the mark of a hand? If it was, Hatch argued, it offered no clue as the intricate lines of the flesh were smeared together, obliterated.

Next, The Thinking Machine critically glanced about him, and finally threw open the window facing east. For a long time he stood silently squinting out; and, save for the minute lines in his forehead, there was no indication whatever of his mental workings. The little room was on the second floor, and jutted out at right angles across a narrow alley which ran beneath them to the kitchen in the back. The dead wall of the next building was only four feet from the Phillips' wall, and was without windows, so it was easily seen how a man, unobserved, might climb up from below, despite an arc-light above the wide front door of a block of flats across the street, visible in the vista of the alley.

"Do you happen to know, Perdue," asked The Thinking Machine at last, "if this west window was ever opened?"

"Never," replied the physician. "Detective Mallory questioned the servants about it. It seems that the kitchen is beneath, somewhat to the back, and the odors of cooking come up."

"How many outside doors has this house?"

"Only two," was the reply. "The one you entered and one opening into the alley below us."

"Both were found locked yesterday morning?"

"Yes. Both doors have spring-locks, therefore each locks itself when closed."

"Oh!" exclaimed the scientist suddenly.

He turned away from the window, and for a second time he examined the still and silent gong. Somewhere in his mind seemed to be an inkling that the gong might be more closely associated than appeared with the mystery of death, and yet, watching him curiously, Dr. Perdue knew he could have no knowledge of the sinister part it had played in the affair. With a penknife The Thinking Machine made a slight mark on the underside of each bell in turn, then squinted at them one after another. On the inside of the top bell—the largest—he found something—a mark, a symbol, perhaps—but it seemed meaningless to Hatch and Dr. Perdue, who were peering over his shoulder. It was merely a circle with three upward rays and three dots inside it.

"The manufacturer's mark, perhaps," Hatch suggested.

"Of course, it's impossible that the bell could have had anything to do——" Dr. Perdue began.

"Nothing is impossible, Perdue," snapped the scientist crabbedly. "Do not say that. It annoys me exceedingly." He continued to stare fixedly at the symbol. "Exactly where was the body found?" he asked, after a little while.

"Here," replied Dr. Perdue, and he indicated a spot near the window.

The Thinking Machine measured the distance with his eye.

"The only real problem here," he remarked musingly, after a moment, as if supplementing a previous statement, "is what made him lock the door and run."

"What made—who?" Hatch asked eagerly.

The Thinking Machine merely squinted at him, through him, beyond him, with glassy eyes. His thoughts seemed far away, and the cobwebby lines in his forehead grew deeper. Dr. Perdue was apparently at the moment too self-absorbed to heed.

"Now, Perdue," demanded The Thinking Machine suddenly, "what is really the matter with Mr. Phillips?"

"Well, it's rather——" he started haltingly, then went on as if his mind were made up. "You know, Van Dusen, there's something behind all this that hasn't been told, for reasons which I consider good ones. It might interest you, because you are keen on these things, but I doubt if it would help you. And besides, I should have to insist that you alone should hear it."

He glanced meaningly at Hatch, whom he knew to be present only in his capacity as reporter.

"There's something else—about the bell," said The Thinking Machine quickly. It was not a question, but a statement.

"Yes, about the bell," acquiesced the physician, as if a little surprised that the other should know. "But as I said, it——"

"I undertook to get at the facts here to aid Mr. Hatch," explained The Thinking Machine, "but I can assure you he will print nothing without my permission."

Dr. Perdue looked at the newspaper man inquiringly; Hatch nodded.

"I expect perhaps it would be better for you to hear it from Phillips himself," went on the physician. "Come along. I think he would be willing to tell you."

Thus the scientist and the reporter met Franklin Phillips. He was in bed. The once masterful financier seemed but a shadow of what he had been. His strong face was now white and haggard, and lined almost beyond recognition. The lips were pale, the hands nervously clenched at the sheet, and in his eyes was horror—hideous horror. They glittered at times and only at intervals reflected the strength, the power which once lay there. His present condition was pitiable and inexplicable to Hatch, who remembered him as the rugged storm-center of half a dozen spectacular financial battles.

Mr. Phillips talked willingly—seemed, indeed, relieved to be able to relate in detail those circumstances which, in a way, accounted for his utter collapse. As he went on volubly, yet coherently enough, his eyes settled on the inscrutable face of The Thinking Machine as if seeking belief. He found it, for the scientist nodded time after time, and gradually the lines in the dome-like forehead were dissipated.

"*Now* I know why he ran," declared the scientist positively, enigmatically. The remark was hopelessly without meaning to the others. "As I understand it, Mr. Phillips," he asked, "the east window was always open when the bell sounded?"

"Yes, I believe it was, always," replied Mr. Phillips, after a moment's thought.

"And you always heard it when the window was open?"

"Oh, no," replied the financier. "There were many times when the window was open that I didn't hear anything."

A fleeting bewilderment crossed the scientist's face, then was gone.

"Of course, of course," he said after a moment. "Stupid of me. I should have known that. Now, the first time you ever noticed it, the bell rang twice—that is, twice with an interval of say, a few seconds, between?"

"Yes."

"And you had had the gong, then, two or three months?"

"About three months—yes."

"The weather remained cool during that time? Late winter and early spring?"

"I presume so. I don't recall. I know the first time I heard the bell was an early warm day of spring, because my window had not previously been opened."

The Thinking Machine was dreamily squinting upward. As he stared into the quiet, narrow eyes, a certain measure of confidence seemed to return to Mr. Phillips. He raised himself on an elbow.

"You say that once you heard the bell ring late at night—twice. What were the circumstances?"

"That was the night preceding a day of some important operations I had planned," explained Mr. Phillips, "and I was in the little room for a long time after midnight going over some figures."

"Do you remember the date?"

"Perfectly. It was Tuesday, the eleventh of this month," and for an instant memory called to Mr. Phillips' face an expression which financial foes knew well. "I remember because next day I forced the market up to a record price on some railway stocks I happen to control."

The Thinking Machine nodded.

"This servant of yours who is missing, Francis, was rather a timid sort of man, I imagine?"

"Well, I could hardly say," replied Mr. Phillips doubtfully.

"Well, he was," declared The Thinking Machine flatly. "He was a good servant, I dare say?"

"Yes, excellent."

"Would it have been within his duties to close a window which might have been left open at night?"

"Certainly."

"Rather a big man?"

"Yes, six feet or so—two hundred and ten pounds, perhaps."

"And Mr. Matsumi was, of course, small?"

"Yes, small even for a Japanese."

The Thinking Machine rose and placed his fingers on Mr. Phillips' wrist. He stood thus for half a minute.

"Did you ever notice any odor after the bell rang?" he inquired at last.

"Odor?" Mr. Phillips seemed puzzled. "I don't see what an odor would have to do——"

"I didn't expect you to," interrupted The Thinking Machine crustily. "I merely want to know if you noticed one."

"No," retorted Mr. Phillips shortly.

"And could you explain your precise feeling?" continued the scientist. "Did the effect of the bell's ringing seem to be entirely mental, or was it physical? In other words, was there any physical exaltation or depression when you heard it?"

"It would be rather difficult to say—even to myself," responded Mr. Phillips. "It always seemed to be a shock, but I suppose it was really a mental condition which reacted on my nerves."

The Thinking Machine walked over to the window and stood with his back to the others. For a minute or more he remained there, and three eager pairs of eyes were fixed inquiringly on the back of his yellow head. Beneath the irritated voice, behind the inscrutable face, in the disjointed questioning, they all knew intuitively that there was some definite purpose, but to none came a glimmer of light as to its nature.

"I think, perhaps, the matter is all clear now," he remarked musingly at last. "There are two vital questions yet to be answered. If the first of these is answered in the affirmative, I know that a mind—I may say a Japanese mind—of singularly ingenious quality conceived the condition which brought about this affair; if in the negative, the entire matter becomes ridiculously simple."

Mr. Phillips was leaning forward, listening greedily. There was hope and fear, doubt and confidence, eagerness and a certain tense restraint in his manner. Dr. Perdue was silent. Hatch merely waited.

"What made the bell ring?" demanded Mr. Phillips.

"I must find the answer to the two remaining questions first," returned The Thinking Machine.

"You mentioned a Japanese," said Mr. Phillips. "Do you suspect Mr. Matsumi of any connection with the—the mystery?"

"I never suspect persons of things, Mr. Phillips," said The Thinking Machine curtly. "I never suspect—I always *know*. When I *know* in this case, I shall inform you. Mr. Hatch and I are going out for a few minutes. When we return, the matter can be disposed of in ten minutes."

He led the way out and along the hall to the little room where the gong hung. Hatch closed the door as he entered. Then for the third time the scientist examined the bells. He struck the fifth violently, time after time, and after each stroke he thrust an inquisitive nose almost against it, and sniffed. Hatch stared at him in wonderment. When the scientist had finished, he shook his head as if answering a question in the negative. With Hatch following, he passed out into the street.

"What's the matter with Phillips?" the reporter ventured, as they reached the pavement.

"Scared, frightened," was the tart rejoinder. "He's merely morbidly anxious to account for the bell ringing. If I had been absolutely certain before I came out, I should have told him. I am certain now. You know, Mr. Hatch, when a thing is beyond immediate understanding, it instantly suggests the supernatural to some minds. Mr. Phillips wouldn't confess it, but he sees behind the ringing of that bell some uncanny power—a threat, perhaps—and the thing has preyed upon him until he's nearly insane. When I can arrange to make him understand perfectly why the bell rings he will be all right again. Do you see?"

"I can readily see how the ringing of the bell strikes one as uncanny," Hatch declared grimly. "Have you any idea what causes it?"

"I *know* what causes it," returned the other irritably. "And if you don't know, you're stupid."

The reporter shook his head hopelessly.

They crossed the street to the big block of flats opposite, and entered. The Thinking Machine inquired for and was shown into the office of the manager. He had only one question.

"Was there a ball, or reception, or anything of that sort held in this building on Tuesday night, the eleventh of this month?" he inquired.

"No," was the response. "There has never been anything of that sort here."

"Thanks," said The Thinking Machine. "Good day."

Turning abruptly, he left the manager to wonder as he liked, and with Hatch following, ascended the stairs to the next floor. Here was a wide, airy corridor extending the full length of the building. The Thinking Machine glanced neither to right nor left; he went straight to the rear, where a plate-glass window enframed a panorama of the city. From where they stood the city's roofs slanted down toward the river, half a mile away.

As Hatch looked on, The Thinking Machine took out his watch and set it two and a half minutes forward, after which he turned and walked to the other end of the corridor. Here, too, was a plate-glass window. For just a fraction of an instant he stood staring straight out at the Phillips' home across the way, then, without a word, retraced his steps down the stairs, and into the street.

Hatch's head was overflowing with questions, but he choked them back and merely trailed along. They reentered the Phillips' house in silence. Dr. Perdue and Harvey Phillips met them in the hall. An expression of infinite relief came into the physician's face at the sight of The Thinking Machine.

"I'm glad you're back so soon," he said quickly. "Here's a new development, and a singular one." He referred evidently to a long envelope he held. "Step into the library here."

They entered, and Dr. Perdue carefully closed the door behind them.

"Just a few minutes ago, Harvey received a sealed envelope by mail," he explained. "It enclosed this one, also sealed. He was going to show it to his father, but I didn't think it wise because of—because——"

The Thinking Machine took the envelope in one slender hand and examined it. It was a perfectly plain white one, and bore only a single line written in a small, copper-plate hand, with occasional unexpected angles:

"*To be opened when the fifth bell rings eleven times.*"

Something as nearly approaching complacent satisfaction as Hatch had ever seen overspread the petulant countenance of The Thinking Machine, and a long, aspirated "Ah!" escaped the thin lips. There was a hushed silence. Harvey Phillips, to whom nothing of the mystery was known beyond the actual death of Wagner, sought to read what it all meant in Dr. Perdue's face. In turn, Dr. Perdue's eyes were fastened on The Thinking Machine.

"Of course, you don't know who this is from, Mr. Phillips?" inquired the scientist of the young man.

"I have no idea," was the reply. "It seemed to amaze Dr. Perdue, here, but frankly I can't imagine why."

"You don't know the handwriting?"

"No."

"Well, I do," declared The Thinking Machine emphatically. "It's Mr. Matsumi's." He glared at the physician. "And in it lies the key to this affair of the bell. The mere fact that it came at all proves everything as I saw it."

"But it can't be from Matsumi," protested the young man. "The postmark on the outside was Paris."

"That means merely that he has run away to escape arrest on a charge of murder."

"Then Matsumi killed Wagner?" Hatch asked quickly.

"I didn't say it was a confession," responded the scientist curtly. "It is merely a history of the bell. I dare say——"

Suddenly the door was thrown open, and Mrs. Phillips entered the room. Her face was ashen.

"Doctor, he is worse—sinking rapidly!" she gasped. "Please come!"

Dr. Perdue glanced from her pallid face to the impassive Thinking Machine.

"Van Dusen," he said solemnly, "if you can do anything to explain this thing, for God's sake do it now. I know it will save a man's reason—it might save his life."

"Is he conscious?" inquired the scientist of Mrs. Phillips.

"No; he seems to have utterly collapsed," she explained. "I was talking to him, when suddenly he sat up in bed as if listening, then shrieked something I didn't understand, and fell back unconscious."

Dr. Perdue was dragged out of the room by the wife and son. The Thinking Machine glanced at his watch. It was three and a half minutes past four o'clock. He nodded, then turned to Hatch.

"Please go into the little room and close the window," he instructed. "Mr. Phillips has heard the bell again, and I imagine Dr. Perdue needs me. Meanwhile, put this envelope in your pocket," and he handed to Hatch the mysterious sealed packet, and followed the others silently to the room where the invalid was.

It was twenty minutes past nine o'clock that evening. In the little room where the gong hung were Franklin Phillips, pale and weak, but eager; Dr. Perdue, The Thinking Machine, Harvey Phillips and Hatch. For four hours Dr. Perdue and the scientist had labored over the unconscious financier, and, finally, a tinge of color returned to the pale lips, then came consciousness.

"It was my suggestion, Mr. Phillips, that we are here," explained The Thinking Machine quietly. "I want to show you just why and how the bell rings, and, incidentally, clear up the other points of the mystery. Now, if I should tell you that the bell will sound a given number of times at a given instant, and it *should* sound, you would know that I was aware of the cause?"

"Certainly," assented Mr. Phillips eagerly.

"And then if I demonstrated tangibly *how* it sounded, you would be satisfied?"

"Yes, of course, yes."

"Very good," and the scientist turned to the reporter. "Mr. Hatch, 'phone to the Weather Bureau and ask if there was a storm about midnight preceding the finding of Wagner's body; also if there was thunder. And get the direction and velocity of the wind. I know, of course, that there *was* thunder, and that the wind was either from the east or there was no wind. I *know* it, not from personal observation, but by pure logic of events."

The reporter nodded.

"Also, I will have to ask you to borrow for me somewhere, a violin and a champagne glass."

There happened to be a violin in the house. Harvey Phillips went for it, and Hatch went to the telephone. Five minutes later Hatch reappeared; Harvey Phillips had preceded him.

"Light wind from the east, four miles an hour," Hatch reported tersely. "The storm threatened just before midnight. There was vivid lightning and heavy thunder."

To prosaic Dr. Perdue these preliminaries smacked a little of charlatanry. Mr. Phillips was interested, but impatient. The Thinking Machine, watch in hand, lay back in his chair squinting steadily upward.

"Now, Mr. Phillips," he announced, "in just thirty-three and three-quarter minutes the bell will ring. It will sound ten times. I am taking pains to reproduce the exact conditions under which the bell has always sounded since you have known it, because, if I show you, there can be no doubt."

Mr. Phillips was leaning forward, gripping the arm of his chair.

"Meanwhile, I will reconstruct the events, not as they *might* have happened, but as they *must* have happened," continued The Thinking Machine. "They will not be in sequence, but as they were revealed to me by each added fact; for logic, Mr. Phillips, is only a sum in arithmetic, and the answer based on every known fact must be correct as inevitably as that two and two make four—not sometimes, but always.

"Well, a man was found dead here—shot. His mere presence indicated burglary. The open window showed how he probably entered. Considering only these superficial facts, we see instantly that more than *one* person might have entered that window. Yet it is hardly likely that two thieves entered, and one killed the other before they got their booty, for nothing was stolen, and it is still less likely that one man came here to commit suicide. What, then?

"The blood-mark on the bell. It was made by a human hand. Yet a man shot instantly dead could not have made it. Therefore, we *know* there was another person. The door locked on the outside absolutely confirmed this. Ordinarily, I dare say, the door is never locked? No? Then, who locked it? Certainly not a second thief, for he would not have risked escaping through the house after a shot which, for all he knew, had aroused every one. Ergo, some one in the house locked the door. Who?

"One of your servants, Giles Francis, is missing. Did he hear some one in the room? No, for he would have alarmed the household. What happened to him? Where is he? There is, of course, a chance that he ran out to find a policeman, and was disposed of in some way by an outside confederate of the man inside. But, remember, please, the last we know of him he was asleep in bed. The vital point, therefore, is what aroused him. From that we can easily develop his subsequent actions."

The Thinking Machine paused and glanced casually at his watch, then toward the east window, which was open, but with the screen in.

"We know," he resumed, "that if Francis had been aroused by burglars, or by a sound which he attributed to burglars, he would have awakened other servants. We must suppose he was awakened by some noise. What is most probable? Thunder! That would account for his every act. So let's say for the moment that it was thunder, that he remembered this window was open, partially dressed himself, and came here to close it. This was, we will also presume, just before midnight. He met Wagner here, and, in some way, got Wagner's revolver. Then the fatal shot was fired.

"From this point, as the facts developed, Francis' acts became more difficult of comprehension. I could readily see how, when Wagner fell, Francis might have placed his hand over the heart to see if he were dead, and thus stained his hands; but why did Francis then smear blood on the fifth bell of the gong, leave this room, locking the door behind him, and run into the street? In other words, why did he lock the door, and run?

"I had already attached considerable importance to the gong, primarily because of the blood, and had examined the bells closely. I even scratched them to assure myself that they were bronze, and not a precious metal which would attract thieves. Then, Mr. Phillips, I heard your story, and instantly I *knew* why Francis locked the door and ran. It was because he was frightened—horribly, unspeakably frightened. Naturally, there was a nerve-racking shock when he found he had killed a man. Then, as he stood, horror-stricken, perhaps, the bell rang. It affected him as it did you, Mr. Phillips, but under circumstances which were inconceivably more terrifying to a timid man. The bell rang six, seven, eight—perhaps a dozen times. To Francis, looking down upon a man he had killed, it was maddening, inexplicable. He placed his hand on it to stop the sound, then, crazed with terror, ran out of the room, locking the door behind him, and out of the house. The outer door closed with a spring-lock. He will return in time, because, of course, he was justified in killing Wagner."

Again The Thinking Machine glanced at his watch. Eighteen minutes of the specified thirty-three had elapsed.

"Now, as to the bell itself," he went on; "its history is of no consequence. It's Japanese, and we know it's extremely old. We must assume from Mr. Matsumi's conduct that it is an object of—of, say, veneration. We can imagine it hanging in a temple; perhaps it rang there, and awed multitudes listened. Perhaps they regarded it as prophetic. After its disappearance from Japan, we don't know how, Mr. Matsumi was naturally amazed to see it here, and was anxious to buy it. You refused to listen to him, Mr. Phillips. Then he went to Wagner and offered, we'll say, some large sum for it. That accounts for Wagner's letters and his presence here. He came to steal the thing which he couldn't buy. His denial of all knowledge of the bell is explained readily by Detective Mallory's statement that he had long been suspected of handling stolen goods. He denied, because he feared a trap. I may add that I attributed an ingenuity of construction to the bell which it did not possess. When I asked if you ever noted any odor when it sounded, Mr. Phillips, I had an idea that perhaps your present condition had been brought about by a subtle poison in which the gong had once been immersed, particles of which might have been cast off when the bell sounded, and drawn into the lungs. I can assure you, however, that there was no poison. That is all, I think."

"But the sealed letter——" began Dr. Perdue.

"Oh, I opened that," was the casual rejoinder; but Dr. Perdue, as he looked, read a warning in the scientist's face. "It related to another matter entirely."

Dr. Perdue gazed at him a moment, and understood. Unconsciously Hatch felt the pocket where he had placed the letter. It was still there. He understood. The Thinking Machine rose, glanced out of the window, then turned to the reporter.

"Now, Mr. Hatch," he requested, "please go across the street to the block opposite, and open the rear window in the corridor where we were. See that it remains open for twenty minutes, then return here. Keep out of the corridor while the window is open, and if possible keep others from coming there."

Without a word or question Hatch went out. The Thinking Machine dropped back into his chair, glanced at his watch, then scribbled something on a card, which he handed in a casual manner to Dr. Perdue.

"By the way," he remarked irrelevantly, "there's an excellent compound for nervous indigestion I ran across the other day. Perhaps you might find it useful."

Dr. Perdue read the card. On it was:

"Letter dangerous. Probably predicts death. Has religious significance. Would advise Phillips not be informed."

"I'll try it some time," remarked Dr. Perdue.

There was a silence of two or three minutes. The Thinking Machine was idly twirling his watch in his slender fingers; Mr. Phillips sat staring at the bell, but there was no longer fright in his manner; it seemed rather a quiet, if keen, curiosity.

"In just three minutes," said The Thinking Machine at last. A pause. "Now two!" Again a pause. "Now one! Be perfectly calm, and listen!" Another pause, then suddenly: "Now!"

"Boom!" rang the bell, as if echoing the word. Despite himself, Mr. Phillips started a little, and the scientist's fingers closed on his pulse. "Boom!" again came the note. The bell hung motionless; the musical clangor seemed to roll out methodically, rhythmically. Three! Four! Five! Six! Seven! Eight! Nine! Ten!

When the last note sounded, The Thinking Machine was staring into Mr. Phillips' face, seeking understanding. He found only bewilderment, and with quick impatience picked up the violin and bow.

"Here!" he exclaimed curtly. "Watch the champagne glass."

He tapped the fragile glass, and it sang shrilly. Then on the violin he sought the accompanying chord. Four times he drew the bow across the strings, and the glass was silent. Then the violin caught the pitch, and the glass, three or four feet away, sang with it. Louder and louder the violin note grew, then suddenly, with a crash, the thin receptacle collapsed, shattered, tumbled to pieces before their eyes. Mr. Phillips stared in the utmost astonishment.

"A little demonstration in natural philosophy," explained The Thinking Machine. "In other words, vibration. Vibration sounded the glass, just as vibration sounded the bell on the gong there. You saw me sound the glass; the note which sounds the bell is a clock on a direct line half a mile away due east."

Mr. Phillips stared first at the shattered glass, then at the scientist. After a moment he understood, and an inexpressible feeling of relief swept over him.

"But the bell didn't always sound when the window was open," objected Dr. Perdue, after a moment.

"The bell can only sound when this window and both corridor windows on the second floor across the way are open—on warm nights, for instance," replied The Thinking Machine. "Then, too, the wind must be from the east, or else there must be none. A gust of air, a person passing through the hall, any one of a dozen things would interrupt the sensitive sound waves and prevent all strokes of the clock reaching the bell here, while some of them might. Of course, any bell on the gong may be sounded with a violin, or, if they are true notes, with a piano, and I knew this at first. But Mr. Phillips had once heard the bell long after midnight—say, two o'clock in the morning. Pianos and violins are not going so late, except, perhaps at a ball. There was no ball across the street that night, therefore we came to the obvious remainder—a clock. It is visible from the rear window of the second floor corridor over there. It's all logic, logic, logic!"

There was a pause. Dr. Perdue, looking into the face of his patient, was reassured by what he saw there, and something of his own professional jocundity asserted itself.

"Instead of being a thing to make you nervous, Phillips," he said at last with a smile, "it seems to me that the bell is an excellent and reliable timepiece."

Mr. Phillips glanced at him quickly, and the drawn, white face was relieved by a slight smile. After a while Hatch returned, and for some time the little party sat in the room talking over the affair. Their conversation was interrupted at last by the clangor of the bell, and every person present rose and stared at it anew, with the exception of The Thinking Machine. His squint eyes were still turned upward—he didn't even alter his position. There were eleven strokes of the bell, then silence.

"Eleven o'clock," remarked The Thinking Machine placidly. "You left the windows open over there, Mr. Hatch."

Hatch nodded.

Mr. Phillips was in bed, sleeping calmly, when Dr. Perdue and The Thinking Machine, accompanied by Hatch, went away.

"Suppose we drop in at my place, and look at that letter?" suggested the doctor.

The Thinking Machine, in Dr. Perdue's office, took the sealed packet from the reporter and opened it. Dr. Perdue was peering over his shoulder. The scientist squinted down the page with inscrutable face, then crumpled up the letter, struck a match, and ignited it.

"But—but——" protested Dr. Perdue quickly, and Hatch saw that some strange pallor suddenly overspread his face; "it said that—that eleven strokes meant—meant——"

"You're a fool, Perdue," snapped The Thinking Machine, and he glared straight into the physician's eyes. "Didn't I show why and how the bell rang? Do you expect me to account for every barbaric superstition of a half-civilized race?"

The paper burned, and The Thinking Machine crumpled up the ashes and dropped them in a waste-paper basket.

Two days later Franklin Phillips was himself again; on the fourth day he appeared at his office; on the sixth the market began to feel the master's clutch; on the eighth Francis was taken into custody and repeated a story identical with that told by The Thinking Machine to account for his disappearance; on the eleventh Franklin Phillips was found dead in bed. On his forehead was a pallid, white spot, faintly visible. It was a circle, with three dots inside, and three rays extending out from it.

A CATALOGUE OF SELECTED DOVER BOOKS IN ALL FIELDS OF INTEREST

A CATALOGUE OF SELECTED DOVER BOOKS IN ALL FIELDS OF INTEREST

RACKHAM'S COLOR ILLUSTRATIONS FOR WAGNER'S RING. Rackham's finest mature work—all 64 full-color watercolors in a faithful and lush interpretation of the *Ring*. Full-sized plates on coated stock of the paintings used by opera companies for authentic staging of Wagner. Captions aid in following complete Ring cycle. Introduction. 64 illustrations plus vignettes. 72pp. 8⅝ x 11¼. 23779-6 Pa. $6.00

CONTEMPORARY POLISH POSTERS IN FULL COLOR, edited by Joseph Czestochowski. 46 full-color examples of brilliant school of Polish graphic design, selected from world's first museum (near Warsaw) dedicated to poster art. Posters on circuses, films, plays, concerts all show cosmopolitan influences, free imagination. Introduction. 48pp. 9⅜ x 12¼. 23780-X Pa. $6.00

GRAPHIC WORKS OF EDVARD MUNCH, Edvard Munch. 90 haunting, evocative prints by first major Expressionist artist and one of the greatest graphic artists of his time: *The Scream, Anxiety, Death Chamber, The Kiss, Madonna,* etc. Introduction by Alfred Werner. 90pp. 9 x 12. 23765-6 Pa. $5.00

THE GOLDEN AGE OF THE POSTER, Hayward and Blanche Cirker. 70 extraordinary posters in full colors, from Maitres de l'Affiche, Mucha, Lautrec, Bradley, Cheret, Beardsley, many others. Total of 78pp. 9⅜ x 12¼. 22753-7 Pa. $5.95

THE NOTEBOOKS OF LEONARDO DA VINCI, edited by J. P. Richter. Extracts from manuscripts reveal great genius; on painting, sculpture, anatomy, sciences, geography, etc. Both Italian and English. 186 ms. pages reproduced, plus 500 additional drawings, including studies for *Last Supper,* Sforza monument, etc. 860pp. 7⅞ x 10¾. (Available in U.S. only) 22572-0, 22573-9 Pa., Two-vol. set $15.90

THE CODEX NUTTALL, as first edited by Zelia Nuttall. Only inexpensive edition, in full color, of a pre-Columbian Mexican (Mixtec) book. 88 color plates show kings, gods, heroes, temples, sacrifices. New explanatory, historical introduction by Arthur G. Miller. 96pp. 11⅜ x 8½. (Available in U.S. only) 23168-2 Pa. $7.95

UNE SEMAINE DE BONTÉ, A SURREALISTIC NOVEL IN COLLAGE, Max Ernst. Masterpiece created out of 19th-century periodical illustrations, explores worlds of terror and surprise. Some consider this Ernst's greatest work. 208pp. 8⅛ x 11. 23252-2 Pa. $6.00

DRAWINGS OF WILLIAM BLAKE, William Blake. 92 plates from Book of Job, *Divine Comedy, Paradise Lost,* visionary heads, mythological figures, Laocoon, etc. Selection, introduction, commentary by Sir Geoffrey Keynes. 178pp. 8⅛ x 11. 22303-5 Pa. $4.00

ENGRAVINGS OF HOGARTH, William Hogarth. 101 of Hogarth's greatest works: *Rake's Progress, Harlot's Progress, Illustrations for Hudibras, Before and After, Beer Street and Gin Lane,* many more. Full commentary. 256pp. 11 x 13¾. 22479-1 Pa. $12.95

DAUMIER: 120 GREAT LITHOGRAPHS, Honore Daumier. Wide-ranging collection of lithographs by the greatest caricaturist of the 19th century. Concentrates on eternally popular series on lawyers, on married life, on liberated women, etc. Selection, introduction, and notes on plates by Charles F. Ramus. Total of 158pp. 9⅜ x 12¼. 23512-2 Pa. $6.00

DRAWINGS OF MUCHA, Alphonse Maria Mucha. Work reveals draftsman of highest caliber: studies for famous posters and paintings, renderings for book illustrations and ads, etc. 70 works, 9 in color; including 6 items not drawings. Introduction. List of illustrations. 72pp. 9⅜ x 12¼. (Available in U.S. only) 23672-2 Pa. $4.00

GIOVANNI BATTISTA PIRANESI: DRAWINGS IN THE PIERPONT MORGAN LIBRARY, Giovanni Battista Piranesi. For first time ever all of Morgan Library's collection, world's largest. 167 illustrations of rare Piranesi drawings—archeological, architectural, decorative and visionary. Essay, detailed list of drawings, chronology, captions. Edited by Felice Stampfle. 144pp. 9⅜ x 12¼. 23714-1 Pa. $7.50

NEW YORK ETCHINGS (1905-1949), John Sloan. All of important American artist's N.Y. life etchings. 67 works include some of his best art; also lively historical record—Greenwich Village, tenement scenes. Edited by Sloan's widow. Introduction and captions. 79pp. 8⅜ x 11¼. 23651-X Pa. $4.00

CHINESE PAINTING AND CALLIGRAPHY: A PICTORIAL SURVEY, Wan-go Weng. 69 fine examples from John M. Crawford's matchless private collection: landscapes, birds, flowers, human figures, etc., plus calligraphy. Every basic form included: hanging scrolls, handscrolls, album leaves, fans, etc. 109 illustrations. Introduction. Captions. 192pp. 8⅞ x 11¾. 23707-9 Pa. $7.95

DRAWINGS OF REMBRANDT, edited by Seymour Slive. Updated Lippmann, Hofstede de Groot edition, with definitive scholarly apparatus. All portraits, biblical sketches, landscapes, nudes, Oriental figures, classical studies, together with selection of work by followers. 550 illustrations. Total of 630pp. 9⅛ x 12¼. 21485-0, 21486-9 Pa., Two-vol. set $15.00

THE DISASTERS OF WAR, Francisco Goya. 83 etchings record horrors of Napoleonic wars in Spain and war in general. Reprint of 1st edition, plus 3 additional plates. Introduction by Philip Hofer. 97pp. 9⅜ x 8¼. 21872-4 Pa. $4.00

TONE POEMS, SERIES II: TILL EULENSPIEGELS LUSTIGE STREICHE, ALSO SPRACH ZARATHUSTRA, AND EIN HELDENLEBEN, Richard Strauss. Three important orchestral works, including very popular *Till Eulenspiegel's Marry Pranks,* reproduced in full score from original editions. Study score. 315pp. 9⅜ x 12¼. (Available in U.S. only)
23755-9 Pa. $8.95

TONE POEMS, SERIES I: DON JUAN, TOD UND VERKLARUNG AND DON QUIXOTE, Richard Strauss. Three of the most often performed and recorded works in entire orchestral repertoire, reproduced in full score from original editions. Study score. 286pp. 9⅜ x 12¼. (Available in U.S. only)
23754-0 Pa. $7.50

11 LATE STRING QUARTETS, Franz Joseph Haydn. The form which Haydn defined and "brought to perfection." *(Grove's).* 11 string quartets in complete score, his last and his best. The first in a projected series of the complete Haydn string quartets. Reliable modern Eulenberg edition, otherwise difficult to obtain. 320pp. 8⅜ x 11¼. (Available in U.S. only)
23753-2 Pa. $7.50

FOURTH, FIFTH AND SIXTH SYMPHONIES IN FULL SCORE, Peter Ilyitch Tchaikovsky. Complete orchestral scores of Symphony No. 4 in F Minor, Op. 36; Symphony No. 5 in E Minor, Op. 64; Symphony No. 6 in B Minor, "Pathetique," Op. 74. Bretikopf & Hartel eds. Study score. 480pp. 9⅜ x 12¼.
23861-X Pa. $10.95

THE MARRIAGE OF FIGARO: COMPLETE SCORE, Wolfgang A. Mozart. Finest comic opera ever written. Full score, not to be confused with piano renderings. Peters edition. Study score. 448pp. 9⅜ x 12¼. (Available in U.S. only)
23751-6 Pa. $11.95

"IMAGE" ON THE ART AND EVOLUTION OF THE FILM, edited by Marshall Deutelbaum. Pioneering book brings together for first time 38 groundbreaking articles on early silent films from *Image* and 263 illustrations newly shot from rare prints in the collection of the International Museum of Photography. A landmark work. Index. 256pp. 8¼ x 11.
23777-X Pa. $8.95

AROUND-THE-WORLD COOKY BOOK, Lois Lintner Sumption and Marguerite Lintner Ashbrook. 373 cooky and frosting recipes from 28 countries (America, Austria, China, Russia, Italy, etc.) include Viennese kisses, rice wafers, London strips, lady fingers, hony, sugar spice, maple cookies, etc. Clear instructions. All tested. 38 drawings. 182pp. 5⅜ x 8.
23802-4 Pa. $2.50

THE ART NOUVEAU STYLE, edited by Roberta Waddell. 579 rare photographs, not available elsewhere, of works in jewelry, metalwork, glass, ceramics, textiles, architecture and furniture by 175 artists—Mucha, Seguy, Lalique, Tiffany, Gaudin, Hohlwein, Saarinen, and many others. 288pp. 8⅜ x 11¼.
23515-7 Pa. $6.95

THE CURVES OF LIFE, Theodore A. Cook. Examination of shells, leaves, horns, human body, art, etc., in "*the* classic reference on how the golden ratio applies to spirals and helices in nature . . . . "—Martin Gardner. 426 illustrations. Total of 512pp. 5⅜ x 8½. 23701-X Pa. $5.95

AN ILLUSTRATED FLORA OF THE NORTHERN UNITED STATES AND CANADA, Nathaniel L. Britton, Addison Brown. Encyclopedic work covers 4666 species, ferns on up. Everything. Full botanical information, illustration for each. This earlier edition is preferred by many to more recent revisions. 1913 edition. Over 4000 illustrations, total of 2087pp. 6⅛ x 9¼. 22642-5, 22643-3, 22644-1 Pa., Three-vol. set $25.50

MANUAL OF THE GRASSES OF THE UNITED STATES, A. S. Hitchcock, U.S. Dept. of Agriculture. The basic study of American grasses, both indigenous and escapes, cultivated and wild. Over 1400 species. Full descriptions, information. Over 1100 maps, illustrations. Total of 1051pp. 5⅜ x 8½. 22717-0, 22718-9 Pa., Two-vol. set $15.00

THE CACTACEAE,, Nathaniel L. Britton, John N. Rose. Exhaustive, definitive. Every cactus in the world. Full botanical descriptions. Thorough statement of nomenclatures, habitat, detailed finding keys. The one book needed by every cactus enthusiast. Over 1275 illustrations. Total of 1080pp. 8 x 10¼. 21191-6, 21192-4 Clothbd., Two-vol. set $35.00

AMERICAN MEDICINAL PLANTS, Charles F. Millspaugh. Full descriptions, 180 plants covered: history; physical description; methods of preparation with all chemical constituents extracted; all claimed curative or adverse effects. 180 full-page plates. Classification table. 804pp. 6½ x 9¼. 23034-1 Pa. $12.95

A MODERN HERBAL, Margaret Grieve. Much the fullest, most exact, most useful compilation of herbal material. Gigantic alphabetical encyclopedia, from aconite to zedoary, gives botanical information, medical properties, folklore, economic uses, and much else. Indispensable to serious reader. 161 illustrations. 888pp. 6½ x 9¼. (Available in U.S. only) 22798-7, 22799-5 Pa., Two-vol. set $13.00

THE HERBAL or GENERAL HISTORY OF PLANTS, John Gerard. The 1633 edition revised and enlarged by Thomas Johnson. Containing almost 2850 plant descriptions and 2705 superb illustrations, Gerard's *Herbal* is a monumental work, the book all modern English herbals are derived from, the one herbal every serious enthusiast should have in its entirety. Original editions are worth perhaps $750. 1678pp. 8½ x 12¼. 23147-X Clothbd. $50.00

MANUAL OF THE TREES OF NORTH AMERICA, Charles S. Sargent. The basic survey of every native tree and tree-like shrub, 717 species in all. Extremely full descriptions, information on habitat, growth, locales, economics, etc. Necessary to every serious tree lover. Over 100 finding keys. 783 illustrations. Total of 986pp. 5⅜ x 8½. 20277-1, 20278-X Pa., Two-vol. set $11.00

CATALOGUE OF DOVER BOOKS